The Edge Of Summer

BOBBI MACLAREN

The Edge of Summer

Copyright © 2024 by Bobbi Maclaren

All rights reserved.

No part of this book may be reproduced in any form or by any electronic or mechanical means, including information storage and retrieval systems, without written permission from the author, except for the use of brief quotations in a book review.

Paperback ISBN: 978-1-7383063-0-5

Cover by Sam at Ink and Laurel

To eleven-year-old me,
We did it.

CONTENT WARNING

Please note that this book does contain: mentions of the death of parents (happens off-page, but a theme throughout), mentions of a house fire (on page in dreams/flashbacks), mentions of revenge porn (not done by main character), and sexually explicit material.

If you would like to avoid the explicit material, the chapters to skip are: 18, 21 and 26.

PS. If you're part of my family, it's not too late to close the book. Seriously.

PROLOGUE
DELILAH

THERE ARE TOO many casseroles in the refrigerator.

I always thought the sheer onslaught of food after someone dies was a bit ridiculous—a Hollywood movie cliché—but after the funeral, people started coming out of the woodwork offering bakeware I'll probably never get around to giving back.

What I could really use help with is navigating wills and final wishes and estates—all the things I didn't think I would have to worry about for decades. Instead all I have is twenty casseroles and no desire to eat any of them. That, and a slew of unsolicited opinions about how I should be handling everything.

Are you sure you can manage two children? You're only twenty-five.

Of course you should take them. It's what your parents would have wanted.

You are so brave. I would be a total mess in your situation!

The biggest thing I have come to realize in the past few

weeks: people suck at navigating death. I wasn't good at it either. I'm still not. No one knows what to say, and when they think they do, whatever comes out of their mouth makes me feel like punching something. Possibly them.

Maybe I just want someone to blame—somewhere to hurl this ugly ball of hurt churning in my chest beneath the film of numbness. One of these days, the numbness will wear off, and I fear then that I will shatter.

There are so many things I wish I could say. So many things I wish I had done differently. Regret has never tasted so bitter. If I hadn't taken that picture, would they still be here? My parents certainly wouldn't have been out driving that afternoon if it wasn't for me and the mess they had to clean up.

The rain slants sideways as it pelts the windows of my family's James Bay home. Rain isn't exactly a novel concept on the west coast, but the torrential downpour and the cracks of thunder feel angry, like the earth is seeking revenge.

I never used to be afraid of thunderstorms. As a kid, each time lightning lanced the blackened sky, I would watch in quiet fascination. Storms are as natural a phenomenon as any; Mother Nature taking back her power. But ever since the night that police constable knocked on my apartment door, that appreciation for the weather has been lost. In its place is a low-level anxiety that lives in the pit of my stomach, making me wonder whose family the natural phenomenon will claim next.

My phone chiming with a text pulls me from my stupor. I realize then that I've been standing in front of the open fridge, staring at nothing. I half expect my mother to appear and chastise me for letting the cold air get out. But I'm alone, like I have been for weeks. I pull the device from my back pocket and check my messages.

> MITCHELL
> Have you come to your senses yet?

Asshole. I came to my senses the day I found out he was cheating on me and proceeded to dump him.

I want to scream. I want to hurl my phone at the wall and let it smash to pieces. But what if someone needs to reach me about my siblings or my parents' estate? My life isn't mine—not anymore. I dropped out of my masters program two days after it happened, back when the numbness was fresh and every task I checked off the list felt like I was one step closer to feeling normal again. Except normal doesn't exist.

> I'm not changing my mind. Leave me alone.

> MITCHELL
> We were together for eight years, Delilah. I deserve more than a shitty excuse of a reason.

> I don't really give a shit what you think you deserve. I didn't deserve to have my private pictures splashed across the internet but life isn't fair, is it?

> MITCHELL
> Baby, I told you that wasn't me.

> And I told you to go fuck yourself.

The slamming of the front door distracts me. The sound of hurried footsteps on the stairs steals my attention altogether. I pocket my phone and instantly forget about my asshole ex. By the time I make it to the foyer, Parker is long gone, though his backpack rests haphazardly at the foot of the steps.

I quickly poke my head into the living room. Sophia is still set up on the couch, watching whatever mind-numbing kids' show is popular right now. Days with her are easy. It's only at night that her emotions wreak havoc. It's only at night that I hear her cry. Sleep hasn't come easy for either of us lately.

Upstairs, I find my brother in his bedroom. He angrily tugs at the tie from his school uniform that is still looped around his neck. His fingers shake, making the task impossible.

"Let me help," I say. I brush his hands away, and then I work to gently loosen the knot. "Want to tell me what's wrong? Why are you home so early?"

Why didn't you tell me you were leaving school? Going out in the rain?

I keep those questions to myself. The last thing I want is for him to see me as overbearing.

The relationship I had with Parker was always an easy one. I was ten when he was born and I loved every minute of having a baby brother. When I got to high school, things changed, but I always made time for him. Our parents' deaths have tested that relationship, bending it so far that I'm terrified one of these days it will break.

In a split second, I went from being his older sister to

being his guardian. Things that I never had to think about before now occupy all my waking thoughts, bleeding into my dreams. If you can even call them dreams.

"I'm not going back there," he replies.

I thought two weeks was too soon to head back to school. To start a new year, no less. But he was insistent, and I didn't want to disrupt his routine any more than it already had been. So he went. I dropped him off this morning, an encouraging and utterly hollow smile on my face.

I nod, tossing the tie onto his bed. "We can wait, Parker. There's no rush. Your teachers will understand."

"*No.*" His voice cracks with emotion. "I'm *never* going back."

"What happened?"

That question feels woefully inadequate. So much has happened, and any number of things could be causing his turmoil.

Frustrated tears gather in his eyes. "Do you know what everyone is saying?"

Dread weighs me down, like cinder blocks tied to my ankles. I fear that his response will be the same reason I haven't been on social media or answered any of my friends' texts.

"They're talking about—" He shakes his head. "They're saying he did it on purpose, Delilah. Because of you."

I was expecting it, but the words land like a blow to the face anyway. When your father is the leader of an entire province, your life is open to a whole host of scrutiny. That only multiplies when word gets out that he was involved in a car accident. I made the mistake of checking my Instagram notifications a few nights after the news broke, and I really wish that I hadn't. I promptly switched my account to private and deleted all my previous posts. I didn't even bother looking at my messages.

The truth is, no one will ever really know what happened that day. According to the emergency crews, it was a simple accident. Though there's nothing simple about death. All I know is that my parents are gone and I have to figure out how to be okay with that. Scratch that—I don't think I'll ever be okay. But for Parker and Sophia, I'm going to have to pretend.

I pull my brother into my arms. His recent growth spurt has left him taller than me, so his chin rests on top of my head. I'm not sure who this hug benefits more—me or him.

"Why is this happening to us?" Parker whispers.

Why? I have been asking myself that question about a hundred times a day for weeks. I haven't yet managed to find the answer.

"I don't know." I swallow the emotion welling in my chest, begging to be let free. "But we're gonna get through it."

We have to. I refuse to let my siblings drown under this weight. I'll carry it all if I have to.

"Are you hungry?" I ask, pulling away. "I could use some food."

A lie. My appetite these days is abysmal, but when you have a picky four-year-old on your hands that likes to skip out on vegetables, you have to set a good example. Even if that means forcing food down your throat when everything tastes like cardboard.

Parker sniffs, wiping roughly at a tear that managed to escape. "Not if you're planning to make it."

"Hey!" A small smile, almost genuine, blooms on my lips. "That's rude."

His answering grin is teasing. The edges are a little rough, tinged in emotion, but the fact that he's smiling at all is a win in my book. "You're the worst cook in this family and you know it."

Family. However imperfect, that's what the five of us were. And now there are only three.

I clear my throat. "There are enough casseroles in the fridge to last us through the apocalypse. I'm sure one of them will live up to your standards."

We descend the stairs and I collect Sophia from the living room. In the kitchen, I go through the motions of doling out portions of casserole and heating them in the microwave. The thought of using the oven is daunting—I'm way too tired. Tired in the way that sleep can't fix.

In the distance, thunder claps, and I jump. It carries on like an avenging angel, setting the earth to rights. But my world has already been tilted off its axis, and it will never be the same again.

CHAPTER ONE
LUKE

"*C'MON*, LADY!"

The telltale whine of someone not getting their way floats through the air as I pull open the door to the restaurant. A month or so from now, a Saturday afternoon in the thick of summer, a line will trail from the host stand, out the door and around the corner of the building. Today, business is leisurely, giving me a front row seat to the scene unfolding at the bar.

My sister, like always, is stationed behind the counter. Dockside has been her home away from home since high school, and rarely does she let anyone else tend the bar. Right now, her arms are crossed as she regards the men in front of her.

On closer inspection, I note that the *men* are really boys. They're both sporting cutoff muscle tanks, cargo shorts and flip flops—the standard uniform of a young Kip Island summer tourist—but all their attire does is highlight their spindly limbs.

"I *said* no," Clara emphasizes.

One of the teens crosses his own arms. "Why do you have to be such a goddamn bit—"

I'd already witnessed enough, but the audacity of this kid to call my sister a bitch has me seeing red. As I step up to the bar beside the boys, I try to rein in my anger. I somehow manage because my voice is level when I ask, "What's going on?"

My sister's lips purse at my interjection, but I pay her no mind. Clara has had an aversion to my help ever since we were kids. As her older brother, it was expected of me, but I'd be lying if I said I didn't enjoy it, too. I like taking care of my family.

The spokesperson for the duo throws his hands in the air. "This chick is refusing to serve us. And she won't give us our IDs back!" He says this in a way that assumes I'll share in his commiseration.

Clara scowls at him. "Because they're *fake*."

"They are not!" His chest puffs out in defiance. "We're twenty-one."

I hold a hand out, and with an eye roll, Clara relinquishes the driver's licences. Being right across the lake from Michigan, I'm more than familiar with their state IDs. Year-round, but especially in the summer months, a slew of American teens like to come to the island to openly indulge, and some get into more than their share of trouble. I'll give it to the boys—these are good, but they severely overshot with their supposed birthdates.

"The good news is the drinking age in Ontario is nineteen," I tell them. "The bad news is that you're definitely not nineteen, let alone twenty-one."

"You said it was the same!" the quiet boy says, shoving the other.

"Shut up!" the loud one hisses.

"Tell you what." I make a show of tucking the fakes into my pocket. "I'll keep these. And you can either ask Clara nicely for a cold pop or be on your way."

The quiet one shrinks in defeat. The loud one, however, sizes me up to see just how serious I am. I arch a brow. When his eyes land on my uniform, he joins his friend.

Once the boys scurry out the door, Clara throws a rag at my chest. "I was handling that, you know," she grouses.

I reach across the bar to ruffle her hair. "*Oh, thank you, Luke,*" I mock.

She crosses her arms as she dodges me. "I'm not *thanking* you for steamrolling me." She glowers. "I'm not a little kid. I don't need coddling."

I sigh. "I know you're not, Clarebear. I was just trying to help keep the trouble out."

She scoffs. "Pretty sure the hooligan ousting is usually handled by the police, not the fire chief."

She's not wrong. But with a police force as small as the one on Kip Island, I've become something of a multitasker. I can keep on top of my own reports, grease the wheels of bureaucracy, and make sure my family is safe.

"Would you accept that I was on my way to beg you to feed me lunch and the well-meaning brother in me didn't like seeing someone give you a hard time?"

A wicked gleam enters her eyes. "Only if you let me decide what you're eating."

I bite back a groan of protest. As I lower myself to a barstool, I point a finger at her. "No kale."

She shakes her head. "When you're fifty and your cholesterol is shit, don't come crying to me."

I simply grin in response. With a parting eye roll, Clara heads over to the computer to send my order to the kitchen. Before she can return my way, a customer grabs her attention, and I watch in evergreen fascination as she expertly mixes their drink.

For as long as I can remember, it's been a widely-accepted fact that Clara was always meant to run Dockside. She started with serving tea to her dolls, and now she pours shots for tipsy bachelorettes. You wouldn't expect it just by looking at her, but Clara can—and often does—command a room full of rowdy drunks with a snap of her fingers.

"I'm meeting the new tenant tomorrow morning," Clara says when she returns, propping an elbow on the gleaming surface of the bar.

I tense. "New tenant?"

She nods. "The pink house. She is *so* nice! And she has a younger brother and sister." She keeps talking, going on about this tenant, completely oblivious to my growing annoyance.

"When were you planning to mention that Muriel moved out?"

Along with Dockside, and the bed and breakfast they run out of our childhood home, our parents own a string of brightly-coloured houses on Hawberry Lane. Mom and Dad have their hands full with the bed and breakfast, so Clara has taken it upon herself to manage the rental properties on top of her duties at the restaurant. For most of my life, the pink house has been occupied by a sweet older woman named Muriel. As far as I knew, it still was.

My sister blinks. "Um, right now? She decided that she wanted to be closer to her grandkids and they both live on the mainland now. She left last week."

I scowl. "You should've told me *before* you drew up the new lease."

Now it's Clara's turn to scowl. "Why? So you could think of a million stupid reasons why she's not good enough to rent from us?"

Her words make me sound like a judgmental asshole. Hell, maybe I am, but you can't do a job like mine without it eroding some of the trust you have in the world—in people. I'm cautious on a good day, but with my family, I take no chances. I already made that mistake once.

"So I could be aware of who's going to be living in the house our parents own for who knows how long."

It's not as if the island doesn't see an influx of strangers. Come summertime, when tourist season is at its peak, we get people from all over. But the rental Clara is talking about isn't a vacation spot—it's long-term. This new tenant, whoever she is, is planning to stick around.

Clara's eyes roll again. "I suppose you also won't like the fact that I'm planning to offer her a job."

"*Clara*," I scold. "Do you even really know this woman?"

She points a finger at me. "Don't you dare patronize me, Lucas Bowman. You forget that I know all the ways to make you cry mercy. Keep it up and I'll put my skills to good use."

For now, I drop the subject, because my food is about to be ready and I honestly wouldn't put it past my sister to spit in it.

As I eat, the customers begin to shift. The leisurely pace from before is lost for a time as more boats dock at the marina and their passengers traipse through the doors looking for a quick bite. Then my favourite customer of all comes barrelling in.

"Clary!"

At the sound of her nickname, my sister rounds the bar and crouches just as a forty-pound ball of energy, disguised in dark curls and a blue polka dot dress, crashes into her. My sister laughs as she falls back on her ass, her arms tight around Abbie's back.

"My favourite niece!" Clara says with a squeal.

Following behind Abbie, with much less enthusiasm, is Clara's twin. Abbie pulls out of Clara's arms and sticks her tongue out at him.

"I win, Daddy!" she taunts.

Gabe grins. "You're too fast, Princess."

Gabe slides onto a stool, leaving one open between us for Abbie. He rubs a hand over his tired face. It seems running around after his daughter has finally caught up to my brother. In this moment, he looks much older than his twenty-eight years.

"Rough day?" I ask.

Gabe sighs. "She woke up *four* times last night, yet she's full of energy while I'm dead on my feet."

I frown. "The nightmares again?"

He shakes his head, a confused frown on his face. "No, she hasn't had those in months. It's just one of those phases where she thinks she doesn't need to sleep."

As Clara lifts our niece onto her stool, I'm reminded of the argument we were in the middle of. I turn back to Gabe. "Tell her it was a bad idea to rent out the pink house and *hire* the new tenant without consulting me first."

Clara butts in before he can respond. "Ugh, this again. Gabriel, please tell *Chief Tight-ass* that I'm a big girl who knows what she's doing. I run a successful restaurant and manage all our parents' properties—I'm not stupid."

Abbie points a finger at her aunt. "*Ooo*, Clary, you said a bad word!"

Gabe rubs his temples. "I am not getting involved with this. Every time I pick a side, it doesn't end well for me."

"Because you always pick the *wrong* one!" Clara counters, stomping her foot. "I'm your twin. You're supposed to be on my side."

I shrug. "Brothers have to stick together."

Clara sticks out her tongue, and then her gaze focuses on Abbie. "Well, so do aunts and nieces," she says. "How would you feel about a sleepover tonight?"

Abbie's eyes light up. "Yes, yes, yes!"

Clara holds a hand to the side of her mouth, as if shielding her words from me and Gabe. "I'll even let you have ice cream before dinner. But don't tell your dad."

Abbie's excited eyes flit to Gabe and then back again. She holds out a palm to Clara. "Deal."

As they shake hands, Gabe looks on in amusement. Then

his head swings my way. "Apparently I have a free night. Want to grab a beer later?"

I grimace. Usually the majority of tourists and cottagers don't start to arrive until after the May long weekend, but already the island is starting to notice an uptick in traffic. With that comes more accidents. More accidents mean more paperwork.

"Rain check?" I ask. "The summer volunteers start next week, and then I'll have more free time."

Gabe snorts. "Free time. *Right*."

"You work too much," Clara says.

I groan. "You sound like Mom."

"You mean we're both incredibly intelligent women? Yes, we are. Thanks for noticing."

I cover Abbie's ears with my hands. "I mean you're both a pain in my ass."

Abbie wiggles in my hold. "I know you're saying bad words, Lukey!"

"Yeah, *Lukey*," Clara chastises, "cut it out!"

I throw a fry at her, but she expertly catches it in her mouth. A lifetime of running around with me and Gabe taught her that.

"What about him?" I ask, pointing to our brother. "You never get on his case about work."

"There's a difference between a little overtime and making work your entire personality," Clara replies.

"I can't just dump my responsibilities. In case you haven't noticed, I'm in charge of an entire fire department."

"Yeah," Gabe says with a roll of his eyes, "we've noticed."

No matter how many times I explain it to them, my

family just doesn't *get* it. The constant worry is a foreign concept. Our parents, Clara, Gabe and Abbie—they're all I have. One misjudgment almost cost me someone I love once before. I can't—I *won't*—make that mistake again. If that makes me the no-fun uncle and the always busy brother, then so be it.

At least I won't have to race through fire again, wondering if it's too late.

CHAPTER TWO
DELILAH

"SISSY, LOOK!"

My brain, lagging from the lack of sleep I've gotten in the past week, is slow to register my sister calling for me. While I'm in desperate need of a bed, Sophia is wired, as if we didn't wake up before the sun in order to catch our ferry from Tobermory.

I've always been a little impulsive. When I decide I want something, I go for it. But I truly never thought a postcard would be the thing to prompt a move halfway across the country.

Two months ago, as I stood in line at the post office, a piece of mail fluttering to the floor caught my attention. Without thinking twice, I picked it up. I have no idea what the postcard said—all I remember is the image of the lighthouse standing proudly on the shore. The owner of the postcard snatched it out of my hand shortly thereafter, but I managed to catch the inscription.

Greetings from Kip Island.

I completed my business at the post office in a daze. To this day, I'm not entirely sure that I sent that paperwork to the right place. All I knew was that I needed to be wherever Kip Island was.

Perhaps it was ill-advised to make a drastic life change based on a stranger's postcard, but I had felt unmoored since the moment I found out about the accident. That lighthouse felt like a tether—something I could reach for to pull myself out of the fog like the ships of long ago.

"Sissy, Sissy, *look*!"

Again, Sophia points across the water. I follow her finger to where the white lighthouse—arguably what Kip Island is most famous for—juts off the horizon, standing proudly. The reds and oranges of the rising sun serve as a picturesque backdrop, exactly like the one off that postcard.

A promise of sanctuary.

My sister's little hands grip the metal rail in excitement as she tries to peer over the edge of the boat, and I can't help but tighten my hold around her middle in response. My mind flashes with images of her falling overboard and me being helpless to stop it. I refuse to lose someone else. Not to mention, the papers would have a field day when they inevitably found out who I am. It's bad enough that our parents' accident was splashed all over the news. They don't need to report that the daughter of British Columbia's former premier got her little sister killed, too.

"Careful, Soph, or you'll be swimming with the fish."

"I wanna swim with the fishies, Sissy," she says. "I wanna be a mermaid!"

Says the girl that can't handle her face getting wet when

it's time for a bath. I'm surprised the spray coming up off the water hasn't bothered her yet. Though that is due, in great part, to the way the island has mesmerized her. Sophia is probably the only one out of the three of us actually *excited* about this move. When I showed her pictures of the lighthouse, beach and quaint downtown, she wanted to pack her bags immediately.

I smile as I tuck a strand of hair behind her ear. While both Parker and I share the same dark brown hair, Sophia's is almost a white blonde. Our parents' decision to foster and then adopt her when she was a baby had taken me by surprise. I was the product of a rather eventful homecoming night, and Parker came along as planned ten years later. The idea of adding a baby to the mix when I was twenty-one had been a little off-putting at first. But then I saw her adorably chubby face and none of my reservations mattered anymore.

"If you want to be a mermaid, then that's what you'll be."

I don't realize what I said at first. Not until my eyes prick with involuntary tears.

If you want to be a photographer, then that's what you'll be.

I wasn't much older than Sophia when our mother said those words to me. I was fooling around with a disposable camera, getting my thumb in all the shots, when she asked me what I wanted to be when I grew up. I thought about it for a second and then declared I was going to be the best photographer in the world. And she smiled.

I swallow thickly as I try to dislodge my mother's words from my brain. Simply because I never managed to follow through. Given everything, a business degree seemed like a more suitable path.

When Sophia looks over her shoulder, beaming up at me, it gets a little easier to breathe. Every time she does, I swear my heart doubles in size. Because it means that she's happy, and that perhaps I'm not messing up as royally as I think I am.

"*Pretty*," she whispers, eyes glazing over as she stares at the horizon.

In the distance, Kip Island, the biggest in an archipelago on Lake Huron, welcomes us. We left the mainland just as the first rays of light were beginning to peek out, scaring the moon into submission. Now sunrise is in full force and I itch for the weight of my camera in my hand, but it's tucked away in the trunk of my car. I settle for my phone, pulling it from the back pocket of my shorts and aiming it one-handed toward the scene beyond the bow. I snap a dozen pictures before I put my phone away. I hope at least one of them isn't blurry.

It's been a long time since I felt the urge to take pictures. Eight months, to be precise. I hardly ever went a day without my camera in hand, but that was before. Before I messed up. Before our parents died. Before I became the guardian of both my younger siblings. It's hard to find joy in a hobby when tiredness clouds your soul.

The breeze cutting across the lake whips Sophia's hair into her face. I smooth it back again and secure it in a ponytail with one of the hair ties that are always on my wrist. My own hair is tucked into a ponytail, up and out of my face the way I like it. I hardly ever wear it down, and when I do, I almost always regret it.

The ferry begins to slow as we approach the shore. I can see the lighthouse looming closer, the marina dotted with boats of all shapes and sizes. It's still early May, but the weather is warm. Even if it wasn't, the island is charming enough to make visitors forget about subpar temperatures. All the articles I read online said that a trip any time of the year was worthwhile. I hope it's all true considering we're going to be here longer than a simple vacation. At least a year, given the lease I signed on our new house.

A voice crackles over the speaker system, instructing everyone to return to their vehicles parked on the lowest level of the boat. I tug Sophia from the rail, setting her back on her feet.

These past few months have not been easy on my baby sister. She is the strongest, most resilient girl I know, but I still worry. That's why we came here. Kip Island may be charming, but it is also symbolic of the fresh start Sophia needs. The fresh start we *all* need.

"Where's Parker?" Sophia asks.

I glance toward the starboard side of the boat. Our brother leans over the rail, much like Sophia had a moment ago. His hood is drawn over his head, likely hiding the earbud playing music that is way too loud.

"Parker!" I call. "Time to head back to the car!"

For a moment, I think he's going to ignore me. He has grown exceptionally good at that over the past eight months. Thankfully, he pushes off the rail and stuffs his hands in his pockets, making his way back to us.

Sophia isn't old enough to know the details of how our parents died, but Parker is. I worry about Sophia, but I'm actively concerned about Parker. I know that sixteen-year-olds aren't perpetual sunshines and rainbows, but my brother has nearly disappeared and I don't know how to get him back.

"Can we get ice cream, Sissy?" Sophia asks.

I grin as I swing her up on my hip and start to migrate toward our car. Sophia has always been small for her age, but I swear all these changes have made her shrink. Still, I know it won't be long until I can't hold her in my arms anymore.

"Ice cream? We haven't even had breakfast yet!"

Sophia offers me a cheeky grin. "Ice cream for breakfast, please!"

I laugh. "I'll think about it. We have to go see our new house first."

I buckle Sophia into her booster, and then I round to the driver's side of the car. Parker is already in the passenger seat, head turned out the window. I don't even try to make conversation.

Before long, the ferry docks, and then I follow the line of vehicles making their exit. When the tires hit solid ground, I breathe a sigh of relief.

To the left of the dock, the lighthouse, situated on the point, is even more impressive up close. At the base, a lakeside restaurant is just waking up, staff bustling about to get ready for opening. I recognize the restaurant as the one owned by our new landlord. To the right of the dock, Main Street runs along the edge of the lake. Storefronts, a coffee shop, a couple banks, the post office and the library—the extent of Kip Island's downtown.

I hang a right, settling into the flow of early morning traffic. I've never been to Kip Island before, but I can't help that it feels distinctly like coming home.

"We're lost."

"We are *not* lost," I insist. "This island is tiny. We can't be lost!"

Parker slumps further in the passenger seat. "We were supposed to be there twenty minutes ago," he grumbles. "We're lost."

I steer my car into the roundabout in front of the little public library for the third time, and *okay*, maybe we're a bit lost. To be fair, the directions given to me by the property manager of our new rental don't make much sense, and even the GPS is confused.

I jab at the built-in navigation screen, eyes darting between it and the road. "Just give me a minute. I'll get us unlost."

Parker snorts. "Good luck with that."

But I don't need luck. Just sheer determination and the will of a woman who is sick of letting her family down.

I ease my foot off the accelerator, slowing the vehicle to a crawl. I know I'm breaking at least a couple laws right now, but I refuse to get this wrong and give Parker another reason to hate me. I keep fiddling with the screen, glancing up every now and then.

"Delilah!"

My head shoots toward the windshield and I realize that we're way too close to the truck in front of us. I slam on the brakes and wince when I hear the sound of metal scraping against metal. *Oh my God. What did I just do?*

"Shit," I curse.

"Sissy!" Sophia gasps. "You're not 'upposed to say that."

"Yeah, *Sissy*, that's a bad word," Parker mocks.

I shoot my brother a sharp look. Now, when my panic is beginning to rise, is not the time for snarky remarks. I bite back another expletive. My hands begin to get clammy as the full scope of my actions starts to set in.

Out the windshield, I watch the truck door open, and then boot-clad feet hit the asphalt. A man steps out and comes to stand by the hood of my car. His brown hair is neatly cut, a little longer on the top and shorter on the sides. A fitted black t-shirt stretches across a broad chest and toned shoulders. Never before have I noticed a guy's *shoulders*. But I notice his.

I also notice the way his brown eyes seem to be assessing me through the glass, the same way that I am him. He's looking right at me, and I'm afraid he sees everything I'm desperately trying to hide.

At this point, I realize I should probably stop staring and actually do something. I scramble to unhook my seatbelt as I ready myself to face the music. When I get out of the car and take a look at the damage, the guy just continues to study me.

Wincing, I turn toward him. "Uh, hi," I say stupidly.

And then I wave.

Please, someone kill me now.

CHAPTER THREE
LUKE

MORNINGS on the island are my favourite.

Quiet blankets the town, and my truck is the only vehicle on the road. The mornings hang on to the crisp chill from the night before, so when I roll my windows down, the fresh air sharpens my lungs.

On my way to the station, I make a point of driving down Main Street. At the end of the road, the lighthouse—and my family's restaurant—looms. Beyond Dockside's steady presence lie the calm waters of Lake Huron. As the day breaks and the town comes to life, so too will the lake. The water that once lapped at the rocky edge of the island will roll, as boats begin to dock at the marina, and the ferry makes more frequent trips back and forth to the mainland.

Some people might feel stuck living on an island—fenced in by water on all sides. I don't share that particular sentiment. I like the insularity. Having grown up here, I know exactly what to expect. This town and its routines are nothing if not reliable. Everyone in my high school graduating class couldn't wait to get off the island. They were under the impression that things were better out there, and they had their sights set on a life beyond this shoreline. I left, too, but I always knew I would be back. A few short years away at college and then I moved home.

The familiarity is a comfort when a large part of my job is battling the unknown. There are aspects to fire that can be predictable, but every situation is wildly different and I never quite know what I'm sending my team into. In the other areas of my life, I do my best to keep careful control of the things I can. I know firsthand what happens when I don't.

At the end of Main Street, I pull into a parking spot right in front of the one and only café. As I hop out of my truck, I watch the barista set the sandwich board up on the sidewalk. When she sees me, she greets me with a smile. The laugh lines around her dark eyes crinkle and the grey-streaked brunette strands of her bob wave.

"Morning, Chief Bowman!" Loretta calls.

I nod. "Morning."

I hold the front door open for her and then follow her inside. We make idle conversation as she rounds the counter to start on my usual black coffee. It isn't long before I'm back in my truck and on my way to work, the same as every other day. Predictable—just the way I like it.

With my window cracked and some old country song playing softly on the radio, I cruise down the street. Yellow and orange paint the sky as the sun continues its ascent.

As I'm coming up to a four-way stop, I look in my rear view mirror and notice a car behind me. Other than my truck, it seems to be the only one on the road. I take my foot off the accelerator and step gradually on the brake, rolling to a halt at the stop sign. The driver behind me doesn't do the same.

I hardly feel the impact, but when I look again in my mirror, I can tell that the car is much too close to my bumper. I curse under my breath as I shift into park and throw my hazard lights on. The last thing I want to do this morning is deal with this, but I feel an obligation to at least make sure the other driver is alright.

I slide out of my truck and head to the back to assess the situation. The driver, a woman in her mid-twenties, still sits in her seat, mouth agape. Her hands grip the steering wheel at ten and two. She isn't someone I recognize which means she isn't from around here. She drives an Audi—some kind of sporty crossover. Her plates indicate she's from out west. *Tourist*, it screams.

I don't think I'll ever get used to the amount of vacationers the island pulls in each summer. We've always been a destination for cottagers and the odd weekender, but about a decade ago, some travel blogger wrote a whole piece on the month she spent here. It went viral, and suddenly people began to flock to our shores. The growth since has been exponential. Both a blessing and a curse.

The woman shakes herself from her daze and finally steps out of the car. As she rounds the hood to inspect the damage for herself, I get an eyeful of the smooth, tempting skin of her legs not covered by her denim shorts. *A goddamn curse indeed*.

"Uh, hi," she says with a small wave.

Before I can say anything, she spins away from me to take

a longer look at the damage. When she bends at the waist, eyeing her bumper, I have to clench my jaw and turn away.

The woman just rear-ended me, for Christ's sake. I should be focused on getting her insurance information, not admiring the long, graceful lines of her limbs. Still, I can't stop myself from turning back and drinking in the sight of her again. This time, I notice more than just her legs. Long, dark brown hair held in a ponytail drapes over her back, but a few strands have come loose and now frame her face. A tight black t-shirt clings to her torso and chest, matching the black Vans she wears on her feet. I can just see the edge of black ink peeking out from the sleeve of her shirt.

She stands to her full height, putting her about half a foot shorter than my six feet. She places her hands on her hips, and I try to stop my eyes from wandering there, too.

"It doesn't look too bad," she says with a nod. "Just a little tap."

Her words pull my focus from admiring her physical attributes. Instead, I find myself scowling. For some reason, what she said irks me. Her unaffected tone has my shoulders tensing. It's true—this accident could have been worse. I've *seen* worse. But the blasé way she dismisses this as a simple near-miss doesn't sit quite right with me.

"Just a *little tap*?" My words come out hardened with irritation. "Your headlight is busted."

If I was in anything other than my truck, like the old Volkswagen Beetle my sister insists on driving, the back bumper would be a mess.

Her eyes widen, and the bone-deep weariness I see in her expression catches me by surprise. It gives me pause. My annoyance shifts from a rolling boil to a slow simmer. The minute shaking I notice in her hands snuffs my irritation out altogether. In my head, I can hear Clara chastising me for being rude. My mother, too. They both think my delivery, at times, leaves something to be desired.

When I take note of the teenage boy in the passenger seat, and the wide-eyed young girl in the back, about Abbie's age, I sigh. Then I let the tension fully run from my body. "Are you all okay?" I ask. My voice, hardly in use yet this morning, comes out gruff. "No one's hurt?"

She shakes her head. "No, we're fine." Her teeth snag her bottom lip. I can't seem to look away. "Are you?"

I nod jerkily. "Fine."

The passenger door of her car opens and the teenager steps out. He tugs the hood off his head, revealing shaggy hair the same shade as the woman's. They're definitely related, then.

The woman sighs. "I'm sorry. I was trying to get our stupid GPS to work and I wasn't paying close enough attention."

Call it run-off adrenaline or pure insanity. Whatever it is, I can't even begin to describe why I decide to blurt out my next words. "Have you been drinking?"

The teenage boy—her brother?—snickers from his spot beside her. I meant it as a joke, but by the way her eyes widen, she doesn't take it that way. Maybe Clara and my mother were on to something about my delivery.

"What? No!" she cries. "It's seven-thirty in the morning!"

Because I can't seem to leave well enough alone, I turn to the boy. "She telling the truth?"

His answering nod is morose. "Unfortunately." Then he glances at his phone. "We're *really* late now."

She turns to glare at him. "*Thank you*, Parker. So helpful."

He throws his hands up in surrender. "I was just saying," he mutters.

Her sigh gives way to hidden frustration. For a second, the unaffected demeanour she presents herself with is torn away. Perhaps she isn't as happy-go-lucky as she likes to make people think.

"Let me grab my insurance stuff," she says.

We exchange information and phone numbers, and then all that's left for me to do is get in my truck and drive away. Instead, I decide to stick my foot in it again. It's none of my business, really, except others' reckless actions make my skin itch.

"You should be more careful," I say. "This could've ended a lot worse."

Her eyes harden at this. *Shit*. I sound like her dad, reprimanding her for hopping a curb when she's learning how to drive. That is the last thing I want to be.

"Noted," she says. She crosses her arms defensively. "If you could just point me in the direction of Hawberry Lane, we'll be on our way."

I should say something. *Fix this, you idiot*.

"Take the next exit off the roundabout and follow the road until it forks. Take the fork or you'll wind up right back here."

"Thank you," she sniffs.

She gestures for Parker to get back in the car and then she does the same. Metal scrapes as she throws the car in reverse and backs away from my bumper. And then I stand there like the idiot I am, watching her speed away.

Delilah Delacroix.

Her name rolls around in my head as I drive the rest of the way to the station. When I arrive, I note that the engine bay door is open as my brother and Connor, one of the guys on our crew, hose down the rig. It's a cold day in hell when my baby brother beats me to work. He usually rolls into the parking lot right at the last second, walking through the door just as his shift starts.

"Good of you to join us, Chief!" Gabe calls with a smirk.

I roll my eyes. "Considering how often you slide in just under the wire, I think I'm entitled to be late once."

"He's not wrong," Connor interjects.

Gabe flips his friend the bird. "I should have left your ass behind in grade nine gym class."

Connor scoffs. "If anyone was being left behind, it was *you*. Couldn't catch a ball for shit."

I leave the pair to their bickering as I head deeper into the station. It isn't long before I hear footsteps trailing behind me, and then my brother is following me into my office. Every other firefighter here knows how to knock. Gabe doesn't.

"Everything alright?" he asks. "You're never late."

That's the thing about Gabe. Even though he could spend all day giving me shit, he actually cares, too. It isn't always easy working together or being his boss, but I know that I can count on him when it matters. I consider telling him about the accident—about Delilah. Knowing Gabe, he would probably have a good laugh at my expense. But for some reason, I can't make the words come out.

"I just slept in. Must've forgotten to set an alarm."

I know it's a bullshit excuse. *He* knows it's a bullshit excuse. Thankfully, he accepts it anyway. He gives me an acknowledging nod, pats the doorframe and then heads back toward the engine bay.

I try to focus on the report I'm meant to be working on, but it's no use. I keep replaying the accident over and over again. I feel bad, chastising her like that. And if we report this accident, her insurance will only get more expensive. Half an hour later, I pull out my phone and send her a text.

> Don't worry about going through insurance. The truck is fine.

DELILAH
> Are you sure?

> Just get that headlight fixed.

She doesn't respond right away. My knee begins to bounce involuntarily as I force myself not to stare at my phone.

DELILAH

Aye aye, Captain.

Sorry, *Chief.

I shake my head. She must've seen the lettering on my truck and put the pieces together. Despite myself, I smile. Although a fender bender isn't the most ideal way to start the morning, I have to acknowledge that it's the most excitement I've had in a while.

Stowing my phone in a drawer, I turn back to my report. But I can't seem to get the image of a certain woman out of my head.

CHAPTER FOUR
DELILAH

GOD, that was embarrassing.

I've been driving for almost a decade and I've never been in an accident before. I've come close, but I have never actually collided with another vehicle. It was just my luck that the person I hit is not only the fire chief of our new town, but he also happens to be the most beautiful man I think I've ever laid eyes on. At first I thought my tired eyes were deceiving me, but no—he really is just that pretty.

And then he opened his mouth.

There's nothing quite like the shame of being chastised. Coming from him, it made me bristle. He unknowingly poked at an old wound, and it ached, like pressing on a bruise just to see if it still hurt. I messed up—I *know* I messed up.

But he also pulled a laugh out of Parker. I've been waiting on that laugh for months. No matter how annoyed I am at the man, I am grateful for that.

Stubbornly, I want to ignore his directions and find the house myself, but Sophia is getting antsy and Parker is back to pretending I don't exist. So I give in and do as he said. Much to my displeasure, it doesn't take us long to pull onto Hawberry Lane. The street is small, tucked away on the outskirts of the downtown area. Trees line either side of the road, dressed in varying shades of summer green.

"Sissy, are we almost there?" Sophia asks from the back.

"Don't ask her, Soph," Parker says. "She just got us lost."

"Hey, I also got us *un*lost, just like I said I would."

Parker snorts. "I think the credit actually goes to that guy you hit."

I look in the rear view mirror at my sister. "We're almost there, Soph."

I hope.

The houses here are smaller than the ones in our old neighbourhood, but the yards are larger. They aren't stacked on top of one another like in the city, but you're still close to your neighbours. Although the sun has risen, the island is still sleeping, savouring this Sunday in late spring. There were hardly any cars on the road in town, and the same can be said for this street. It's an eerie kind of quiet, but one I could picture myself getting used to.

I am more than ready for a change of pace.

When I pull into the driveway, Sophia gasps from the backseat. The house—*our* house—is tiny and coloured a light pink. It matches the neighbouring houses in architecture, though each one is painted in varying shades of pink, green, blue and white. The front porch, painted white to match the house's trim, looks almost brand new. There's even a porch swing, which is what drew me to the house in the first place.

"We're gonna live in a Barbie house, Sissy!" she squeals.

I hide my grimace. The house itself is perfect for us, but pink is certainly not a colour I would normally go for. Though in a place like Kip Island, long-term rentals are few and far between, so I learned rather quickly to take what I could get.

"What do you think?" I ask Parker.

The old version of my brother would crack a joke about the house. This version of him only grunts. My hands tighten on the steering wheel. I want to assure him that this is hard for me, too, but every time I even remotely try to relate to how he's feeling, it doesn't go well.

Once I exit the car and help Sophia out of her seat, I note the woman standing on the front step. She waves as we approach, meeting us halfway down the short driveway. Parker trails behind.

"Hi!" The smiling blonde bounces on the balls of her feet, giving away her excitement. "I'm Clara. It's so nice to officially meet you!"

Clara looks every bit as sweet in person as she sounded over the phone. Her long hair is plaited in two braids and the cardigan she's wearing over her summery dress gives off girl-next-door vibes. She is effortlessly everything that my ex tried to mould me to be.

When I settled on Kip Island as our new home, the listing for this rental didn't pop up right away. The ones that did, I was turned away for one reason or another. I was about to give up—I was barely hanging on by a thread as it was—and then I saw Clara's listing.

After our initial phone call, she and I messaged back and forth. First, with my inquiries about renting, and then with all the details about our arrival. She also made a point to give me a rundown of everything the island has to offer—restaurants, stores, parks. And then our conversations spiralled into unimportant things.

They tell you not to talk to strangers. To be cautious of the people you meet online. But I needed someone who didn't already know me or what my family had been through. Being in Clara's presence now, I feel inclined to fall at her feet in thanks. She'll never know just how much I needed her. How much her hand, extended into the dark, gave me the strength to step into the light. Like my lighthouse in human form.

I've never been short on social relationships, but I don't think I've ever truly had a friend.

I return her smile. "Delilah." I tug my sister against my side. "And this is my sister, Sophia, and my brother, Parker."

"Hi, Parker." She grins at him, but he doesn't respond. Clara's smile gentles on Sophia as she presses shyly into me. "Hi, Sophia. You know, my niece is about your age. Maybe you and Abbie could have a play date."

A play date where the other adults in the room don't look at me with pity? I could weep at the thought alone. It would be nice not having to wonder whether the looks I'm getting are because they've seen my nudes or because they're sorry my parents are dead. Or a delightful combination of both.

"Soph would love that," I say.

"Abbie would, too. She's always looking to make new friends," Clara replies. Then she gestures toward the front door. It's painted a soft white to match the porch. "I'll just show you around quickly, and then I'll leave you to get settled."

Clara unlocks the door, and then she ushers us inside. Parker opts to sit on the front step and pull out his phone.

Her tour of the small house is very thorough. The front door opens into the living room and kitchen. Heading down a narrow hallway, you hit the back of the house where the biggest bedroom and its matching en suite is. Up a set of stairs, you are met with two small bedrooms and another bathroom. There is also, thankfully, a closet with a stacked washer and dryer. Most of the house is unfurnished, but there are a few staples already here.

The majority of our furniture got sold with the house when our childhood home was listed. The rest is being sent later this week to fill in some of the gaps.

In the grand scheme of things, this house isn't much, but it's more than what we had before because it comes with something precious: *freedom*. No one on this island knows who we are or the situation we came from. I crave the anonymity.

"Thank you, Clara," I say as I take the keys.

She beams from her spot on the front steps. "Thank *you*. I was kinda worried this gorgeous girl might sit empty for a while. I'm glad you're giving her a purpose."

I chuckle. "Soph has already started calling it the Barbie house, so it will be well-loved while we're here."

Clara winks at Sophia. "I like the way you think, little miss."

Sophia offers her a small smile. Over the course of our tour, my sister began to slowly warm up to Clara. She still hasn't said anything, but she isn't hiding behind me anymore. Progress.

Something—one of the *many* things—that keeps me up at night is the worry that everything Soph has been through has made her retreat into her shell. I don't want that for her. I don't want that for Parker either.

"If you need anything, just let me know," Clara offers.

My phone buzzes in my pocket. I give her an apologetic look as I fish it out and click open my notifications.

> **UNKNOWN NUMBER**
> Don't worry about going through insurance. The truck is fine.

> Are you sure?

> **UNKNOWN NUMBER**
> Just get that headlight fixed.

I roll my eyes.

> Aye aye, Captain.

> Sorry, *Chief.

"Good news?"

I look up, startled. "Huh?"

Clara smirks. "You're smiling at your phone."

Am I smiling? Sure enough, my lips are still stretched up in a grin. I shake my head, shoving my phone back in my pocket. "It's nothing."

She raises a brow but thankfully chooses not to press me for details. I wouldn't even know what to say if she did.

"Alright, I'll see you later. Don't hesitate to reach out for literally anything."

This time when I smile, it's in thanks. "I really appreciate all this." As she moves down the steps, a sense of awareness prickles my skin. I glance over my shoulder and spot an elderly couple standing a few houses down, quite obviously looking in our direction. "So...am I always going to have an audience now?"

This feels different than the eyes I had on me back in Victoria. At home, everyone knew my story and was already judging me for it. Here, it feels more like a gentle—albeit nosy—curiosity.

Clara notices the same couple I did and she laughs. She begins to walk backwards toward a cherry red Volkswagen Beetle parked on the street as she calls, "Welcome to Kip Island, Delilah!"

The stopper keeping my emotions in check weakens by the hour. After spending the past week driving halfway across the country, the tiredness has seeped into my bones and has left me feeling more than a little raw. When the quiet hits and the night finally settles, I lock myself in my bathroom, the only place I truly have privacy. The rest of my existence is spent being accessible to my siblings, in case they need me.

The past few years, there was an underlying tension between me and our father. I was bitter about everything he missed and he wasn't satisfied with all the choices I had made. As a result, I distanced myself, and I wasn't around for

Parker and Sophia as much as I should have been. After the accident, I didn't even give myself time to think before I was figuring out what it would take for me to get custody of them. They were staying with me—end of story.

I'm sure that normally, a twenty-five-year-old with a bit of a murky future wouldn't be an ideal candidate. But thanks to the money we stood to inherit from our parents, I guess none of that mattered. From then on, I've done everything for them.

And I am *so* tired.

I turn the shower on, and the water hitting the tiles acts as a buffer with the thin walls. I haven't even unpacked my toiletries yet—not that I have the energy to bathe right now anyway. I fold against the counter as a sob works its way free. Buried deep by my incessant need to stay positive, it only emerges now that I'm alone.

While I unpacked earlier, I set Sophia up with some paper and crayons. It wasn't until I was tidying up after she had gone to bed that I realized what she drew—a picture of us. Our family. Not as it should be, but as it is. That wrecked me.

Questions—the usual suspects—slide through my mind. Have I done the right thing? Was moving really what was best for us?

Yes.

Living in Victoria felt like wandering through an open field, just waiting for a land mine to blow. Everywhere I went, it was only a matter of time before someone recognized me—by face or name, it didn't matter. They thought they were inconspicuous, but sound travels farther than people realize. Whispers ring louder than any shout.

The tears fall recklessly, not caring that I want to keep them in. That I don't want to feel. Not tonight—not ever. Sometimes, something threatens to peel back that layer of numbness, but I don't want to let it go. I want to hang on. I fear that if I fall apart, I won't be able to put myself back together. And that can't happen. Parker and Sophia need stability. I need to be that for them.

I roughly wipe the wetness from my cheeks and stand from the floor. I turn the shower dial until there is nothing but a trickle. Soon, nothing at all. Like a dam stopping the flow of water, I force my emotions in check.

Then I find myself in the mirror. My face is free of makeup—I haven't had the urge to use it in months. My eyes are dull. My hair, which is in desperate need of a wash, hangs limply in the low ponytail at my back. I look like a poor imitation of the Delilah I used to be. Like a dress you order from a sketchy website that falls to pieces the first time you wear it. It looks alright from afar, but up close you can pick out the inconsistencies—the structural flaws.

Tonight, I let myself crack. But tomorrow is going to be better.

It has to be.

CHAPTER FIVE
LUKE

THERE SHOULD BE a special place in hell for the person who invented budget reports.

Admittedly, I climbed the ranks rather quickly in my decade with the Kip Island Fire Department. I'm the youngest chief the department has had since its inception, and I was the only one up for the promotion a year ago.

Now I know why. Fucking budget reports.

The mayor and the town council have been on my ass about cutting costs this quarter. The only problem with that is the tourist season is creeping in, and with tourists come more fires, accidents and drunken false alarms. We already have to recruit more volunteers for the busy months. I don't need to be wasting my time counting every staple used and pencil broken.

Just as I have decided to throw my computer out the window, a knock sounds on my open door. Jodi Booth, my deputy chief, sticks her head in. Her blonde hair is twisted into a bun at the back of her head, military style. Like the rest of the crew, she is wearing a navy blue t-shirt with the KIFD's logo printed on the left side of the chest.

Jodi has been part of the department since before I was even in high school. When I first joined as a probationary firefighter, she took me under her wing and called me out whenever I did something stupid. Which, as a probie, happened often. I owe a lot to her, and I've often wondered why she isn't sitting in this chair instead of me. Her only response is that I'm far better at schmoozing than she is.

"Everything alright?" she asks, taking note of my scowl.

"Goddamn budget reports," I mutter.

Jodi lets out a low whistle. "Better you than me."

Shaking my head, I shove my computer mouse to the side. "I'd like to see Mayor Otis do this job for a day. Then maybe she wouldn't be breathing down my neck."

Jodi grins. "I would pay good money to see that. Preferably with a bucket of popcorn."

I snort. "Don't get your hopes up. That woman hasn't set foot in this building once. She probably thinks she'll catch a disease. Or a better work ethic."

Saying that I dislike Kip Island's current mayor would be a bit of an understatement. But I have to suck it up because I'm supposed to work under her for the rest of her term. It's going to be a long three years.

"So..." Jodi trails off, rocking back on her heels. "Someone has to go to the store. We drew straws." She then produces a shopping list from behind her back. "Congratulations, you're the lucky winner!"

I raise a brow. "And they sent you to deliver the news?"

She shrugs. "They figured you would be nice to me."

"I'm nice," I say. At the unconvinced look she gives me, I cross my arms. "What?"

"Have you ever heard the saying *kind but not nice*? Yeah, that's you, Bowman."

I want to tell her she's wrong, but I don't think I can. I know I'm not always the most welcoming guy there ever was. With a sigh, I push away from my desk and stand. I snatch the list from Jodi's hand, and then she follows as I leave my office.

"How's Vera these days?" I ask, tucking the slip of paper into my pocket. "I haven't seen her around town lately."

Jodi and her partner, Vera, live on a small farm on the outskirts of town. Vera handles most of the day-to-day operations, so free time is in short supply. Still, she usually stops by the station to leave Jodi some food, often made with produce from their backyard garden when it's in season. And because she loves the rest of us so much, she always brings extra.

"We think our foster cat might be ready to give birth soon, so she has been watching her like a hawk," Jodi explains. "Any chance you would be interested in a kitten?"

I chuckle as I head for the door. "Sorry, Booth!" I call. "You know I'm a dog person."

By the time the automatic doors of Kip Island's only grocery store slide open for me, a crowd is gathered in the produce section. Curiosity gets the best of me, so I gently shove my way through the throng until I reach the centre.

Gordon, a balding man with a too-red face, looks even

closer to blowing a gasket than usual. Sunnyside Market's store manager is infamous on the island for crying wolf. He seems to thrive on the attention. Most everyone does their best to steer clear of him, but it seems today that some unfortunate soul has been caught in the crossfire.

I don't immediately recognize the woman with her back to me—the fall of long, dark hair that reaches halfway down her spine; the cutoff denim shorts that cup her ass; the floral tattoos that swirl her left shoulder blade and travel down her bicep.

I *do*, however, recognize the little girl cowering at her side.

"This is *ridiculous*," Delilah argues, her free hand gesturing in the air. The other is curled around the little girl's shoulder.

"What is *ridiculous* is you thinking that you weren't going to be caught!" Gordon counters.

"Caught? It was an *accident*!"

Gordon raises a finger to shake in her direction, but when he spots me, he straightens. A smug look settles on his face, and he crosses his arms over his chest. Somehow, my presence bolsters him. I want to wipe the expression right off him.

Don't get involved. Just get what's on your list and get the hell out of here.

"The police should be on their way," he says.

"Seriously?" Delilah looks incredulous. "You called the *cops* for this?"

Ah, hell.

My feet are moving before I even register what I'm

about to do. I sidle up beside Delilah, effectively inserting myself into the situation. *Goddamnit, Bowman.* This is none of my business. I really should turn around and walk away.

"Causing trouble already, Ms. Delacroix?" I ask. "You've only been in town...what, twenty-four hours?"

I shouldn't be needling her—riling her up—but she is an enigma I seem to be hardwired to unravel. Aside from my general suspicion of people I don't know, there is something about Delilah that tugs at me.

She whirls, her eyes sparking with anger. When they settle on me, the blaze intensifies. This only endears me to her more. That fire should make me want to get as far away as possible. Instead, I choose to risk the third-degree burns. My lips threaten to quirk in amusement, but I force them into a neutral frown.

With a shake of her head, Delilah turns back to Gordon. "This is all being blown *way* out of proportion!"

"Why don't you start at the beginning?" I ask.

Gordon adjusts his tie. "She—"

I hold a hand up, silencing him. "I'd like to hear it from her, Gordon."

His expression sours, though he backs down. He may act like he's tough shit, but deep down, he's just a coward who likes to take his anger out on those he deems lesser than him. Delilah looks surprised, like my not automatically siding with Gordon is the opposite of what she expected. Still, she tightens her hold on the girl at her side and then tips her chin up.

"Sophia and I were shopping, and she got hungry,"

Delilah begins. "While I was looking at the apples, she took a banana from the display and started eating it."

Gordon scoffs. I cut him a hard look.

"She's five years old." Delilah turns her glare on Gordon. "She's never been grocery shopping before. When I noticed, I explained that we had to pay first. I was *about to* grab a bunch of bananas, so I could pay for the one she ate, but then Paul Blart over here started yelling at me."

It's silent for a minute as her words settle. As the jab at Gordon registers. The crowd, though thinner, is still gathered around, and I watch as everyone tries to bite back a smile. The urge to laugh hits me like a ton of bricks. I clamp down on it, keeping my cool mask of professionalism in place.

I turn to Gordon. "Did Ms. Delacroix try to head for the door without paying for her groceries?"

"Well, no," he sputters, "but—"

I point to the sign above the tiered table of bananas. "That price accurate?"

Gordon eyes me warily. "Yes, of course."

I dig in the pocket of my pants, pulling loose a few coins. I find a quarter and toss it toward him. He fumbles but ultimately manages to catch it. "That should cover it," I say. Then I turn to Delilah. "Do you have more shopping to do?"

Her cheeks are now a dusty pink colour. I try not to let it distract me.

She shakes her head. "No, I think we're done here."

I gesture for her to walk ahead of me, toward the registers. Now that explanations have been made, the crowd disperses, the gossip not as juicy as they once thought.

Gordon's mouth opens and closes like a fish looking for food as Delilah takes hold of her shopping cart and marches forward.

"Next time you're in the mood for drama," I say to Gordon, leaning close so my voice doesn't carry, "turn on a goddamn soap opera. Don't waste people's time embarrassing a little girl over something that costs less than twenty-five cents."

The older man's face turns a violent shade of crimson. I swivel on my heel, following in Delilah's wake. Her groceries are all piled on the belt and she's making idle chitchat with the teenage cashier. But my focus is on Sophia.

The little girl has a finger tucked in one of the belt loops on Delilah's shorts. She clings, looking like she could, at any moment, burst into tears. I'm annoyed at Gordon for wasting everyone's time, but I'm *pissed* that he used Sophia to do it.

I round to the end of the register, helping the cashier pack the groceries and then loading them back in the cart. Meanwhile, Delilah's eyes burn holes in the side of my face. Scrutinizing me. I choose to ignore her.

When the final bag is placed in the cart and Delilah has her receipt in hand, I accompany her and Sophia to their car. Wordlessly, I help place the paper sacs in the trunk. Her movement is stifled by the child at her side, so I do most of the heavy lifting.

"Soph," Delilah says gently, trying to pry her away, "it's okay. You're not in trouble."

More tears glisten in Sophia's eyes, and then they start to fall. *Fuck*. In this moment, she reminds me so much of

Abbie, my heart squeezes. I don't even think before I drop to a knee on the asphalt. I wait until she lifts her chin to meet my eyes.

"Hi, Sophia. I haven't introduced myself yet. I'm Luke. I work at the fire department."

She looks like she wants to shy away from me, but then, despite the tears, her big blue eyes grow curious. "Like a firefighter?" she asks quietly.

"I'm actually the boss," I say with a wink. "I get to tell all the firefighters what to do."

She lets out a small giggle. Some tears still track down her face, but she looks happier than she did before.

I gesture with a thumb over my shoulder, back toward the store. "What happened in there was a mistake. Good people make mistakes. I've made mistakes, and I'm sure your sister has, too."

Sophia's eyes widen as she looks up at Delilah. "Really?" she whispers.

Delilah nods. "Oh, yeah, I've made *loads* of mistakes. You didn't know the rules, so it's not your fault that you broke them. But now that you *do* know, it's your job not to do it again. Okay?"

Sophia nods. "Okay."

Delilah squeezes her shoulder. "Can you get buckled in your seat? I have to talk to the chief for a minute."

Sophia agrees, finally releasing her hold on Delilah's shorts. Once she has shut herself in the vehicle, the woman in front of me finally meets my gaze. It's probing, the way her grey-blue eyes search mine. Like always, I let nothing slip.

"Thank you," she eventually says.

I tip my chin in acknowledgment. "Gordon is a renowned shit disturber, but he shouldn't bother you again. You will, however, likely receive an icy glare the next time you're here."

She shrugs. "Nothing I'm not used to. Paul Blart can try, but he's not going to run me off."

I allow my lips to quirk upwards at the nickname.

"I'll, uh, see you around," she says.

"See you around," I echo.

I stay rooted to the spot even after Delilah gives me her back, ducking her head into the passenger side of her vehicle to check on Sophia. It isn't until she rounds the hood that I finally move, heading back toward the store.

She's just a tourist. She'll be gone before I know it. Yet a million thoughts volley in my brain. A million questions. One, however, sticks out among all the rest: who the hell is Delilah Delacroix?

And why do I want to find out?

CHAPTER SIX
DELILAH

OUR FIRST WEEK on the island has been nothing short of interesting. The incident at Sunnyside Market made me miss ordering groceries online and having them delivered. Perks of now living in a small town and shopping at a mom-and-pop grocer instead of a chain.

The moving truck with our belongings arrived two days after we did. Although the place is a bit cramped, it feels more like home now that it's full of familiar things. The pink house is a whole lot smaller than ours in James Bay, so most of our furniture sold with the house or was given away. The rest of our stuff was shipped across the country to our new home.

After Parker refused to go back to school in September, he was enrolled in an online program instead. Our internet isn't set up yet, so Parker, Sophia and I have spent time each day at the little library downtown so he could finish the last of his assignments.

We exit the library, Sophia's arm swinging our joined hands between us. We veer left while Parker veers right.

"Where are you going?" I call. "I thought we were getting something to eat." Dockside, the restaurant attached to the lighthouse, has been calling my name since we arrived on Kip Island.

My brother kicks at the sidewalk with the toe of his running shoe. "Not hungry," he says. "I'm going back to the house."

Bullshit, I want to yell. But I swallow it down. I've learned to pick my battles with him, and this is one I won't win.

"Are you sure? Do you want us to bring you back anything?"

He shakes his head. "I'll make something later." Then he stuffs his hands in his pockets and gives us his back, starting on the short walk toward Hawberry Lane. I watch him go, wondering what I have to do to get him to talk to me.

"*Sissy*," Sophia whines as she tugs on my hand, "I'm hungry! Can we go?"

I spare Parker's retreating form one last glance, and then I paste a smile on my lips for my sister's benefit. "Yeah, Soph, let's go."

The walk to the lighthouse is a short one, Main Street acting as a straight path that leads right to the base of the structure. Up the sidewalk, I spot a familiar blonde coming toward us. A dog—a German shepherd, if I had to guess—bounds diligently by Clara's side, the leash slack between them.

When she finally spots us, she waves, a smile stretching across her lips. "Hey!" she calls.

Sophia grins when she sees the dog. "Puppy!"

I don't think there's anyone on this planet who loves dogs as much as my sister. As Clara gets closer, Sophia squeezes my hand to the point of breaking it. I hold my breath as I watch my painfully shy sister work through her nerves.

To my surprise, she boldly looks up at Clara and blurts, "Can I *please* pet your puppy?"

Clara chuckles. "Go ahead," she says. "His name is Riot. I have to warn you though: he might decide to give you a kiss."

Sophia giggles as she reaches a hand tentatively toward the dog. True to his owner's words, the dog's tongue lashes out, swiping across Sophia's palm. She shrieks in delight. "That tickles!"

"I didn't know you had a dog," I say.

While Clara and I haven't known each other long, we covered a lot of ground in the weeks leading up to our move to the island. I'm surprised something like this didn't come up.

"Oh, I don't," she says. "Riot belongs to my brother. I just take him for walks once in a while when he gets caught up at work."

One thing I've learned about Clara is that she is constantly running around helping her family. Whether her parents need help at the bed and breakfast they run on the other side of the island or her brother needs someone to watch his daughter—or, apparently, when a dog needs walking—Clara is the one on call.

"What are you guys up to today?" she asks.

"We were just heading to your restaurant to check it out."

Her eyes light up, showing the great pride I know she takes in her job. She gestures toward the restaurant. "Don't let me keep you, then. Go enjoy!"

I laugh at her enthusiasm. "Before you go, I have a question. Do you happen to know anywhere that's hiring?"

Perhaps it would have been smarter to find a job first before uprooting our lives and trekking across the country, but all I could think about was being *away*. Between the sale of our old house and the money our parents left behind, we have more than enough to get by, but I want to keep as much of that money for Parker and Sophia as I can. When they're old enough, they can choose to spend it how they want. In the meantime, I need a job.

Clara grins. "Just about every business on the island is looking for summer help. But I take it you're looking for something more permanent?"

I nod. "Maybe if I get in somewhere for the summer, I can convince them to keep me on."

"No convincing necessary. Come work for me."

"You?"

She gestures to the building behind her. "I'm used to working around parents' schedules, so accommodating for time you need to spend with your siblings won't be an issue. And honestly, you'd be doing me a favour. One of my usual summer hires got an internship in her field and had to quit, so I'm short a server."

"Don't you want to interview me first? Ask about my experience?"

Clara's grin widens. "Nah. I'm more of a trial by fire kind of girl."

I want to press more, but our conversation is interrupted by the sound of shoes slapping on the sidewalk. "Clary!" a little girl shouts.

A blur of motion streaks past me, and then Clara is hauling the little girl into her arms. Her features are somewhat similar to my new boss's, but where Clara is fair-skinned and blonde-haired, the girl's skin is a light olive and her hair hangs in tight brunette curls.

"Abbs, this is my new friend, Delilah," Clara says. "Delilah, this is my niece, Abbie. She's my brother Gabe's daughter."

I smile down at her. "Hi, Abbie." Unlike Sophia, she doesn't seem shy at all. "This is my sister, Sophia."

At the mention of her name, my sister looks up from where she is still busy with Riot, her fingers buried in the tan fur around his collar.

"Hi!" Abbie smiles at Sophia. "How old are you?" She holds her palm up, fingers splayed, along with the thumb on her other hand. "I'm this many!"

Sophia glances at me, and when I give her an encouraging nod, she mumbles, "Five."

"I was five, but then I had my birthday in—" She turns to her aunt. "When did I have my birthday, Clary?"

Clara shakes her head with a chuckle. "Your birthday was in April."

Abbie's head bobs. "And now I'm six!"

A woman—the spitting image of Clara, though about thirty years older—pushes outside from the restaurant. When she spots Abbie standing with us, her taut frame relaxes. "That girl is going to give me a heart attack one of these days," the woman mutters.

Clara wraps an arm around her. "She keeps you young, Ma."

She shakes her head, and then her gaze latches onto mine. She straightens. "Oh!" she exclaims. "You must be Delilah. I'm Maggie." She jerks a thumb toward Clara. "I'm this one's mother."

"That's me," I reply. "Nice to meet you."

"You, too! Clara has told us so much about you. You should really come by the house for brunch on Sunday," Maggie says. "You can meet the rest of the family, and then you'll know a few more friendly faces around town."

Both she and Clara look at me expectantly. The depth of their kindness is a touch overwhelming.

"Oh, that's okay." I offer her a polite smile. "Thank you, though."

"Just think about it," Maggie says. Then she places a hand on her granddaughter's shoulder. "C'mon, Miss Abigail. Let's get you home."

The pair say goodbye and then start heading down the street. Clara follows not long after. Sophia is sad to watch Riot walk away, but Clara assures her that she'll see him again. Then Sophia and I head into Dockside for our promised lunch.

Despite my best efforts, neither Maggie nor Clara would accept no for an answer. So on Sunday morning, my siblings and I climb into my car with Clara to drive to her parents' house for the Bowman family's weekly brunch.

"I feel like we're intruding," I say to Clara as my car rolls through a set of open gates.

Out of the corner of my eye, I can just make out the unimpressed look she's giving me. "My parents turned my childhood home into a bed and breakfast. They literally invite strangers into their space every day," she reasons. "Trust me, you're not intruding."

I want to protest more, but the words die right on the tip of my tongue when the bed and breakfast in question comes into view. Affectionately known as Haven House, according to Clara, the Bowmans' home is a sprawling red-brick farmhouse with a large wraparound porch. It looks straight out of someone's aesthetic Pinterest board with its cobblestone walkway and the flower pots lining the front steps.

"You grew up here?" I ask.

It's not the size of the house that stuns me—the one we lived in back in Victoria was more than big enough—but the way that it so obviously looks like it has been lived in. It may be a bed and breakfast now, but it was a family home first, and it shows.

"Haven House has been in my dad's family for a few

generations now. When my parents got married, my great-grandparents gifted it to them."

I'm still busy admiring the house as Clara, Parker and Sophia exit the car. I haven't put much thought into what my dream home would be, but I think this might be it.

The house is set back from the road which, if not for the guests staying here, would afford the Bowmans some privacy. And privacy is something that, up until recently, I hadn't realized had become a commodity. When my dad became premier, our family was thrust into the public eye. We certainly weren't on the level of the Kardashians or anything, but there was an element of anonymity that had been taken away from us. When Mitchell released my pictures, it felt like the shreds of privacy I had managed to hang on to were suddenly stripped away. Now the allure of a quiet life is too tempting to ignore.

I shake myself from my stupor and hurry to catch up to the group.

"Have no fear, your favourite child is here!" Clara calls once she pushes through the front door.

Sophia grabs my hand, taking her usual spot as my little shadow, and we trail after my new friend. Parker begrudgingly follows behind. He wasn't too happy when I told him about our plans for this morning, but his presence here is a hill I was willing to die on.

Maggie appears in a doorway down the hall, shaking her head at her daughter. "Clara, you know I don't have favourites."

Clara bats her lashes. "But if you did..."

Maggie's eyes roll good-naturedly, and then she smiles

when her gaze settles on us. "It's lovely to see you two again. And you must be Parker! It's nice to meet you," she says. "I'm Maggie."

My brother forces a smile. "Nice to meet you, too."

We follow Maggie into a kitchen that would make a chef salivate. Gleaming stainless steel appliances are placed amongst sleek white countertops and light green cabinetry. Everything looks new, like it was recently remodelled, which makes sense considering they only opened their home to the bed and breakfast a couple years ago.

"The food will be ready shortly," Maggie promises.

"Can I do anything to help?" I ask.

Parker doesn't even try to hold back his snort of derision. I shoot him a glare—one that tells him, in no uncertain terms, to shut the fuck up. I may not be a Michelin Star-worthy cook, but I have come a long way since being put in charge of feeding not just one but three people.

"Mom doesn't let anyone in her kitchen except Dad," Clara says. "You and your siblings set the oven on fire as kids *one time* and suddenly you're a safety hazard."

The annoyed-but-affectionate smile that Maggie gives her daughter sends a pang of longing through me. I bite my tongue to focus on that pain instead of the sting of jealousy. It isn't Clara's fault that my mom isn't here to look at me like that.

Maggie points a spatula at Clara. "Go show them around and let me cook in peace."

Clara sticks her tongue out at her, but she does as she was told. Parker, Sophia and I dutifully follow her as she takes us on a tour of the house. She gives us a quick rundown on the family quarters, and then she takes us to the side of the house that is reserved for guests.

When we make it back to the kitchen, three new people stand in the room. One—a tall man with cropped salt and pepper hair—stands beside Maggie at the stove. Likely Clara's father. The other two men appear to be about my age.

One of them turns, and time seems to stand still when I realize that this man is none other than the fire chief I crashed into on my first day here. The same one that came to my rescue at Sunnyside Market earlier in the week. I knew Kip Island was small, but *fuck me*, I didn't realize it was *this* small.

"Delilah, this is my older brother, Luke. Luke, this is Delilah and her siblings, Parker and Sophia."

When his eyes meet mine, there is no mistaking the fact that he knows exactly who I am. And judging by the tick of his clenched jaw, he doesn't like it.

Not one bit.

CHAPTER
SEVEN
LUKE

RIOT PANTS as he sticks his head out the open passenger window, the wind ruffling his fur. The drive out to my parents' place is his favourite because the speed limit kicks up to eighty, which means he can properly let his tongue wag in the breeze.

With a laugh, I reach a hand out and pat him on the back. He doesn't so much as spare me a glance, too engrossed in watching the scenery pass us by.

Riot and I have been thick as thieves since he came to live with me. I got him three years ago, after an injury forced him to retire from his K-9 unit on the mainland. His former handler is a buddy of mine from school. Under normal circumstances, Riot would've stayed with Randy and lived out the rest of his days as a loyal pet, but a perfect storm of events led him to me.

Riot was shot during a drug raid, and as a result, his recovery was pretty intense. At the same time, Randy's wife went through a complicated birth, and both her recovery and the care of their newborn left Randy with no time to tend to Riot. So he called me.

Those initial days weren't easy, but I wouldn't trade them for the world. My ex tried to get me to give him up—she claimed the constant shedding was too much for her to handle, even though I took care of it—and I almost went through with it. I'm thankful every day that I removed her from my life instead.

When I pull my truck through the gate at Haven House, Riot's tail whips against the back of the passenger seat. He begins to whine, eager to see the rest of his family. While my niece is undoubtedly his favourite, he still gets overly excited when he spots one of my siblings or my parents.

I put my vehicle in park beside Gabe's truck, right in front of the house. As soon as I open my door, Riot climbs over me and jumps down, bounding toward the porch. The door swings inward and Abbie appears, giggling as Riot licks her cheek. I make it up the front steps just as my brother appears in the doorway behind his daughter.

"Dude," he says to Abbie, "quit opening the door by yourself. It could've been a stranger on the other side."

"But I'm not by myself, Daddy," she replies, stroking Riot's fur as she looks up at her dad. A cheeky smile plays on her lips. "It was just Lukey."

I fight my own grin. I don't love the idea of her going against the rules, but I also can't fight the satisfaction I get knowing that Gabe is going to be paid back in kind for his younger self's smart mouth.

My brother crosses his arms. "Well, maybe *Lukey* can explain why you should leave the doors to the adults, then."

I finish climbing the porch steps, then pick Abbie up and throw her over my shoulder. She giggles as I move through the house. Riot yips, hot on my heels.

When I set my niece down in the living room, I level her with a serious look. "Listen to your dad, Abbs. No answering the door unless one of us says it's okay. Safety is the number one priority, right?"

She cocks her head. "What's a prior-ery?"

I chuckle. "*Priority*. It means something that is very important. Something you do first before anything else. Okay?"

She nods. "Okay."

I hold out my hand for a high five. Abbie gives my palm a hard slap, and then she takes off with my dog. Her laughter and his excited barking trail after them.

Gabe sighs as he leans in the doorway. "Why the hell does she listen to you so well?"

I shoot him a smug grin. "Because I'm her favourite." When Gabe's expression doesn't lighten, I sober. "She pushes your buttons because she can. Because she knows that no matter how much shit she gives you, you're still going to be there every night to tell her you love her."

He sighs again. "I guess."

I point a finger at him. "Don't act like you didn't pull the same shit with our parents. As far as I'm concerned, this is your payback."

Gabe flips his middle finger up in response.

When Gabe announced, at eighteen, that he wanted to become a firefighter, Mom just about shit a brick. Don't get me wrong, she was worried about me when I decided to follow in our dad's footsteps, but Gabe is her baby. She has mostly accepted it now, but about once a year she tries to convince him to pick a different career path. Knowing my brother, that will never happen.

In the kitchen, Mom has already gotten a head start on breakfast. Our Sunday morning ritual started when Clara and Gabe both moved out, leaving our parents with an empty nest. To compensate, Mom instated weekly brunch. And when brunch still wasn't enough to occupy her, she convinced Dad to open a bed and breakfast.

With mine and Gabe's jobs being what they are, we can't always make it to brunch, but we do our best. Both of my siblings and I would do just about anything for that woman.

"Morning, Mom," I call over the music. It's not a Bowman family meal without the speakers being cranked just a touch too loud. "Where's Clarebear?"

Usually my sister is the first to arrive at Haven House. Like every Sunday is an unspoken race between the three of us that she is determined to win.

Mom smiles at me over her shoulder. While my sister is undeniably her twin, I have been told that I have her smile. Hers is on display a lot more than mine is, though.

"Morning, sweetie!" she says. "Your sister is around here somewhere. Sorry, she still got here first."

Footsteps stampede on the floorboards as Riot bounds into the room, Abbie hot on his heels. Those two could chase each other for hours, and quite often, they do. By the time we head home, my dog will be tuckered out and ready for a nap on the couch he's not supposed to be on.

"Hi, Lukey!" Abbie calls, greeting me a second time.

I chuckle. "Hi, Abbs."

A hand lands on my shoulder. "Morning, son."

"Hey, Dad."

John Bowman is a man of few words. We are a lot alike in that way. While Mom loves to entertain—whether bed and breakfasts guests or friends—Dad is content to sit back and observe the chaos. Most of the time, he doesn't speak unless spoken to, choosing to listen instead. He was one of the best in the KIFD before he retired.

I may have gotten Mom's smile, but everything else is all Dad. I have a couple inches on him and the sets of our shoulders are broad. More than that, though, he's someone I've always looked up to.

"I see you finally decided to join us," Clara teases as she enters the room.

"Hey, I've been here. Where were *you*?"

"Being a good host and giving my new bestie a tour, *thank you very much*."

It's only now, as I turn toward my sister, that I notice the woman trailing behind her. Today Delilah is wearing another pair of ass-hugging denim shorts with daisies embroidered on one of the pockets. Her dark hair is fashioned into a ponytail. This time, it's held together by a long white ribbon.

Fuck. Me.

What is she doing here, in my family's home? The memory of Delilah rear-ending me comes flooding back, and I know any hope I had of this woman only sticking around for the summer is gone. My jaw tightens when I put the pieces together. This woman is going to be living in Muriel's old house for who knows how long. And now she's here, spending time with my family.

"Delilah," Clara says, "this is my older brother, Luke. Luke, this is Delilah and her siblings, Parker and Sophia."

Her little sister grips her hand tighter. Behind Delilah stands the teenage boy I recognize from the other day, his face giving away the fact that he'd rather be anywhere but here. *You and me both*, I want to say.

Delilah offers me a tentative smile. She can clearly see the displeasure on my face.

Ever the peace-keeper, Mom jumps in. "Delilah, sweetie, this is my husband, John," she says. "And my youngest son, Gabriel. He is Abbie's father."

Delilah's smile is much more sure this time. "It's really nice to meet you. Thanks again for letting us intrude on your family time."

Like we were given a choice.

My mother shoots me a disapproving look and points toward the table like she did when I was in trouble as a kid. Then she forces a beaming smile onto her lips. "Food's ready!"

We all squish into the space around the kitchen table. It's an okay size for the six of us, but nine is a bit of a stretch. And of course, I wind up sitting right next to Delilah. The food gets passed around and we pile it on our plates. Before we can all dig in, Delilah decides to open her mouth.

"Luke and I have actually already met," Delilah says out of nowhere.

My head whips up from my plate.

Mom's face is full of surprise. "Oh. At Dockside?"

Delilah's eyes flit to mine, and then she sets her mouth into a sheepish smile. "Oh, no. I actually rear-ended him our first morning on the island. Even though I'm sure I made him late to work, he was super nice about it."

Gabe coughs in a *that's bullshit* sort of way. I kick my foot out, nailing him in the shin. Clara just sighs as she rolls her eyes. Dad looks on in quiet amusement. And Mom looks like she doesn't quite know what to do with all of us, even though she's had thirty-odd years of practice.

"I'm *hungry*," Abbie whines, cutting the weird tension that has settled over the rest of us. "Can we *eat* now, Grammy?"

After Abbie's begging, we all abandon conversation and tuck into the food. Mom makes an assortment of things, from pancakes or waffles to scrambled eggs to bowls of fruit. It's like a hotel buffet breakfast, but ten times better.

Sophia started out in a chair beside Delilah, but rather quickly she climbed into her older sister's lap, still painfully shy.

Brunch went by as it always does: with great food and ample banter. Still, I couldn't shake the tension in my shoulders from having *her* there. Gabe and Clara seemed unaffected, carrying on ribbing each other as usual, but I was caught up in knowing that Delilah's eyes were on me.

After they were full, Abbie coaxed Sophia into playing with her dollhouse, and then two pairs of tiny footsteps thundered up the stairs.

We're in that phase after everyone has finished eating where no one has found the energy to get out of their chair when Gabe starts to fiddle around on his phone. The music was turned down considerably when we sat at the table, and it still plays quietly in the background. The current song abruptly stops. Then the familiar opening chords of "Hey There Delilah" begin to filter through the room.

And then, something kind of magnificent happens. Delilah laughs. The sound catches me completely off guard. Her eyes crinkle as her head tips back, and her cheeks flush that pretty pink colour I've seen once before.

"Stop, please!" she pleads, covering her face with her hands. "This song *haunts* me."

Beside her, Clara cackles. "How many promposals?"

Delilah peeks out between her fingers. "Too many."

This sends my family into another fit of laughter. I try, but I can't help the chuckle that escapes me. And it doesn't go unnoticed by Delilah. I clear my throat, averting my eyes.

"So, Delilah," Dad starts after the laughter has died down, "what brings you to Kip Island?"

It's a standard question. Anyone would ask this of someone new to town. But Delilah looks almost pained as she formulates her answer. Beneath the table, she fiddles with the frayed edge of a hole in her distressed shorts.

"Truthfully," she says eventually, "I saw it on a postcard and just thought it was pretty."

My family smiles, and Delilah looks relieved. Still, she twists a thread of denim around her finger so tight it cuts off circulation. Before I can stop myself, my hand shoots out to still her movements. She looks how I feel: startled. Her whole body tenses as I unwind the strand from her finger, but she doesn't call me out. I retract my hand quickly before someone else notices.

"I need to go," Parker declares suddenly. He stands from his seat like his ass is on fire. Then he looks sheepishly at Mom. "Uh, thanks for the food, Mrs. Bowman."

Mom smiles. "You're most welcome, sweetie."

Delilah clears her throat as she stands, too. "We should probably all get going," she says. "Parker, can you go find Sophia?" When her brother heads for the stairs, Delilah turns back to the rest of us. "Thank you for everything."

Mom and Clara offer Delilah a round of hugs, and then a few minutes later, she and her siblings slip out the door.

Brunch at Haven House has never been a quiet affair, especially since the addition of Abbie, but I admit that there's something different about Delilah being here. Sophia and Parker, too. That little girl is Abbie's opposite in almost every way, but I don't think I've ever seen my niece smile as much as she has today.

This, though, has my insides twisting. The ease with which my family—even Dad, who is known to be more reserved than his wife and my siblings—has folded the Delacroixes into our routine is alarming.

The last person they invited into our circle left wreckage in her wake. And it was all my fault.

CHAPTER EIGHT
DELILAH

"ARE you *sure* you've never worked in a restaurant before?"

Two days after we crashed the Bowman family's Sunday ritual, Clara had me set up to start working at Dockside. The only clothing requirements for servers are a branded t-shirt and denim, so I'm happy that I won't have to spend the summer wearing some stuffy uniform.

Despite what Clara said when she first offered me this job, though, I knew as soon as I stepped inside the doors of the restaurant that I would need to tell her I had no experience in the food industry. I've had a string of random jobs, some that paid better than others, but none have been working with people like this.

I laugh as I brush a strand of hair off my sweaty forehead. The breeze coming off the lake and through the open windows does little to cool me. A mid-May heatwave has settled across the province, leaving me sticky in all the worst places.

"I'm positive," I tell Clara.

Clara started me easy, first showing me the ropes of opening duties before customers arrived and then having me bus tables when the restaurant opened for the day. But then one of the other waiters called in, and I was thrown into the deep end with a notepad and a pen. Clara kept a close eye, but I had a sneaking suspicion this was that trial by fire she had mentioned.

Thankfully, the customers today were mostly regulars who took pity on me and didn't mind when I accidentally gave them Coke instead of iced tea. I'm sure I've cost Dockside hundreds of dollars in misfilled orders, but Clara just waves me off whenever I try to apologize.

Behind the bar, my new boss grabs the soda gun and fills a glass with water. She slides it across the surface to my waiting palm. I tip it to my lips, devouring the cool liquid.

"You're a natural, then," she says. "Now I don't know what I'll do if you ever decide to leave me."

I laugh again. "It's only been six hours. I hardly think I'm indispensable yet."

Clara's eyes twinkle. "I don't know, that pocketful of generous tips says otherwise," she singsongs.

To say I was surprised about that aspect of the job would be an understatement. I know that servers get tips all the time, but I wasn't expecting the sheer amount of loonies and toonies that now weigh my apron down. I even acquired a few dollar bills from a group of Americans who hadn't bothered to exchange their currency.

"Let's not forget that I also dropped a plate of food and almost spilled a full tray of drinks on a customer's lap."

Clara shakes her head, waving me off. "Semantics. You're doing great, Dee."

Dee.

A memory, long buried, reaches the surface. When Parker was first learning to speak, he had a hard time with Delilah. He eventually settled on Deedee, and from then on, my whole family adopted the nickname. I haven't heard that name in eight long months.

I offer her a shaky smile, trying to rid myself of the picture in my head. "Thanks."

She seems like she is about to say more—like maybe she recognizes the look on my face—but the ringing phone in her back pocket steals her attention. She fishes it out, checking the caller ID.

She groans. "*Ugh*. I'll be right back. I'm just going to take this in the office."

While Clara is gone, I make myself useful. There are rings of condensation on the bar top, so I grab a cloth and begin to wipe them up.

When the front door swings inward, I expect to see a new group of hungry diners, but instead a lone woman walks in. In her arms is a stack of flyers. My mother used to own a collection of vintage fashion magazines, and this woman looks as if she has walked off the page of one of her seventies-era lookbooks in her long skirt and shirt with billowing sleeves paired with her go-go boots. As she walks deeper into the restaurant, toward where I stand at the bar, she smiles and waves to different tables full of locals. Her earrings—giant bright orange geometric shapes—sway with her movement.

As she reaches me, her friendly smile intensifies. She looks to be about sixty, with laugh lines around her mouth and greying hair pulled back into a claw clip to show for it.

"Hello, there," she says. "Is Clara around?"

I set the wet rag aside and dry my hands on a towel. "She just stepped out to take a call. Is there something I can help you with?"

"My name is Carole Dramus." She extends a palm over the bar for me to take. "You must be new around here."

"Delilah Delacroix," I reply as I shake her outstretched hand. "I guess I give off city girl vibes, huh?"

"Not at all!" Carole waves me off. "I just happen to have lived here my whole life. I know everyone and everything to do with this place. That, and I never forget a face, especially one as lovely as yours."

I laugh, slightly taken aback by the compliment. "Oh, uh, thank you." Then, to take the heat off myself, I gesture to the stack of papers in her arms. "Are you advertising something?"

"Oh, yes! I most certainly am." She pulls a page from the stack and slaps it on the bar top. "The Kip Island Business Improvement Association is hosting a photography contest. The winner will receive a contract to produce the photos for the island's updated tourism website."

I slide the paper off the counter and begin to peruse the details. The island's BIA is taking portfolio submissions from seasoned and amateur photographers alike, with a focus on landscape photography and photojournalism. A panel of judges will then vote for a winner who will have the opportunity to sign a six-month contract with the BIA.

The contest sounds like a photographer's wet dream.

Okay, maybe only *this* photographer's wet dream. But it sounds like an amazing opportunity.

The younger me would have handed Carole her portfolio without hesitation. She would have jumped at the chance to prove the people that doubted her wrong. But I have responsibilities that I can't shirk just to chase a pipe dream. Maybe it is just a silly contest, and I probably wouldn't even win, but it would only serve to remind me of what I can't have.

I offer Carole an approving nod, setting the flyer back on the bar. "That sounds like a really great opportunity for someone."

"The winner will also have their photographs featured in my art gallery during the next exhibition."

Now this piques my interest. "The island has an art gallery?"

Despite Kip Island's downtown being a fraction of the size of our old city, I haven't had the chance to explore all it has to offer yet. Sophia and I have only made it through about half of the businesses.

Carole beams. "We sure do. We're just on Main Street. You should drop by sometime!"

Mitchell and my old friends used to laugh at me for the gallery openings and photography exhibitions I attended. They never understood the appeal and they found them boring, instead favouring nightclubs and staying out all night to shake off the monotony of the workweek.

I love the art at the exhibitions, but I also know what it's like to have no one show up for you. Putting your blood, sweat and tears into a project only to have no one to share it with.

It's hard when everyone in your immediate circle is so different from you. They don't think like you—their brains wired for numbers and business and straight facts, not creativity. They don't understand you, and half the time they don't even try.

It feels like shouting into a chasm and not even hearing an echo in reply.

I nod. "I just might take you up on that."

"I'm not too good at all that social media hooey, but I have a Facebook page where I post current events. Feel free to give it a thumb."

This makes me laugh. "I'll have to check it out."

"Clara is a doll and usually hangs my flyers up somewhere in here," she says, gesturing in a circle with her finger. She taps the flyer. "Can you give this to her?"

"Of course!"

She then looks at her watch and winces. "I have to run, but it was lovely meeting you, Delilah. I hope to see you at the gallery soon."

Carole leaves just as she arrived, waving to fellow townspeople like a queen would her loyal subjects. When she disappears outside, I take hold of the flyer again. And for a moment, I let myself think about what would happen if I entered. In an ideal world, my portfolio would earn me a first place spot, and I would not only have my photos displayed for the town to see, but I would also have my first paid photography gig. This would give me exposure—a chance to get my name out there. Then maybe people would hire me for personal photography and I could make a business out of it.

But all of that hinges on winning, and I'm pretty sure I've used up all my luck.

"*So...* Are you going to enter?"

The sudden voice at my side makes me startle. The paper falls from my grasp and flutters to the floor on the opposite side of the counter. My hand rests on my chest, right over my rapidly-beating heart. "God, Clara. You scared me!"

"Well?" she asks. "Are you going to?"

I don't talk about photography with a lot of people. I learned a long time ago that people outside of the community don't really care—until they want you to take a picture of them. They don't want to listen to you ramble about the mechanics; they just want you to capture the perfect shot. But Clara is easy to talk to, and one day it just slipped out. She seemed genuinely interested and has asked multiple times to see my portfolio.

I round the bar to find the fallen page. As I crouch to retrieve it, my gaze lands on a pair of black boots. When I look up, I'm surprised to find Luke—though I shouldn't be. His parents own the restaurant and his sister manages it, so really, it was silly of me to think that he wouldn't be hanging around.

Not that *I* mind, but after our Sunday morning spent having brunch with the Bowmans, it is shockingly clear how much Luke does not like me. You rear-end a man's truck once and suddenly you're the bad guy. I thought that we had put it all behind us. Especially after the fiasco at Sunnyside Market, I thought things would be fine. Apparently not.

Caught up in Luke's gaze, I find myself staring at him. The man is simply too good-looking. Even with his face set in perpetual scrutiny, I'm not afraid to admit—to myself, at least—that I like what I see. When I don't make a further move to reach for the flyer, Luke bends to retrieve it himself. Instead of handing it back to me, he begins to study it.

Embarrassed, I stand to my feet and spin to face Clara, trying to ignore the heat in my cheeks. "Uh, no," I reply. I awkwardly fold my arms across my chest. "Why would I?"

I try to sound nonchalant. Like I couldn't care less about it. Like entering a photography contest is the most ridiculous thing I've heard in my life.

"Why *wouldn't* you? It's harmless! If you win, great. If not, no biggie."

Clara and I may have talked about photography, but we haven't even touched the rift it created between me and my father. He was disappointed I didn't choose it as my major in university, and that led to a lot of tension. Nothing about this contest would be harmless. I can't get into all the reasons while Luke is here, though.

I glance at the floor, biting the inside of my cheek to hide my frustration. She doesn't know that she's dredging up old issues that were never afforded any closure.

Tugging the flyer from Luke's hands, I declare, "I'm going to tape this on the front door. If that's okay?"

Clara studies me. After a moment, she nods. "Sure," she says. "And then why don't you take your break? You deserve it."

I don't waste any time walking away. I tack the poster to the door, and then I push out into the clean air. I don't even bother taking my apron off.

On the far end of Dockside's outdoor patio, there is a set

of stairs that lead down to Anchor's Bay Beach. When I reach the bottom, I let the rocky sand shift beneath my feet as I leave the restaurant behind. Just for a little while.

> Checking in.

PARKER
> We're good.

Some of the tension knotting my shoulders is released at his response. Since our parents died, Parker and I have made it a point to keep in touch every few hours. You answer that text, no matter what. Today he is home watching Sophia. I hate putting that responsibility on him, but with starting this job so quickly, I haven't had a chance to find other arrangements for her. But I will.

I spend my break relishing the sun and reinforcing the wall I've erected around my emotions. If they stay contained, they can't hurt me.

But with each passing day, I feel like the past is quickly catching up to me.

CHAPTER NINE
DELILAH

SLEEP HAS BEEN ELUDING me this week. I managed to secure a sitter for Sophia, someone Clara recommended, after my first shift at the restaurant. And everything else seems to be falling into place, but every time my head hits the pillow, my brain goes into overdrive.

When I close my eyes, my to-do list flashes behind my eyelids like a moving picture. And then when I try to distract myself from that, all I see is Luke. I feel like my mind is playing tricks on me. Very cruel tricks.

It's utterly ridiculous, right? I should not be hung up on a man that doesn't like me. It isn't like he's mean, but I can tell whenever he stops by Dockside while I'm on shift that he's picking me apart with his gaze. I hate that.

My eyes are half-open when I blearily stumble down the hall from my bedroom. The house is quiet, the way it always is before Sophia and Parker wake up. I try to rise before them, to have a few uninterrupted moments to myself. Usually that involves making myself a cup of coffee.

I round the corner into the kitchen and head toward my saviour—the coffee maker. My brain is still clouded with sleep, so I don't notice anything is wrong until I have to grab hold of the island when my feet come out from under me.

"*Shit*!"

When I look down, I find that there is a steadily-growing puddle on my kitchen floor that could rival the lake this island sits on. The room was pristine when I went to bed last night, and it still is—minus all the water.

I wonder if this is a sign. Finding this house and connecting with Clara, it all seems a little too good to be true after the shit I've had to deal with the last nine months. The house itself is perfect. At least, it looks like it on the outside. Maybe this leak is the universe's way of saying it's on to me. It knows that I am in way over my head and I'm struggling to keep it all together. This is a glaring reminder of that.

The first thing I do is call Clara. Despite often staying at Dockside until close, she's still an early riser and has probably already been awake for an hour. Hopefully she has a plumber on speed dial because I am *way* out of my element here.

"Good morning!" she sings when the call connects.

"It's certainly morning, but I wouldn't call it good," I grumble. "We have a bit of a situation."

"What's going on?"

"How would you feel if the house had a swimming pool in the kitchen?"

"Oh, shit."

I grab the tea towel hanging on the oven handle and throw it on the puddle. It soaks through immediately. "That's exactly what I said."

I crouch in front of the cupboard under the sink and open it. I can't tell where the water is coming from, but it doesn't seem to want to let up anytime soon. I notice a knob that looks like it would stop the water from reaching the sink, but when I try to turn it, it won't budge.

"*Ugh*. I'm at Dockside receiving our produce shipment right now. I'll find someone to come help you."

"I'll do my best to save the floors."

After I set my phone on the island, I exhaust every single towel we have in the house, trying to sop up the mess so it doesn't migrate to the living room. Meanwhile, the water still streams from the open cupboard. I try the knob again, just in case something magically changed in the last few minutes. No such luck.

I'm thinking about starting to use blankets now that all the towels are soaked when a knock sounds on the front door. This has me breathing a sigh of relief. *Thank God.*

When I open the door, I find an unimpressed Luke standing on the porch. I cross my arms over my chest as his gaze drops to my bare legs, my sleep shorts, and then my old t-shirt. I lay a hand self-consciously over the now-messy braid I slept in. Luke's jaw clenches and he averts his eyes.

When he speaks, his voice is strained. "Clara said there's a leak."

I open the door wider, making room for his broad frame to enter. When he does, his eyes sweep the room, almost like he expected it to be completely destroyed.

"I think I caught it early," I say. "It hasn't managed to make it past the kitchen."

He takes in the heap of towels and the still-gushing pipe

from under the sink. He stalks over, and then he turns to me incredulously. "You didn't think to shut the water off?" he snaps.

While I'm certainly no plumber, I'm not stupid either. "*Of course* I did!"

"You must've thought about it real hard, then, seeing as water is still gushing out of the pipes."

I glower. "*Thank you*, Captain Obvious. If you took two seconds to step off your high horse, you would know that the knob is stuck!"

He looks somewhat taken aback by my outburst. But this is what happens when I am running on little sleep and haven't been able to have my caffeine fix—I get a little confrontational. I inhale a deep breath, trying to reel my temper back in.

This, of course, is the perfect moment for my t-shirt—stretched at the collar and a size too big—to slide down my left shoulder. It exposes a large portion of my tattoo, but it also exposes my bare skin. I pull it back up, and then look back to Luke. Though it's now covered, his gaze is still trained on my collarbone. And his jaw is locked tight.

"Luke?"

He shakes his head and averts his stare. When he finally settles back on the task at hand, he takes a moment to assess the kitchen sink. Then he reaches up and flips his baseball cap backwards, rendering me speechless. He shouldn't look that damn good doing something so innocuous.

I stand by, watching as he crouches down to get a good look under the sink. I can hear him struggling with the water shut-off knob and then—

"*Fuck!*"

Water begins to gush even harder, and what was once a steady trickle is now a rushing stream. When Luke emerges from underneath the sink, the whole front of his white t-shirt is soaked. The material is translucent now, almost transparent, and the ridges of his abs are *very* visible.

I'd like to say this has no effect on me, but I try to live my life without lying. And *that* would be a big fat one. My mouth runs dry.

"I have to shut the water off for the whole house," he says. He begins to move out of the kitchen, toward the back of the house.

I follow him. "For how long? I have to—"

I gasp as the heel of my foot slips on a slick puddle of water. Unlike earlier, I can't seem to find my balance, and I make peace with my ass hitting the hard floor. I brace for the sting of impact, but it never comes.

Instead, strong arms band around my waist. A rough hand caresses the small of my back where my t-shirt has ridden up in the chaos. Chest to chest with Luke, I am acutely aware of the fact that I'm not wearing a bra. My nipples have hardened to peaks, and they are currently brushing against him with every strangled breath I take. My hands, which have fallen to Luke's biceps, give an involuntary squeeze. And it is at this point that my cheeks flush a bright crimson befitting of my embarrassment.

Still, up close like this, I let myself study Luke. Dark stubble coats his jaw, and I have the strong urge to let my fingertips trace it. His eyes, a deep brown, have swirls of amber in them. And, like always, they're guarded.

I've always had a hard time accepting that some people might not like me. But with Luke, it's not even just that. I want him to like me, but more so, I want to understand why he's so determined not to. Ever since I showed up at his family's house, he has been steadily trying to ignore my presence.

"Thank you," I croak.

Luke's hands drop from my body like my skin has turned into a live stove element. His touch made me feel hot all over, but now all I feel is cold.

"I'm going to shut the water off. Just—" His sigh is tinged with irritation. "Stay here. I don't need you breaking your neck."

The command in his voice brooks no argument. But I'm not very good at doing what I'm told. "No," I say. "What if this happens again? I want you to show me."

Luke looks like he wants to argue. His eyes roam my face, searching for something. Whatever he was looking for, he must find, because he lets out a resigned sigh. "Okay," he says. Then his hand is extended toward me. "Careful."

For a moment, my brain doesn't compute. Then it dawns on me, and I place my hand in his. He may have agreed to show me the ropes, but he doesn't trust that I can navigate the minefield of water on my own. Which, to be fair, I have slipped on twice in the span of forty-five minutes.

His hand is warm in mine. Not clammy, like I'm afraid mine might be. He leads and I follow. We pick our way across the wet floor, carefully circumventing any slips. Only when we make it to the hallway—firmly on dry land—do I realize that our hands are still connected.

I have the brief urge to leave my hand there, just to see

how long he'll continue to hold it. Does it feel as good to him as it does me? But I'm not in a position to piss him off further—he's my ticket to a functioning kitchen sink.

My palm slides out of his reluctantly. Luke looks down, almost like he's surprised, and then he flexes his hand before closing it into a fist. I look away, feeling like an intruder on a moment not meant to be mine.

He clears his throat. "The water shut-off valve is in the closet over here," he says, bringing us back on track. He shows me where the valve is and how to switch it off.

"There goes my morning coffee," I mutter.

"What?"

I sigh. "I can't make my morning coffee. It's completely unhealthy, but I haven't gone one morning for the past five years without coffee of some sort."

"You're right," he says. "That is wildly unhealthy."

At first, I think he's being a judgmental asshole. But when he looks over his shoulder at me, I catch the spark of amusement in his eyes. I'm not sure why he tries to hide it—why he won't let himself laugh. Or maybe he just won't let himself around *me*.

I shove at his shoulder. Of course, he doesn't move a muscle. "Oh, *whatever*. Leave me to my codependency and just help me fix my sink."

At this, he sobers, like he has been reminded why he is here in the first place. For business, not fun.

"I have to get to the station. Now that the water's off, the leaking should stop. I'll get my dad to come by later to fix it. He'll have to bring some new parts."

He nods, like everything is settled. He adjusts the bill of

his baseball cap to face forward—a goddamn shame, really—and then starts to head for the front of the house. To the front door so he can escape. But I don't want him to leave just yet.

If someone was studying my behaviour, they would be thoroughly confused. I don't even understand it myself. All I know is that Luke Bowman intrigues me as much as he unsettles me. Before I can confirm whether this is a good idea, I reach for his hand. He stops in his tracks and then turns to me, giving me his full attention.

"Thank you," I say. "I know this is probably the last thing you wanted to be doing before work. So…thank you."

Luke clears his throat, and I have the good sense to drop his palm. "It's nothing, Delilah. Don't worry about it."

Small footsteps thunder down the stairs, cutting off further conversation. A few seconds later, Sophia rushes into the room. "Hi, Luke!" She smiles. "Did you bring your puppy?"

All sense of shyness is gone as she looks up at him expectantly. Her hair is a mess from the tossing and turning she does in her sleep, and her blue eyes seem impossibly big. At the sight of her, Luke's demeanour visibly softens. It's fascinating to me how he can seem so impenetrable in my presence, but turn into a whole other person when Sophia is involved. Which is understandable—my little sister is adorable and hard to say no to.

Luke chuckles. "Sorry, not today, Soph."

"That's okay," she assures him. Then she tugs on the hem of my shirt. "Sissy, I'm hungry."

"I'll get out of your hair," Luke says, and then he disappears out the front door.

I help Sophia put together some breakfast, and then I do the same for myself. It doesn't feel the same without my regular cup of coffee, but I'll just have to make do and pick one up later.

Just as I sit down to eat, someone knocks on the front door again. Luke said he would send his dad by, but I wasn't expecting him so soon. Except it isn't John Bowman standing on my front porch; it's an employee from the café downtown.

"Delilah?" she asks.

I take note of the to-go cup in her hand. "Uh, hi?"

"This is for you." She shoves the cup into my hand. "Have a good one!"

She then descends the porch and climbs into the car parked on the street in front of the house. I stand in the doorway, still dumbfounded. I was just hand-delivered a coffee from the café that, as far as I know, does not deliver.

> Did you have coffee sent to me??

CLARA
No?

Clara knows how much I value my caffeine in the morning. Her asking the café to bring me a drink after a rough morning is totally something she would do. But she didn't. The only other person that knows I missed my cup of morning coffee is the very grumpy fire chief that showed up on my doorstep earlier. Which means...

Luke bought me coffee. But why?

CHAPTER TEN
LUKE

WHEN I MAKE it to the station after leaving Delilah's house, I am in no mood for pleasantries. The building, once alive with chatter, goes eerily still as I stalk toward my office. I never set out to be the kind of guy whose employees are intimidated by him, but it has become increasingly obvious that I am.

I roll my shoulders, trying to shake some of the tension. But I can't seem to get a certain brunette out of my head.

Seeing Delilah standing in the doorway, wearing the clothes she must have slept in... Those shorts—if you could even call them that, given how well they moulded to her body—showed off the expanse of her toned legs. That t-shirt, which slipped just enough to expose her shoulder and collarbone, begged me to trace that tattoo with my lips, then my tongue. Her pale cheeks were flushed the prettiest pink and her eyes still held a sleepy sheen, like she wasn't fully awake yet.

Fuck, I need to get a grip.

I don't want her. I don't want anything to do with Delilah Delacroix and the way she says my name. What I do want is to steer clear of her. If I could manage it, I'd attempt to get Clara to keep her distance, too. But I know better than to try to force my sister into anything.

My mind runs in circles over my morning. Now the disappointed look that flashed across Delilah's face when she realized she couldn't have her coffee floats across my mind.

Damn it.

I tug my phone from my pocket and pull up Loretta's contact, sending her a quick text. I'm a very loyal customer at the café, so I'm fairly certain she'll grant me this favour.

When I finally make it to my office, I sigh in relief. I need some time to get my head on straight—to focus on work instead of my newest distraction. Just as the door is closing behind me, Jodi slides inside the room. She holds up a mug of coffee as a peace offering when she registers my foul mood.

"Rough morning?" she asks.

I take the coffee and then round my desk, sinking into my chair. "Something like that."

Jodi eyes me over her own mug. She plops down in the seat across from me. "You going to tell me who pissed in your Cheerios, Chief?"

"Wasn't planning on it." Jodi hums, but she doesn't say anything. "What? I've just had a bad morning."

She raises a brow. "I thought you didn't want to talk about it?"

I rub my temple. "Did you do that on purpose?"

"Depends." She grins brightly. "Did it work?"

"You're a pain in my ass. You know that?"

To this, she simply shrugs. "It's what I live for. Now hurry up and spill."

"The kitchen sink at the pink house sprung a leak this morning. Clara asked me to go over and fix it."

"Ah," Jodi says, pointing a finger at me, "that explains the wet t-shirt contest submission." I glare, but all she does is laugh. "Wait, the pink house... That's where that pretty young thing is living, isn't it?"

I know exactly where she's going with this. It's the same direction my mind has been sprinting since I showed up at the house this morning. Hell, probably since I first saw Delilah.

"No."

I set my coffee on the desk and then rifle through the bottom drawer where I keep a change of clothes. It isn't often that I need them, but they come in handy for moments like this when I don't have time to head home to change. I stand and pull my t-shirt, still wet, over my head. I replace it with a dry one, and then I set the old one aside to air out.

"*No*, as in, I'm wrong? Or *no*, as in, you don't want me to be right?"

"*No*, don't go getting any stupid ideas," I amend.

Jodi takes another pull from her coffee. Despite the fact that she doesn't have any children, she pulls my mom's signature look off really well. The one that calls you on your bullshit without so much as a word. When she uses it on our rookies, I find it amusing, but when she turns it on me? Well, I don't like it quite as much.

She shrugs. "I just heard Forrester and Greenaway talking

about her earlier. She seems to have made *quite* the impression when they saw her at Dockside the other day."

Quite the impression indeed. Delilah seems to have made her mark on the whole island in the short time she's been here. You can't step one foot outside without hearing about the restaurant's new waitress. With the exception of Gordon, everyone is singing her praises.

But something about some of my guys talking about Delilah and the *impression* she made on them makes an unfamiliar feeling unfurl in my chest. Whatever it is, I don't have time for it, so I stuff it away. If I'm lucky, it won't crop up again.

"I don't think I care who the guys gossip about, Booth," I say. "So long as they get their jobs done."

Jodi hums again. "If you say so..."

Thankfully, my phone begins to buzz, saving me from this god-awful conversation and Jodi's scrutiny. When I flip it over, *Mom* is splashed across the screen. She is usually good about not calling when she knows I'm working, which means my mind immediately jumps to a potential emergency.

"Mom," I say. "Everything okay?"

"Hi, sweetie," Mom says. "Everything's perfectly fine. I just have a little favour to ask you."

If this favour includes Delilah, she can count me out. I've had my fill of that woman for today. The memory of her nipples straining through the thin fabric of her shirt while they brushed against my chest is still at the forefront of my mind. The root of a good portion of my frustration this morning, if I'm honest.

"Okay..." I say warily.

"You know those donations Carole was collecting for the department? Well, she needs you to go pick them up this morning."

"Does it have to be done this morning? Can't I swing by later?"

Mom sighs. "Luke, you know Carole. If you don't take them now, she'll misplace them, and then you won't see them until next spring."

Carole Dramus is a household name on the island, but she is also known to be synonymous with the word *scatterbrained*. I love the woman, and she means well, but sometimes it's hard to work with her.

I tip my head back with a sigh. "Fine. I'll head there now."

"Thank you," she says. "Now I have to go. I have to finish breakfast before I head into town to do some shopping. Love you!"

"Love you, too."

Maybe if I didn't, I wouldn't get roped into so much shit. Caring about people is exhausting. Even more so when you can't turn that part of yourself off. But I suppose I couldn't do the job I do if I didn't give a shit at least a little.

When I hang up the phone, Jodi is patiently waiting.

"Apparently I'm needed at the art gallery," I say as I stand.

She salutes. "Good luck. We'll hold down the fort."

Kip Island Fine Arts and Photography has been run by Carole for as long as I can remember. My mom and Carole have been friends since they were kids, so I've known the woman all my life. Every town has a resident busybody, and Carole is ours. She makes it a point to know everything being done on the island and if she thinks there's a better way to do it, she isn't shy about letting you know. That said, you won't find a kinder woman on Kip Island. Scatterbrain and all.

When I pull up to the curb outside the gallery, Carole is standing out on the sidewalk. She looks, as she always does, like she walked straight out of the seventies. Today she is sporting her signature bell-bottom jeans, a yellow flowy top, and Birkenstocks. Her greying hair is held back with a psychedelic-patterned headband.

"Luke," she says with a smile. "Thank you for coming!"

She holds her arms open for a hug and I fold into them. It's a little awkward, given how short she is in comparison. As we embrace, her familiar floral perfume invades my nose.

"Nice to see you, Carole."

She eventually releases me and then nods toward the gallery. "Alright, let's go find those donations."

She leads me inside, and I stand patiently as she looks for the box of donations. When she said she had to *find* them, she meant it. I glance at the clock, noting each minute that passes. I know everyone at the station will be fine without me, and I know that if they get called out, I'll be notified. Still, that doesn't stop the anxious energy from flowing through my veins.

"Aha! Got 'em."

Carole produces the box with a flourish. I take them and

tuck them under my arm, more than ready to get out of here. "Thank you, Carole. The department really appreciates this." Then I take a step back, prepared to make a run for it.

"Hold on," she says. "This would be a perfect opportunity for a picture!"

I stop in my tracks. "A picture? For what?"

"For the Facebook!"

She hustles around the front counter again and grabs her phone from underneath. It's an iPhone, cracked and a few generations behind. She then excitedly bounds toward me as she fiddles with the device. I stand awkwardly, wishing I was anywhere but here.

Just as I've convinced myself to grin and bear it, the bell above the door jingles and Carole lowers her phone. Her smile stretches as she spots the newcomer. "Delilah! What a wonderful surprise!"

Oh, you have got to be fucking kidding me.

I whip around and sure enough, the one woman I was hoping to avoid is standing just inside the entrance. Her sister is with her, their hands intertwined.

The braid in her hair from this morning is gone, replaced with what I have come to know as her signature ponytail. Her sleep shorts have been replaced with denim and the t-shirt she now wears clings to her torso, hiding the tattoo on her shoulder but accentuating her chest.

"Hi, Carole." Delilah's eyes sweep over us. "I take it this is a bad time?"

Yes.

"Oh, nonsense." Carole waves off her worry. "Look around. Make yourself at home."

When Delilah and Sophia start perusing the displays, Carole turns back to me. I brace for the picture, but she starts fiddling with her phone again, holding up a finger in the universal *one minute* signal. As I wait, I can feel Delilah's eyes on me, curious.

"Luke," Carole says, drawing my attention sharply to her. "You look a little tense, hun. Are you alright?"

"Fine," I grumble.

She raises her phone for the third time. "Alrighty, here we go!"

I wait, but nothing seems to be happening. "Carole? I've gotta get back to—"

"Oh, *shoot*. I just can't seem to..." Carole blows out a frustrated breath. Then she rounds on the only other adult in the building. "Delilah, would you be a dear and take the chief's photo for me? I want to put it on the Facebook."

When I allow myself to look at her, I find Delilah trying to suppress a grin. Her teeth snag her bottom lip as the edges of a smile curve her pretty mouth.

"Sure, Carole," she manages to say, despite the blatant laughter in her eyes.

She sets her purse on the front counter and then takes the device from Carole's hand. I shift from foot to foot, increasingly more uncomfortable as she studies the screen to line up the shot.

"How do you want me?" I ask.

Delilah's head shoots up, and if I didn't know any better, I would say that her gaze heats at my words. "Just like that," she says. Then, "You gonna smile for me, Chief?"

I raise a brow. "Just take the damn picture, Shutterbug."

I'm not sure where that nickname came from, and the surprise on Delilah's face is likely mirrored on my own. Still, she snaps a few pictures and then hands the phone back to Carole. Carole—the woman with a shit-eating grin on her face.

"Thank you so much, Chickadee," she says to Delilah. "You're a lifesaver."

Delilah points to the phone. "When you post that, don't forget to tag our beloved chief over there. We wouldn't want him to miss it."

I roll my eyes. Delilah's grin only stretches in response. She has a beautiful smile. It makes her eyes turn more blue than grey. Like the ocean, changing with the tide.

And on that note, I need to get out of here before she fully sweeps me away. Because with each passing minute of distraction, my control crumbles. I avert my eyes and say goodbye to Carole before pushing out the front door.

I don't look back.

CHAPTER
ELEVEN
DELILAH

WITHOUT REALLY MEANING TO, I stumble into a comfortable routine in the weeks following our arrival on the island. May bleeds into June, and with every day that passes, it begins to feel more like home here. Being surrounded by people that don't know the old me is refreshing. I don't have to pretend not to see the barely-contained pity in strangers' eyes.

I've also taken to spending my lunch breaks down on the beach. The water lapping at the shore mixed with the call of seagulls and the shouts of children down the sand have become my soundtrack as I let the fresh air invade my lungs.

Beside me, resting on my apron, my phone begins to ring. When I notice the Vancouver area code, I debate not answering. So far, my life back home hasn't followed me here, and I'd really like to keep it that way. I used to get regular messages from my ex, but even those have seemingly stopped. Just as the call is about to drop, my curiosity wins out and I accept.

"Hello?"

"Hi, is this Delilah?"

"It is," I say carefully. "Who is this?"

"My name is Tanya. My partner and I bought your family's home," the woman says. "I got your number from one of the neighbours. Sorry to cold call you like this, but I finally got around to sorting out the office today and I found something in the desk that I think might belong to you."

I swallow. "That was my father's office. It's probably just work stuff."

I should know—I was honoured with the painstaking task of clearing it all away. If it was up to me, I would have chucked the whole lot. None of it mattered anymore. But there were some important documents that Dad's assistant took off my hands.

"This doesn't seem like work. It was stuck to the top of one of the drawers, so it would've been easy to miss. But it looks like it's a letter addressed to you from your father."

My mouth goes dry. "What does it say?"

"When I realized how personal it was, I stopped reading," she says. "I'd be happy to mail it to you so you can see for yourself."

"Be honest," I say. "Do I want to read it?"

I wait with bated breath. I'm not sure which answer I would prefer. I just need someone to tell me what to do. I've been making it up as I go for months and I'm tired of second-guessing myself. What if she says that I don't want to read it? Does that mean that he didn't forgive me for what happened with Mitchell?

"If it was me…I would want to."

Anxiety swirls in the pit of my stomach. I simultaneously want to get my hands on that letter while also wishing that I never knew it existed.

"Thank you for telling me," I croak.

I relay my new address to Tanya and she promises to drop the letter in the mailbox later today. Then, after checking in with Parker and with Sophia's sitter, I return to Dockside.

"Everything alright?" Clara asks. "You look a little like you've seen a ghost."

I feel a little like it, too.

But I simply nod, tying my apron around my waist. "I'm alright. Just a little tired."

I decide not to mention the letter that Tanya found. For some reason, I can't bring myself to put words to whatever it is that I'm feeling, let alone admit it to Clara. So I shove it aside and pretend it doesn't exist. That strategy has yet to fail me.

In order to put the letter out of my mind, I jump back into work. We get a surge of diners—a class full of grade eights from the mainland on their graduation trip to the island. Serving them keeps me busy and on my feet, effectively putting everything else out of my mind as I try to keep their orders straight.

All that concentration goes out the window when Luke walks in.

My mouth runs dry as I watch him nod to people in greeting. How dare he have the audacity to come into my place of work looking like that. How am I supposed to do my job when the fire chief is posted at the bar wearing a button-up shirt that fits him so perfectly? It's truly unfair.

The past couple Sundays, Luke has been absent from the Bowmans' brunch. If I didn't know any better, I would say that he was doing it to avoid me. If not for the fact that Gabe was also absent, I wouldn't have known that the influx of tourists as summer progressed made the station busier than the month before. Still, whenever we are in the same room, he avoids making eye contact with me.

Maybe I wouldn't notice so much if I wasn't already looking at him.

It's a habit I know I should break. It isn't doing me any favours. But I can't help feeling drawn to him.

"*Delilah*. Are you sure you're okay?"

I jump, tearing my gaze away from Luke and pinning it on my boss. Clara's expression is one of concern, wary eyes scrutinizing me. I shake off my distraction, forcing myself to focus on her instead.

"Sorry." I offer her a sheepish grin. "What did you say?"

Clara rolls her eyes, though she still laughs. "I'm just going to take the garbage out. I'll be right back."

I nod, and she takes off through the door. This leaves me to turn my attention back to Luke. He is seated on a stool now, his forearms resting on the bar as his eyes scan his phone. I wait until he sets it aside to speak.

"You're late," I say.

His brow arches as amusement colours his features. This is the closest I've come to a laugh from him. "I wasn't aware we had an appointment," he replies. "Worried about me, Shutterbug?"

No, I think. *Yes. Just a little.*

Receiving the worst news of your life tends to condition you to be prepared for it to happen again, and the guy all but has a standing meeting with that barstool every day. Sue me for being concerned. It definitely doesn't have anything to do with the fact that I *may* enjoy seeing his stupid face while I work.

"I was just wondering who would play the role of Stoic Man Sitting On Stool if you weren't here to fulfill your duties."

He looks down, and I *think* I catch the barest hint of a smile. The asshole is trying to pretend that he doesn't find me funny. If he wants to ignore it, then *fine*. I wordlessly slide a glass of water—all he ever drinks is water—across the bartop. Then I input his usual lunch order into the computer.

His lips tip into a smirk. "Seems I'm not the only one beholden to routine."

I refuse to be embarrassed that I know his usual order. Good waitresses know their regular customers, and even though Luke isn't paying, that's what he is. A customer. Never mind the fact that I don't pay half as much attention to Dockside's other diners as I do him.

"How come you're all dressed up?" I ask instead, avoiding his supposition.

He sighs. "Another meeting with the mayor."

I want to ask more, but I get distracted by the unpleasant smell that begins to waft through the air. Then Clara appears, looking worse for wear. The front of her once-pink shirt is now soaked through and is some kind of suspicious brown colour.

My jaw drops. "Oh my God, what happened to you?"

She grimaces as she pinches her shirt and pulls it away from her midsection. "The garbage bag tore," she explains. "I have unidentified *juices* all over me."

"Holy hell, Clara," Luke curses with a wince. "That's disgusting."

She glares at her brother. "Gee, thanks. As if I don't already know that."

"Go home and shower," I say, patting her—thankfully dry—shoulder. "I've got the bar covered."

Most of the other waiters working today are new summer hires, and they, like me, haven't been trained on the bar. I learned rather quickly that that is Clara's domain—she only relinquishes control to a very specific set of people. But desperate times and all that. No way can Clara finish out her shift drenched in garbage juice.

She arches a brow, clearly not convinced. "You know how to bartend?"

"Well...not exactly. But you've said yourself that customers love me. They can learn to be patient while I figure it out."

I've been to enough parties in my life to know the basics. I'm sure it's not that hard. Clara, however, does not seem to share my sentiments. She turns pleading eyes on her brother.

"Can you stay?" she asks. "I know you probably need to get to the station, but I *really* would like to shower and I don't want to put this all on Delilah."

At this, I laugh. "What, you think Mr. Fire Chief will be better at slinging drinks than me?"

Luke crosses his arms, unimpressed. Then again, I don't think I've ever actually seen him impressed, so maybe that's just his face.

"I know how to make drinks. I worked here in the summers when I was in college," he says indignantly.

Clara ignores me as she directs her pout toward her brother. "Pretty please?"

That look is the embodiment of a younger sister's guilt trip. Sophia does it well, but Clara has perfected it. I can tell the exact moment that Luke decides to give in because his whole body locks, strung tight with the knowledge that he'll be stuck with me until she gets back.

"Fine," he eventually grumbles.

I clap my hands together. "Now that's the spirit!" I say sarcastically.

The chilliness of his answering glare would put the polar ice caps to shame. I simply smile in response. Clara blows Luke a kiss, mouths a *thank you* in my direction, and then she heads out the back door.

Now that it's mid-afternoon, the restaurant has died down considerably. Things will start to pick up again as it nears dinner, but for now we have a comfortable lull.

I turn to grab my glass of water and when I spin back around, I find Luke flicking open the button on his shirt sleeve. I unabashedly watch as he deftly rolls the fabric, exposing his forearm. He then repeats the process on the other side. I want to say the sight doesn't affect me, but that would be a goddamn lie. I've tried to ignore it, but Luke Bowman is undeniably a very good-looking man. And I am a weak, weak woman.

"Alright," I say. I set my water back on the counter and then plant my hands on my hips. "Where do we start?"

Luke sends me a questioning look. "We?"

I nod. "Yes, *we*. You're going to teach me how to make drinks."

He crosses his arms over his chest. This only pulls my attention to his arms even more. "I don't recall agreeing to that."

"You agreed to help your sister. Teaching me would be helping her."

"Helping her would be ensuring that you don't destroy her bar."

Now I cross my arms in defence. "Despite what you seem to think, I'm a fairly capable woman," I say quietly. "Not everything I touch turns to ashes, you know."

Is that what he thinks? That I'm going to wreck his family's restaurant like I wrecked my car? If he was Mitchell, the automatic answer would be yes. He never trusted me—not really. When Luke sighs, I can almost feel the resignation settle in his bones.

"Okay," he says, just like the day he came to help with my leaking sink.

The drink orders start off easy enough—just a couple pints of lager. They soon morph into mixed drinks and I begin to realize that bartending is perhaps harder than I thought. Luke is true to his word, walking me through each drink step by step.

I spin, reaching for a bottle of vodka on the back shelf. In the process, my elbow knocks into another bottle that I forgot to put back after the last drink. Time moves both fast and slow in the way it does when you wait for something to hit the ground.

But the bottle never makes it that far. Luke reaches out, his hand grasping the neck. He successfully stops it from careening to the floor and smashing at our feet. The only problem is that his body is now insanely close to mine, his chest pressed impossibly close to my back.

I can feel every breath he takes. I can sense the way his body tenses. I wait for him to move away. Yet he doesn't. Now time shifts and bends around me. I'm reminded of that day in my kitchen when he stopped me from falling. Only then, I could see his face. Right now I have no idea what he's thinking, and *God*, I want to. What I wouldn't give to know what is running through his head.

When he draws his body away from mine, I suddenly feel cold. He sets the bottle safely back on the shelf and clears his throat. "We need more lemons," he declares.

Before I can say anything, he takes off toward the kitchen. I would have believed him, if not for the full bowl of citruses on the counter.

Okay, he officially hates me.

I finish making that drink, and then I grab a cloth and begin wiping down the bar top. When I get to a particularly stubborn spot, I scrub—hard.

"You know what?" I mutter to myself. "*No.*"

He doesn't get to run away. I want an explanation—a reason why he can't stand to be in the same room as me for more than a few minutes. I throw the cloth down on the counter, and then I follow after him. I march right past the cooks and push into the walk-in refrigerator, letting the door smack closed behind me.

CHAPTER TWELVE

LUKE

FUCKING STUPID.

The cool air of the walk-in does nothing to dissuade the heat crawling up my spine thanks to her. *You're an idiot, Bowman. A goddamn idiot.* I shake my head at myself. At my foolishness. Why am I letting her get under my skin? I've only known the woman for a month.

When the door swings open and then slams shut, I look up. I shouldn't be surprised to find that she followed me. "What are you doing?" I demand.

Delilah stands guard in front of the exit. There is a stubborn set to her frame that tells me I'm not going to get out of this metal box easily. "Getting answers."

I give her my back, pretending to focus on the lemons I didn't really need to grab. I just needed a minute to breathe—to extricate myself from the sphere of *her*. Having to watch her strut around in those goddamn cutoff shorts is its own brand of torture, but physically being close to her, like that day in her kitchen, muddles my brain. I can't afford that.

Kristina made my head spin, too, and look how that ended. Abbie had nightmares for months, and I let my family down. Nothing good comes from me being distracted. Not then and certainly not now.

"Luke," she says, softer now. "Why do you hate me?"

The quiet plea in her voice breaks me. In setting out to protect myself, I've made her feel like I don't like her. That's not the problem. The problem is that I do—too much. But fuck, I never want to hear that sad quaver of her voice again.

I roll a lemon in my hands, still with my back to her. "I don't hate you."

She scoffs. "Fine, maybe you don't hate me, but you sure as hell don't *like* me. I'm just asking for some constructive criticism here, Chief."

That does me in. People call me Chief about a hundred times a day, but hearing it from her lips—right here, in this moment—sets something off inside my chest. I spin to face her, and Delilah looks startled at the move.

"What do you want from my family?"

What do you want from me?

All Kristina ever did was take, take, take. So the question launches from my mouth without any grace. It encompasses all the things I can't say out loud; all the things I wish I had asked Kristina. Before it was too late. I've always prided myself on being able to read people. But somehow, I managed to miss all the signs in the woman I thought I loved —the woman I thought loved me. And my niece paid the price.

Delilah's eyes turn quicksilver, more grey than blue. "*Nothing*. Despite what you seem to think, I didn't seek them out. I didn't ask for them to take pity on me. If you don't like it, take it up with them, but I'm not going to apologize."

This gives me pause. "You think they pity you?"

Her laugh is humourless. "Of course they do. Most days, I'm just trying to keep my head above water, and it's painfully obvious."

In this moment, I *do* feel sorry for her. Because she has evidently lived a life where genuine care and affection can so easily be mistaken for pity. If I know one thing, it's that my family has welcomed Delilah with open arms because that's just the type of people they are. Not because they think she is incapable of handling things on her own.

"You're too hard on yourself," I say. "You wanted constructive criticism. There it is."

Without meaning to, I've drawn closer. This woman is like a goddamn lighthouse calling me home. The chill of the refrigerator has nothing on the heat coursing through my veins.

"*I'm hard on myself*," she mocks. Her eyes narrow. "*That's* why you don't like me?"

I sigh. "You keep saying that."

"Because it's true."

This is when I do something stupid. Stupider than the things I've already done. I let the words slip that I've been doing everything in my power to keep in. "I don't like that you make me feel."

"Feel what?"

I don't answer at first because the truth is, I don't know. Attraction, yes. That's painfully obvious in the way that my body begs to be near her. But it's something else, too. Like parts of me—the ones that are a little jaded; a little broken—recognize those same parts in her. Like calls to like, and in a lot of ways, Delilah and I are the same.

"Things I haven't felt in a long goddamn time."

As the weight of that admission settles between us, Delilah takes a step closer to me. It seems I'm not the only one affected by the magnetic pull between us.

"You want to know what I do hate?" I ask. My voice is low.

Delilah's tongue darts out, licking her lips. My eyes can't help but fall at the action. "A lot of things, I'm sure."

My answering grin is wicked. "Many things, yes," I agree. "But most of all, I hate that I can't get you out of my head."

At this point, all sense has gone out of my brain. Truthfully, I'm not sure it ever existed when it comes to Delilah. The tether of my restraint snaps like a frayed rope. In one fell swoop, I have her sitting on a stack of crates, her thighs parted so I can slot myself into the space. I relish the gasp that leaves her.

"What are you saying?" she asks.

"I'm saying, Delilah—" My hand finds her dark ponytail, and I wind it around my fist. I test it by tugging slightly, eliciting another gasp. "That against my better judgment, you have tattooed yourself on all my senses. So all I want to touch is *you*." My other hand curls over one of her thighs. "All I can see is *you*." I let my eyes rove her body. "Taste." At this, I lean in. I nip the lobe of her ear, chasing it with my tongue. "Smell." I inhale deeply, my lungs expanding with whatever floral perfume she wears, but also something uniquely *her*.

"You forgot one." Her voice is breathy.

I release her ponytail, letting my fingers trail along the column of her throat. She tips her head slightly, giving me better access.

"Your voice. It haunts me," I admit.

"You know what *I* hate?" she asks. I meet her gaze. It swirls with want, just as my own. "I hate that you think you have any right to know me. That your reasons are more important than mine. But you don't have a right to my pain."

It is the briefest glimpse—a quick glance through a closing door—but I see everything she hides behind that mask of hers. She paints herself like a porcelain doll never meant to be played with, but beneath the surface, cracks are beginning to form. Have been for a while, if I had to guess. So I do the only thing I can: I swallow that pain whole.

My hand finds Delilah's throat. As I apply delicate pressure, I haul her mouth to mine. We clash like two opposing sides of a battle that are both determined to win. My palm on her thigh is punishing in its grip, but she just tightens her legs around my hips in response.

My veins hum with electricity, a steady current passing between us. When my tongue slides against hers, I feel a shock to my system, like I've been electrocuted. I didn't realize just how much my body had been craving Delilah until the feel of her was imprinted on my lips. The flavour of her cherry lip balm will linger for days.

After Kristina, I didn't let myself indulge in anyone. But one taste of Delilah and I know exactly what I've been missing out on.

When she pulls back, her lips are already swollen. She

looks at me. Looks *into* me. And then she surges forward, fisting the front of my shirt to bring my mouth back to hers. My palm slips further up her thigh, my fingers dipping beneath the hem of those denim shorts I hate to love so much. She responds in kind, hooking her finger through one of my belt loops and urging me closer.

The hand that was once at her throat now trails over her shoulder and down her arm. Goosebumps settle on her skin in its wake. I find the hem of her shirt and slip my palm beneath, curving around her back. Her skin is smooth beneath mine.

Kissing Delilah is nothing like I thought it would be. Stupidly, I assumed that once I had a taste, that would be enough to sate me. But as her tongue tangles with mine once again, it is becoming increasingly apparent that isn't the case. I want to savour her. More than that, I want to slip my hand inside those shorts and feel her.

Behind us, the refrigerator door swings open. My lips break from Delilah's, and I look over my shoulder to find the line cook staring at us, open-mouthed. It was easy to forget where we were when I had Delilah all to myself, but now everything comes crashing back. Not only are we far from alone, but we're also supposed to be running the bar.

A distraction. This woman is a goddamn distraction. She makes me feel reckless and I can't afford that. I take one step back and then another, putting distance between us. Maybe the farther I get, the easier it will be. I faintly register the door closing again, our audience now gone.

Delilah, undeterred, pats my chest as she slides off the stack of crates. "Back to work, Chief," she says in a normal tone. As if what just happened had no effect on her. Then she looks pointedly at my crotch. "Feel free to take a minute."

And then she's gone.

I stare at the spot where she was standing just a moment ago and run a hand over my mouth, disbelieving that that just happened. *What the hell did I do?*

What I do know for sure is that I am so fucking screwed.

CHAPTER THIRTEEN
DELILAH

I MANAGE to make it a whole day without acknowledging what happened between me and Luke. But at some point between the start of my shift at Dockside this morning and Clara arriving at my house, she grows suspicious.

"Okay," she declares. "I have to ask. Are you okay?"

"Of course." The flat look on her face indicates I'm going to have to be more convincing. "Why wouldn't I be?"

"I don't know. You're just acting...weird."

"I'm not acting weird," I insist.

Clara raises a brow. "You're acting *really* weird."

To evade her likely line of questioning, I take a sip of my margarita. Having a bartender for a friend comes in handy when you want a fancy drink but don't have the energy to go to a bar—or a babysitter. One text and Clara brought what seemed like the whole bar setup to my kitchen island. Which is perfect because after the past few days I've had, I really need this drink.

"You've been really fidgety today," she continues. She pops an olive in her mouth mid-sentence. Along with the alcohol, she brought a charcuterie board heaping with cheeses, meats and various pickled things. "You don't fidget. And I don't think you've made proper eye contact with me once. So again, *weird*."

Perhaps my friend isn't as oblivious as I hoped. Skirting by without acknowledging the elephant in the room seems less and less like a viable option.

"Would you believe me if I said I was just tired?"

Clara laughs. "Well, I maybe would have if you hadn't said it like *that*. What's going on? Is it that douchebag ex of yours again?"

I've only shared a little bit about my relationship with Mitchell, but from what she has heard, she is *not* a fan. That makes two of us.

I exhale deeply. "No, not this time."

She sets a hand on my arm, her gaze growing concerned. "Then what is it?"

I'm not sure how Luke would feel about his sister knowing the real reason why I've been off all day. We didn't exactly have time to discuss it. But I don't think I can keep it in any longer. I don't think I want to. My head is a messy place to be and Clara is the first friend that's made me feel comfortable enough to share everything, even if it is messy.

"Your brother...kissed me."

Clara leaps off the couch, nearly spilling her drink and knocking the charcuterie to the floor. Her face is a mix of shock and a little disappointment. "Oh my God. *Gabe*?"

"*What*? No!" I set my glass on the coffee table and cover

my face with my hands, my cheeks flaming. Why did I decide to tell her this again? It definitely wasn't one of my brightest ideas. "*Luke*. Luke kissed me."

"Not Gabe?"

I shake my head, still hiding. "Not Gabe."

"And you're sure it was Luke? *My* Luke?"

I groan. "I think I know who kissed me, Clara!"

When I peek out between my fingers, I'm not sure what I expect to find on her face. What I certainly *don't* expect is the sly smirk stretching across her pink-painted lips. It's at this moment that the regret really starts to settle in.

"When did this happen? Where?"

I cringe. "Remember when that garbage juice got all over you and you ran home to shower?"

"Delilah Delacroix!" she mock scolds as she retakes her seat beside me. "The boss steps out and you decide to have a make out session with her brother?"

"It wasn't a *make out session*." Okay, it kind of was. "And *he* kissed *me*!" My voice comes out shrill, and I realize too late that that only makes me seem more guilty.

"But the real question is: did you kiss him back?"

When I don't respond right away, she raises a brow. I groan, covering my face again. "I shouldn't have brought this up. I really don't think I should be talking about this with you."

"Let's forget that he's my brother for a second. This is what friends do, Dee. Hallie and I used to talk about stuff like this all the time. It's not the same with her living in Toronto now, so I *need* this. You are my only friend here besides my brothers." She exaggerates her frown and puts her palms together in prayer. "That's *sad*. Please?"

"Well, you're my only friend, period," I counter. I didn't have many to begin with, and the few that I did have had no idea how to act around me after what happened with Mitchell. My parents' deaths only made things worse, so I stopped reaching out. "We can be sad together."

"Deal." Then she looks at me expectantly. "*So...?*"

"I may have accidentally kissed him back. Just a tiny bit."

"*Accidentally?* Delilah!" She shoves my shoulder and I pretend to topple over from the embarrassment.

"Clara!" She bites her smile, but an excited hum still manages to escape her. I can see her brain churning as she tries to spin this into one of her romance book plots. I shake my head as I point a reprimanding finger in her direction. "Don't get your hopes up. It was just a kiss."

A *really good* kiss. A kiss I'm going to measure all kisses, past and present, against. But that's all it was. When Jimmy walked in on us, the look on Luke's face was one full of regret. So even if I wanted it to mean something, he obviously doesn't. The only way forward is to pretend it never happened.

"Sure. That's what all the main characters say."

"Seriously, Clara! This is not one of your books. There is no happily ever after in the cards for me and Luke. There is no *me and Luke*."

She pouts. "Ugh. But your tropes would be so *good!*"

"I don't even know what that means, but no. Just no. Can we talk about something else?"

"Fine," she agrees. She takes another sip of her drink

before narrowing her eyes at me. "When are you going to enter Carole's photography contest?"

I should have known that changing the subject would backfire on me. Clara has the uncanny ability to pick out exactly what I'm trying to avoid and then talk about it until I can't escape. It's very annoying when I'm trying to ignore all my problems.

"Any chance we can talk about another something else?"

Clara shakes her head. "Sorry, lady. It's either Luke or the contest."

I slump in my seat. "I hate you." She only grins in response. I take a healthy sip of my drink before speaking. "I'm not entering," I declare.

"But—"

"I know how you feel about that, and I really appreciate the confidence you have in me. But I just don't think it's a good idea right now."

I can't exactly put into words why I feel so hesitant. What happened was years ago now. It shouldn't matter anymore. But it does, and I hate that it still affects me. Clara would probably think it's a stupid excuse. Even *I* think it's a stupid excuse, yet here I am, using it as a way to justify not doing something that I want to do.

My friend studies me for a moment. I worry that she can see straight through me, as if I'm made of glass. I squirm under her scrutiny—fidgeting just as she said.

"Okay." I breathe a sigh of relief as she accepts this. "I get it. You've got a lot going on."

That is the understatement of the century. I thought I had everything under control, but now every day feels like more is being piled on. Hell, I still haven't gotten around to getting my headlight fixed. It has become a permanent fixture on my to-do list.

This time last year, I only had myself to take care of. Don't get me wrong, I do not regret taking my siblings for even a second. But going from a mostly functioning single adult to suddenly having two people depending on me for almost everything is exhausting. Still, I would do it again a hundred times over.

"What about you?" I ask, desperate to *actually* change the subject this time.

At this, Clara blushes. The natural scarlet compliments the pink headband she has on. "What about me?"

"I don't know... Do you have a *special someone* you haven't told me about?"

"Okay, one," she says, holding up a manicured finger. Her nails are oval-shaped and painted a light pink—her favourite colour. "You sound like my grandma. Two, no, I don't. There aren't exactly a lot of guys who are *special someone* material on the island. I went to high school with just about all of them and they might as well still go there for all that they've matured."

"What about *off* the island?"

She blinks, looking as if the thought of dating somewhere other than Kip Island hasn't even crossed her mind. Eventually, she shakes her head. "I don't want to leave. I mean, I've got Dockside, and my parents always need help with one thing or another."

"Do you really not want to? Or do you just think that you can't?"

Not that I want her moving away from me after I just found her, but if that was something she wanted, I would support her one hundred percent. From the expression on her face, though, I can tell that I've struck a nerve.

She sucks in a breath and then pastes on a grin. "What I need is one of my book boyfriends to show up on the island, small town romance style, and then all my problems would be solved."

Alright, so we're deflecting with jokes. I can take a hint. I'm not exactly in a position to argue when I'm doing my best to evade answering hard questions myself.

"If you could pick any set of tropes, whatever those are, what would they be?"

Clara looks excited, as if she has been preparing all her life to answer this question. "Small town romance, obviously."

I roll my eyes with a smile. "*Obviously.*"

"I love reading enemies to lovers. The tension is always off the charts, so I think that would be fun. Bonus points if it's spicy."

I arch a brow. "Enemies? I couldn't see you being enemies with anyone. You're too nice."

She fluffs her hair. "That's what I want you to think. Everyone in this town sees me as sweet little Clara. But if you wrong me or someone I love, all bets are off."

I chuckle. "Remind me not to get on your bad side."

We leave the uncomfortable topics behind and delve into much more important matters: town gossip. Back in Victoria, we hardly knew our next door neighbours, let alone most of the city. Here on the island, unless you're a tourist, you can't really get away with anything. Even then, it's hard to evade notice. I sure didn't miss the looks that I received when I first arrived. Now that I've lived here a while, I've become old news and I can enjoy the gossip mill for what it is.

Most of Kip Island's gossip is funnelled through Maria, one of the parents in charge of the PTA at the elementary school. I'm not sure where she gets it all from, but she disseminates news faster than the newspaper, the Island Chronicles.

"Oh!" Clara says a while later. She plucks her phone off the coffee table and starts tapping away. "Look at this picture Hallie sent me. The lucky bitch got to visit Paris when her nanny family took her to freaking *France* with them!"

I chuckle. "Jealous?"

"Only a little," she admits. "France is number one on my travel bucket list."

As I look at the photo of the Eiffel Tower all lit up at night, the front door swings open. Parker walks in, his head down and his earbuds in. Par for the course these days.

"Hey!" I call. I wave a hand in his direction, but he swiftly ignores me. "Parker."

Without sparing me a glance, he grabs an apple from the fridge and then trudges up the stairs. I slump back on the couch, blowing out a frustrated breath. And when my eyes land on Clara again, my cheeks flame. God, it's embarrassing that she witnessed that—how utterly inept I am at all this. I can't even get my own brother to like me enough to acknowledge me.

She offers me a small smile, one tinged with pity. "Want me to make you another drink?"

I thrust my glass toward her. "Yes, *please*."

CHAPTER FOURTEEN
LUKE

RUNNING USED to be nothing more than a game. A bit of tag in the backyard when Clara, Gabe and I were kids. Then it became a competition. Who, between the three of us, could reach an arbitrary finish line first. Although our parents tried their best, we all grew up with a bit of a competitive streak.

Recently, it has become a distraction. When I bury myself up to my eyeballs in the stacks of paperwork on my desk and it's still not enough to quiet my brain, I run. Most of the time I head out on my own, but sometimes—days like today—Clara or Gabe join me.

"You really *are* the favourite grandchild, huh?" my brother muses.

While Gabe and Clara both got left a generous sum of money when our maternal grandparents passed away, I was gifted their house. My grandmother would probably have a heart attack if she saw what had become of her beloved home, but there wasn't a whole lot of good left after the fire. Better to tear down the ruins and start again.

I pop the tops off two bottles of beer and then settle into one of the Muskoka chairs on my back deck. My property backs onto a small wooded area. Early in the morning, this is the perfect spot to catch a glimpse of the wildlife. And in the evening, it is the optimal place to unwind after a run where I not only hit a personal best, but also effectively dethroned my brother.

"Done licking your wounds?" I ask, holding one of the bottles out to Gabe.

He grabs it, promptly taking a swig. With his free hand, he flips me the bird. I grin.

"You claim I'm a sore loser, but you haven't let a minute go by without gloating. You're a showboat, dear brother," he replies.

I laugh. Sure, I'm milking this a little, but Gabe has been terrible at losing since we were kids. There were many a thrown Monopoly board—so many that Mom banned board games in our house for a while. It's fair to say my brother has gotten better with age, but he still doesn't take too kindly to seeing someone else have what he wants.

With a ball in his mouth, Riot bounds up the steps. He drops it at my feet expectantly. I bend and retrieve it, and then I lob it across the yard. He takes off like a shot and I relax back in my chair.

"What's Abbs up to tonight?" I ask. Shifting the conversation to my niece is a surefire way to improve my brother's mood.

"Clara took her for a sleepover again." He cocks his head,

mulling something over. "Not that I'm ungrateful, but she's been spending a lot more time with Abbie lately…"

I rest my bottle on the armrest of my chair, totally focused on my brother. "Why is that bad?"

"It's not necessarily bad," he assures. "It's just different. Haven't you noticed that *she* is different? I don't know. I can't put my finger on it; I just have this feeling. Maybe it's a twin thing, but I'm worried about her."

Guilt gnaws at me. What does it say that I *haven't* noticed a change in our sister?

It says I've been too distracted, that's what. A certain dark-haired beauty enters my life, and suddenly I'm dropping the ball left and right. Something I can't afford with my family.

"I'll keep an eye out," I assure him.

I may not have noticed before, but like hell am I going to let anything get past me now. Clara tends to keep her secrets locked up tighter than Fort Knox, and I generally respect that, but if she's struggling with something, I want to know. I want to help her. Need to.

We settle into a comfortable silence, watching as the sun slides lower in the sky, bathing everything in golden hour light. I get so lost in my thoughts that I almost miss when Gabe speaks.

"So," he drawls, picking at the label on his bottle, "Delilah, huh?"

His mention of her name brings me crash landing back to earth. I grunt. "What about her?"

His eyes bore into the side of my face. I set my jaw, opting for a neutral expression. Still, in my peripheral vision I can see his lips tug into a knowing grin.

"You've got a crush," he accuses.

I scoff. "What are you, twelve? I do not have a crush."

My knee begins to bounce—a telltale sign that I'm not telling the entire truth. I cross my ankle over the opposite knee, hoping that Gabe won't read much into it. Of course, that's too much to ask for with my nosy brother.

"I don't blame you, you know," Gabe continues. "For having a crush on Delilah. She's..."

Don't take the bait, Bowman. Gabe has been a class-A shit disturber since the day he came home from the hospital. This is no different.

"She's *what*?" My tone is sharper than a knife.

My brother smirks, and then he takes a slow pull from his beer, drawing out his response. "She is a very intelligent woman," he finally says. "Which is unfortunate for you because it means she's going to realize sooner rather than later that she can do better."

I shove at the side of his head. All he does is laugh in response.

"There's nothing to do better at because there's nothing going on between us."

Gabe shakes his head. "If you say so."

"I do say so. Delilah is a fine woman." I cringe internally at my wording. "But I'm not interested."

He laughs, undoubtedly at my expense. "It's really funny you believe that."

"Alright," I huff. "I *can't* be interested."

This catches him off guard, and he's silent for a minute.

"Man, Kristina really did a number on you, huh?" he says eventually.

My jaw clenches, my molars grinding together. My ex is my least favourite topic, and I'm already on edge after he brought up Delilah. Talking about Kristina feels akin to picking apart every last mistake I've ever made until I'm raw and bleeding.

His expression softens. "It wasn't your fault, Luke. You've gotta let it go. I'm not burying you with someone else's guilt."

If only it was that easy.

The once comfortable silence is now riddled with tension. I let out a slow breath. I don't generally like being at odds with my brother, even if he is a pain in the ass. I'm usually the one that extends the olive branch, and today is no different.

"You seeing anyone lately?" I ask.

I'm not sure why I do. We don't often talk about the women in our beds, and keeping on this topic is bound to circle back to Delilah, if I know my brother.

He huffs a laugh. "Dating on Kip Island is hard enough without the added perk of being a single parent."

He and Abbie's mom were only together long enough to create her. Larissa was a friend of a friend, and a simple one night stand later, she was pregnant. The first couple years weren't easy by any means, but they managed to come out the other side as friends who happen to share a daughter.

He isn't wrong about the dating scene, though. The pool of singles on the island is not so much a pool as it is a puddle that consists of old classmates and middle-aged divorcées.

The only reason I met Kristina was because she came here on vacation and never left. Maybe that should have been my first red flag.

For Gabe, it's undoubtedly harder, given the time he dedicates to his daughter and his work. But I have a feeling that isn't the only thing holding him back.

"Hm," I hum. "How's Hallie these days?"

Gabe stiffens. "Hallie?"

"Yeah, you know. Hallie, the short blonde that used to follow you around with hearts in her eyes. Have you spoken to her lately?"

"She's Clara's best friend, not mine. Why would *I* have spoken to her?"

I shrug. "I don't know. Didn't stop you in high school."

His jaw tightens. He glances away, out toward the trees. For a moment, I think maybe he's going to ignore me. Then he says, "Well, newsflash: we're not in high school anymore."

Ever since Hallie Foster left the island, just days after their high school graduation, she's been a touchy subject. Clara and Gabe met Hallie in kindergarten, and ever since, Clara has been friends with her. But there always seemed to be something between him and Hallie. Except graduation came and went, and she left for university. She hasn't really been home since.

Clara is still friends with her. They talk every day. But when Gabe is around, she never mentions Hallie. No one knows exactly what happened between her and Gabe before she left, but we do know it wasn't good. Our brother wasn't the same after.

I decide not to press the subject. Instead I let the silence settle over us again.

The sound of glass shattering rouses me from sleep. I'm alone in my bedroom at the back of the house. Another crack, this time like the house is settling into place.

I throw off my covers and pad across the room. Opening my bedroom door, I lean out into the hallway. Everything is dark, but slivers of moonlight illuminate the floor. I move to investigate, but then more glass fractures. My pulse quickens in response. The sound is distant, coming from the front of the house. What the hell?

Another loud smashing of glass. This time, it's my bedroom window.

A flash of light, and then fire. I step back as it licks at the edge of my bed like a match taking to a fresh wick. Out. I need to get out.

I make my way to the front door, but the moment I try to turn the handle, it doesn't budge. I tug and tug, but it's no use. Dread settles in my gut.

Back in my bedroom, a red brick lies on the rug, pieces of glass littered all over the floor. Most of the pane is gone, but some jagged pieces jut out from the frame. The house is steadily going up in flames, so the window is my only choice of escape.

I swing my legs over the sill. As I lower myself, my shoulder snags on a piece of glass. I bite back my groan as it rips my skin and blood trickles down my arm. It's warm and sticky, the metallic stench mixing with the smoke rapidly filling the air.

Finally, I drop to the ground. The house only has one storey, so the jump wasn't far, but the shock of my landing still reverberates through my legs. I try to drag air into my lungs as I move away from the wall of the house.

"Lukey!"

My steps falter. No. That's not right. She isn't supposed to be there.

"Lukey, help me!"

I wake with a start. My chest is tight, like the smoke I saw in my head was more than just an illusion. Gabe left hours ago, and now the house is dark around me. Sitting up, I realize that I fell asleep on the couch. I reach over and switch a lamp on, the warm light illuminating the space. Riot stirs from his bed in front of the fireplace.

I scrub a hand down the side of my face. My heart still pounds, the nightmare feeling much too vivid and real for my liking. It wasn't real—at least, not most of it. There were fragments that were memories, interwoven with the nightmare. Just enough to remind me what's at stake when I let my guard down.

For a time, these nightmares were a nightly occurrence. Abbie's seemed to be the same, which made the guilt settle bone-deep. My niece is doing better—back to the carefree kid she should be. I thought I was better, too. But lately I've been backsliding, and I'm sure it has to do with that kiss.

Kissing Delilah was like a dream. One I didn't want to wake up from. But I don't get to live in dreamland. I tried that once and it almost got my niece killed. My brother may want me to let it go, but I can't.

Riot stands from his bed and walks over to me. He

nudges my hand with his snout, and I oblige, my fingers sifting through the soft fur at his neck. In another life, Riot could have been some type of support dog. From the beginning, he has been in tune with me, and he can tell when I've had a rough day.

"I just have to put her out of my head," I say aloud. "That can't be too hard, right?"

Riot's head cocks to the side as he snorts. As if he's saying, *Yeah, right. Good luck with that.*

I relax into the couch and tip my head to the ceiling. As much as I want to deny it, Gabe may have had a point earlier. I don't like my brother being right on any given day, but especially about something like this. It just means I'm going to have to work extra hard at staying away from her. It's the only way. But staying away is hard to do when my family has taken her in and given her a standing invitation to brunch.

Riot lets out a pitying sigh.

I groan. "*Fuck.*"

CHAPTER
FIFTEEN
LUKE

AVOIDING DELILAH WORKS—FOR two days. I knew it was futile, but I had to try anyway. Giving up—giving *in*—is not an option. Though in a town the size of Kip Island, it was only a matter of time before our paths crossed again.

Sometimes I take Riot to the dog park in town so he can let out some energy with other dogs his size. The fenced-in space is close to the playground where all the kids like to hang out when it's sunny. Today, of course, is the one day that Delilah and Sophia happen to be there the same time we are.

When Riot spots Delilah, he whines. Then he begins to pull, and the loose grip I had on his leash is no match for his strength. He bounds toward her, a tennis ball clamped firmly in his jaw. As soon as he reaches her, he drops the ball at her feet. Even from a distance, I can hear her melodious laugh.

"Now where did you come from?" she asks as she takes hold of his dangling leash. "I don't think you're supposed to be over here, buddy."

Riot gives himself away, looking guiltily in my direction. As I approach, Delilah's gaze pans to me. And she looks... surprisingly normal.

It isn't like I want her to tear into me, wondering why I haven't been around after that kiss. But I was expecting a little bit of a reaction at least. Instead she just wears her usual smile as she strokes between Riot's ears. This sets me on edge. If she was Kristina, I know she would have been pounding on my door, demanding an explanation. Wanting us to talk.

"First my family, now my damn dog," I say. "You seem to bewitch everyone."

I try to sound annoyed, but it doesn't quite have the intended bite. This causes her to laugh again and fuck, I really love that sound. Delilah is captivating in a way that begs for my attention—but I've been deluded before. Lulled into complacency. And it was all a lie.

"Sorry. I can't help that I'm just that lovable."

She says it sarcastically, as if she honestly doesn't realize how true that statement is. But ever since she decided to make Kip Island her home, the people have embraced her with open arms. My family isn't the only one invested in her success here.

From the set of swings, Sophia spots us. A beaming smile stretches across her lips as she waves. Delilah and I both wave back. Then the silence sets in.

I'm not entirely sure why I'm still standing here except for the fact that I can't seem to leave. Riot and I should be well on our way to the off-leash area. Yet here I stand. Maybe it has something to do with the fact that everything between me and Delilah feels unresolved.

"Look—"

"About the other—"

We both speak at the same time. She lets out an awkward chuckle.

"You go," I say.

"Oh, um, okay. I was just going to say that this—" She gestures between us. "Doesn't have to be weird."

I arch a brow. "Weird?"

"Yeah." Her head bobs on a nod. "You know, *weird*. We're both adults who can recognize that what happened the other day was just a little...blip."

In other words, a mistake.

This should be a relief. It *is* a relief. All she's doing is putting words to everything I've been thinking since that day. So why does it feel so *wrong* to hear?

"A blip?"

"Are you just going to repeat everything I say?"

I scowl. "Explain."

She rolls her eyes. "You may be someone's boss, but you certainly aren't mine, so you can tone down the attitude." I cross my arms, trying not to give away how much I enjoy her putting me in my place. "Yes, a *blip*. We both got caught up in the moment, and we said and did some things that we normally wouldn't have. But it's not a big deal, so let's not make it one. You can go back to mildly tolerating my existence and that'll be that."

That'll be that.

She seems like she has it all figured out. However, I'm not so sure I want this role I've been given. I can't be with her—can't kiss those lips I've been dying to taste again—but I don't like her thinking that I hate her. I need to get a better handle on myself. Maybe then I won't act like an asshole when I'm trying to keep myself from doing something I shouldn't.

I can be nice. I *should* be nice. On top of being Clara's friend, she's my parents' employee. The expectation is that I'm *not* a complete douche. For all the reasons why I shouldn't care what she thinks of me, there are a million more for why I do.

"Alright," I agree, "it was a blip. But mildly tolerating your existence isn't going to work for me."

"Oh, right. I forgot. You don't like me at all."

I hum. At this point, I won't be able to convince her of the truth, so I ask, "What if I said that I changed my mind?" Her eyes narrow on me in response. "Counter offer: we forget the kiss—"

"The blip."

"We forget the *blip* and carry on like two civilized people who are going to be in each other's lives for the foreseeable future. Think you can handle that, Shutterbug?"

She grins. "Oh, I can take it, Chief."

The words are innocent enough, but the gleam in her eye certainly isn't. *Ah, fuck.* I should have known she wouldn't make this easy on me.

Thankfully, she averts her gaze a moment later to check on Sophia. The little girl is climbing the stairs of the play structure to get to the spiral slide on the opposite end. This gives me time to think about anything other than the heat in Delilah's eyes.

When her attention is back on me, I jerk my chin toward

the camera slung over her shoulder by the strap. "So you're a photographer."

She rests a protective hand on the device, like my talking about it might make it disappear. "It's mostly just a hobby. Pretty amateur stuff."

Something tells me that's not entirely true. From the way my sister was acting, it seems like Delilah is stuck on selling herself short.

"Have you thought about that photography contest?"

She looks a little surprised that I asked, though she schools her expression quickly. Her cheeks, however, turn pink. "What photography contest?"

I raise a brow. "Carole's contest. The one you got all flustered about when Clara suggested you enter."

"Oh," she says halfheartedly. "That one."

I chuckle. "Yeah, *that one*."

She sighs. "Fine, I've thought about it. And it's not happening."

"Why not?"

I probably shouldn't pry. We barely know each other, and we only just agreed to play nice. But I ask anyway. Her lips part, ready to respond, but my phone interrupts her. I swear I see her sigh in relief as she gestures for me to answer.

As I listen to Jodi on the other end of the line, Delilah tries to pretend she isn't paying attention to me. But I notice the way her eyes trace the changing expression on my face.

"Everything alright?" she asks after I hang up.

I shove my phone back into my pocket. "I have to go. There's a bad accident on the causeway and they need me."

"Oh. Of course." Worry softens her expression. "I hope everyone is alright."

I nod in acknowledgement, ready to head back to my truck. But then my eyes land on Riot. Delilah still has a hold of his leash and now he's lying in the grass at her feet, chewing on his ball. My next words are out before I can stop them, but I don't take them back.

"Can you do me a favour?"

If I thought she was surprised before, then she is even more so now. Which is fair. I really haven't been the nicest guy lately. The familiar ache of guilt churns in my stomach. I'll just have to fix it. Not sure how yet, but I will.

"Uh," she stammers, "sure."

"Do you think you can take Riot? I don't really have the time to stop at home."

She doesn't hesitate to nod. "Of course," she says. "I've got him."

"You're sure?"

"*Go*. He'll be fine, Luke. I have no doubt you would track me down if he wasn't."

As I back away, I point a finger at her. "I know where you live, Delacroix."

She mock gasps. "Is there *actually* a sense of humour hiding in there?"

When I glance over my shoulder, I let her catch a corner of my smile. And then I walk away, choosing to trust her in a way I'm not sure she entirely understands.

Later that night, I find myself steering my truck onto Hawberry Lane. The last time I was here, I had to deal with a leaking sink and Delilah dressed in those goddamn sleep shorts. Keeping my hands off her was decidedly difficult. I'm hoping this encounter goes a whole lot smoother.

Though the sun is still casting a faint glow across the sky, the porch light is on at the pink house. And when I ascend the steps, I'm surprised to find Delilah outside.

She sits on the porch swing my dad and I installed for Muriel two summers ago. One foot is tucked beneath her while the other, bare, skims the wooden slats below, controlling the pace of her back and forth movement. Riot lies on the porch, chin resting on his front paws. He barely opens his eyes on my approach.

"Hey," she says with a smile. A smile I've begun to look forward to.

I lean back against the railing, bracing my hands on either side of my body. The chipping white paint digs into my palms. I make a mental note to mention it to Dad. Technically, this is Clara's domain, keeping an eye on the rental properties, but if I can give her one less thing to worry about, then that's what I'm going to do.

"Thanks for taking him," I say. "Sorry it's so late. I meant to ask Clara to pick him up, but it slipped my mind."

"It's okay," she assures. "Is everything alright? With the accident?"

For a moment, I'm too stunned to answer. I clear my throat. "It wasn't pretty, but it could have been worse. After some time in the hospital, everyone should make a full recovery."

She looks...*relieved*. She doesn't even know the people that were involved, yet she clearly cares. Enough to ask about them anyway. I can't help comparing her to Kristina. My ex hated when I had to blow her off for work. It wasn't often, and my job isn't exactly something you feel good saying no to, yet it always caused a fight. If I had left her with Riot, it would've been even worse.

Delilah bends and strokes the dog's back. "Well, feel free to need a favour more often. Soph had a blast, and I think Riot did, too."

That explains why he hasn't even acknowledged my presence. Usually I get a tail wag at the very least, but he looks like he's dead to the world. I might even have to carry him to my truck. "I owe you one."

Beside her on the swing, Delilah's phone buzzes in swift succession, indicating a handful of texts have come through. When she glances at it, her shoulders stiffen.

"You okay?" I ask.

She flips her phone face down. By the smile she pastes on her lips, you wouldn't think anything was wrong. But I can tell by the crease in her brows that something is up. "It's nothing," she says. She leaves her phone on the swing as she stands and moves closer to me.

I fold my arms across my chest. "I don't know if I believe that."

She rolls her eyes. "Fine. It was my ex boyfriend. Happy now?"

No, I think. *Not a fucking chance*. It's certainly not my place to care, but that hasn't stopped me before. I don't like the thought of her being uncomfortable because of this guy.

"Why is your ex texting you?"

"You know, that's an *excellent* question. Why don't you ask him?"

My mouth curves upwards in response. "Don't tempt me."

She shakes her head. This time, a genuine smile stretches across her lips. "I'm a big girl, Chief. I can handle my own problems. Especially ones named Mitchell."

I nod. "Understood."

We lock eyes, and the intensity in hers makes my head spin like one of those midway rides at the town's fall fair. I need to go. I'm on the brink of breaking all the rules I've laid out for myself. The most important of which is keeping my hands to myself, no matter how good she looks in those cutoff denim shorts. Delilah's tongue traces her lower lip and my traitorous eyes track it.

"It was a blip," she says after a long moment, as if she needs convincing.

"A blip," I agree.

"So we definitely shouldn't do it again."

"Definitely not."

She regards me for a second more. Resigned, she retrieves her phone from the swing. And then I watch as she slips through her front door. Before it closes, she pokes her head back out and issues me a soft smile.

"Goodnight, Chief," she says.

"Night, Shutterbug."

CHAPTER SIXTEEN
DELILAH

SOMETHING IS DIFFERENT ABOUT LUKE.

He left my house with Riot two hours ago, and still, he's on my mind. Specifically, our interaction at the park. I remember the sharp whistle cutting through the air as Luke tried to call Riot back to him. I turned toward the sound, and my eyes instantly widened. If I was a cartoon character, hearts would have been circling my head. Because Luke Bowman came striding in my direction wearing a baseball cap. A *backwards* baseball cap. I wondered briefly if he knew how good he looked.

Maybe it was the sun shining on him just right, or perhaps I was still drunk from our kiss, but there was an unmistakable shift in the air around him.

Now as I lie in bed trying to sleep, my mind drifts to that day at Dockside. *Against my better judgment, you have tattooed yourself on all my senses*, he said. I can play it off to Clara as just a simple kiss all I want, but the truth is that I'm still hung up on it days later. I can't see myself getting over it anytime soon either. Especially not when Luke goes off script.

His behaviour today is in direct opposition of everything I thought I knew about the man and his feelings toward me. Before today, I could have sworn that he wanted nothing to do with me. Even after the kiss, which any rational person would chalk up to pure physical attraction. But then he asked about my photography and genuinely seemed interested in my response. And when he asked me to look after Riot? All my preconceived notions flew out the window.

This isn't what I wanted. Leaving Victoria, coming here—I didn't plan to find a distraction in someone like Luke. But maybe... Maybe it wouldn't be so bad.

I strike the thought down as soon as it manifests. We already agreed that the kiss was a one-time thing. Besides that, I have my siblings to focus on. Luke should have no place in my brain when I have more important things to think about. I need to let him go, no matter how much I wish I could feel his weight between my thighs again.

After tossing and turning for what feels like forever, I give up on sleep. My hope of getting an early night has long since been quashed anyway. I slip out of my bedroom and head to the kitchen for some water, flipping on the overhead light as I go. When I reach for a glass in the cupboard, I spot movement in my peripheral.

I abandon my mission and turn to face the front door. My brother stands by the exit, his fingers twisted around the door handle. He instantly freezes, caught in the act of sneaking out. I'm equal parts mad that he is trying to slip out unnoticed and disappointed that he is being so obvious about it. In another life, I probably would have helped him.

But that isn't the life we live. I have a new role to play now.

I raise a brow as I cross my arms over my chest. My water can wait. "Where the hell do you think you're going?" I ask.

"Out," is his blunt reply.

I sigh. "It's one in the morning, Parker. You can't just go *out*. Especially without telling me."

He crosses his own arms in defiance. "Watch me."

"I won't have you wandering the streets in the middle of the night just because you're angry at me. You can be angry in your bedroom."

"I'm not a little kid, Delilah. Stop treating me like one!"

I clench my jaw, trying not to lash out in response. "Parker, I—"

"*Mama!*"

Parker and I both pause. We stare at one another, not entirely sure that we heard right. Then another loud cry punctures the silence and my stomach drops. Usually we have this trouble when Sophia is settling into bed. After I read her a story, she sometimes asks for our parents. It breaks my heart every time. Tonight there was none of that, and I thought things would be okay. I should have known better.

Parker and I move at the same time, ascending the stairs and heading straight for our sister's bedroom. Although we may be at odds most of the time lately, there is one thing we will always agree on: keeping Sophia happy.

Throwing open the door, I assess her bedroom. The soft glow of the pink night light reveals Sophia hiding under her comforter, her knees tucked up to her chest. Her face is screwed up in pain and her eyes are closed.

"Soph," I call gently as I kneel at her side.

"Sissy?" she whispers.

I stroke her soft cheek. "It's me, Soph. I'm here. You're okay."

Her eyes slowly open, and then they fill with tears. Her bottom lip quivers. "I want Mommy and Daddy."

Her words are like a dagger to the heart. White hot pain, so piercing it would bring me to my knees if I wasn't there already, hits me in the chest. "Sophia, I—"

I choke on my words. I don't know what to say to make her feel better. Not when I know that I'll never live up to them. I don't want to. Replacing them is certainly not my intention, but just knowing that I'm not even a fraction as good at this as they were paralyzes my voice.

Parker sinks to his knees beside me. "It's okay to miss them, Soph," he says. "I do."

I miss them, too.

I urge the words to leave my lips. *I miss them, I miss them, I miss them.* But the connection between my heart and my mouth has been severed, and I can no longer manage speaking from the deepest parts of myself. My existence has been relegated to surface level.

Parker's eyes fall shut, and then a lone tear streaks down his cheek. Without thinking, I reach over and set my hand on his, offering him a reassuring squeeze. He doesn't return it, but he doesn't pull away either. Is it sad I count that a success?

When Sophia calms considerably, I read one of her

favourite books. Her eyes slowly begin to droop and her breathing evens out. Still, she manages to grip my hand when I try to leave.

"Sissy, stay," she pleads.

I am powerless to resist her, especially after being unable to offer her comfort earlier. So I crawl into bed beside her, tucking her against my side. She snuggles into me, her body relaxing.

To my surprise, Parker stuck around through story time. Now he stands beside the bed, watching us.

"Are you still going out?" I ask him quietly. I can't physically stop him, but I am hoping that he has changed his mind.

"No," he eventually says.

"Parker, stay?" Sophia asks groggily.

He obliges, sliding onto the other side of her bed.

Relief sweeps through me. "Thank you."

"I'm not doing it for you." He turns away from me and stares up at the ceiling. "I'm doing it for Sophia."

In the morning, I wake up to find Parker gone. His spot on Sophia's bed is rumpled, so I know he must have stayed a while, but sometime while we both slept, he crept out of the room.

Despite the hours of rest I managed to get, my brain is still clouded in a fog of weariness as I get Sophia ready for the day. After she is picked up by her sitter, I slowly begin to make myself presentable for my day shift at Dockside. I can already tell it's going to be a long one based on the amount of times I've yawned.

With a travel mug of coffee—my very own liquid gold—in hand, I step out my front door. And then I immediately start to panic. My car, which was parked in the driveway just last night, is nowhere to be found. *What the hell?*

I spin in a circle, as if that will magically make the vehicle appear. Parker is still asleep in his room, so I know he hasn't taken my car for a joyride. At a loss for what to do, I pull my phone from my bag and start typing.

> I think someone stole my car?

Clara doesn't waste time texting me back. Instead, she initiates a call. "What do you mean, someone stole your car?" she asks.

"I don't know!" I reply. "It was in my driveway last night and now it's not!"

"Text Luke. He might be a little pissy, but his feelings of moral obligation will soon kick in and he'll be forced to help you."

I snort. "I don't really see what the fire chief could—" My words cut off when I spot a familiar vehicle parked up against the curb. "On second thought, I very much will be texting your brother. I'll see you at work, Clara."

"Um, okay, then..." She hesitantly hangs up, caught off guard by my change in tone.

And I pull up the contact I told myself I wouldn't use again.

> You stole my car!

CHIEF
> Who is this?

> Do you make a habit of stealing women's cars, Chief? Who do you think this is?

CHIEF
> I didn't steal it.

> Then why is your truck on the street in front of my house? And my car is nowhere to be found?

He doesn't respond. I wait, tapping my foot anxiously on the front porch. At least I'm friends with my boss. Getting written up for being late to work is the last thing I need right now. A few moments later, I watch my car roll leisurely down the street and pull into my driveway. My car—sans the damage on the front bumper from when I rear-ended Luke's truck.

The man in question emerges from my vehicle looking way too good for this early in the morning. It's not even that early, but still. He's sporting his fire department uniform, and the way his navy blue t-shirt clings to his chest almost has me distracted.

Almost.

I adjust my ponytail self-consciously as I wait for him to approach. He stops just in front of the steps, giving me the height advantage for once. I strangely feel a little drunk on the perceived power it gives me.

"You got my car fixed?" I ask. It comes off like an accusation.

He nods. "I did."

He doesn't offer any other explanation, and I'm simply left staring at this enigma of a man. This man that I'm still convinced only slightly tolerates me on a good day. Our kiss the other day was an anomaly, and the truce we brokered at the park seems like even more of one.

"Why?" I finally ask.

"So I don't have to keep pretending not to see your busted headlight." He shifts on his feet, uncomfortable. "You shouldn't be driving like that. It's not safe."

The Delilah that first arrived on Kip Island would have bristled at that comment. She would have taken offence. Hell, I did take offence. Except I know Luke now. Not entirely, but I know him enough to understand this. Clara wasn't wrong about his sense of moral obligation. The man doesn't know how to *not* help.

"Thank you," I say, and I mean it. "Let me know how much it cost and I'll reimburse you."

"Don't worry about it."

My jaw drops. "*Don't worry about it*? I can't just not worry! That had to be a lot of money, Luke."

He shakes his head. "It's fine, Delilah. My friend at the body shop owed me a favour."

And because I really don't know when to leave well enough alone, I decide to open my big fat mouth. "You have friends?" I blurt.

My cheeks heat. I'm not sure where that came from, but when I look up at Luke, his lips are twisted like he's trying not to laugh. I have absolutely no regrets if it means a chance of seeing that.

"Contrary to popular belief, I do," he says. "Finn and I went to high school together."

I sigh. I know he isn't going to relent and let me pay, so I nod. I can feel his eyes assessing me then, perhaps searching for the things that need fixing. Unlike my car, however, I can't just be taken in and repaired in one morning.

"Are you okay?" he finally asks.

I must look like a mess. I *feel* like a mess. I want to say no. My brother hates me, and I don't blame him. I can't even comfort my sister properly. By all accounts, I'm failing. I don't say any of that, though. He doesn't care about my baggage.

Instead I offer him a tired smile. "I'm fine. Just on my way to work." My eyes flit to the driveway and back again. "You know, before someone *Grand Theft Auto*'d my car."

His eyes roll. "Next time I'm tempted to return a favour, I'll think better of it."

This time, my grin is downright goofy. "Careful, Chief, or I might start to get the feeling that you actually like me."

Luke shakes his head in exasperation. "God forbid."

He takes a couple steps back, putting an end to our conversation. Not that I would admit this out loud, but I'm sad to see him go. What a glutton for punishment I must be.

Luke tosses my keys back to me. "Try not to hit anyone else, yeah? The friends and family discount tends to only apply the first time you do expensive damage."

I ignore his jab, instead focusing on the fact that he had my keys. Not my spare set either, but the ones with all my keychains fastened to them. I hadn't even noticed they were gone.

"How did you even get these?"

He shrugs. "I have my ways." Then he turns on his heel, throwing me a wave over his shoulder. "See you around, Shutterbug."

Even though my car has been returned, safe and sound, I'm left even more unsettled than I was when I walked out my front door. And it's all thanks to Kip Island's beloved fire chief.

CHAPTER
SEVENTEEN
DELILAH

FIRSTS ARE ALWAYS THE HARDEST.

First Thanksgiving, first Christmas, first birthday. The Delacroixes were never big on Thanksgiving, so the holiday passed us by with only a mild pang of longing. Christmas, on the other hand, was our mom's favourite. I tried to keep her traditions alive—decorating the house to the nines, baking cookies with Sophia, going hard on the Santa rouse. I like to think Soph had fun, but everything had a melancholic hollowness to it that kept me from enjoying it. Parker chose not to participate at all.

Sophia's birthday came next at the beginning of February, and then Parker's shortly after at the end of March. By then, a certain numbness had settled over us all, so the days passed with little fanfare. Sophia requested ice cream for breakfast, and like always, I was powerless to resist.

I haven't told anyone on the island that today is my birthday. Truthfully, I'm trying to forget about it altogether. But as I walk into the Bowmans' kitchen, ready for another Sunday brunch, that is much easier said than done.

A homemade banner that reads *Happy Birthday, Delilah!* hangs on the wall opposite the doorway I'm frozen in. Based on the colour palette, I can only assume Abbie and Sophia had hands in making it. And there are balloons *everywhere*. John is still a little red in the face, leading me to believe he spent the better part of his morning inflating them.

"Surprise!" Clara exclaims.

She was strangely insistent that we make it to brunch today. I chalked it up to her general mission to make us feel welcome here, but evidently that wasn't the whole story.

"Sit, sit," Maggie says, ushering me, Sophia and Parker to the table.

Still too stunned to object, I take my usual seat. Right beside Luke. He catches my bewildered gaze and he smiles. *Smiles*—something that goes against everything he stands for when it comes to me.

"Happy birthday, Shutterbug," he murmurs.

"Thanks," I whisper. Then I turn my eyes away from him and his stupidly pretty smile. They land on Clara. "How did you know?"

She grins sheepishly. "Your rental application. I couldn't let the day pass without acknowledging it."

I shake my head. "This is a lot more than just acknowledging it, Clara. You didn't have to do any of this."

I wish you didn't do this.

I feel instantly guilty as soon as the thought crosses my mind, but I can't help it. This day was already hard enough, and now I have to grin and bear it in front of the nicest family I've ever had the pleasure of knowing.

From across the table, Gabe laughs. "Try telling Mom that. Celebrations are compulsory in this house."

A rush of emotions hits me all at once.

I didn't always have a complicated relationship with my birthday. When I was a kid—when it was just my parents and me—we used to spend the whole day together. As a surprise gift shortly after their high school graduation, they weren't prepared for me. But that didn't stop them from doing their best to give me everything I wanted. Our life wasn't easy, but it was *good*.

Things shifted when Dad decided he wanted to get into politics. Generally speaking, he was young, but he had a way with words that gave him carte blanche to climb the ranks. After that, I was often paraded around as proof of his success. If he could make it out the other side of young parenthood alright, surely he could run a province. As if those things are actually comparable. But when it comes to optics, it doesn't really matter, does it?

I think what hurts the most isn't that things changed. Things changed, and I got left behind. When asked to subscribe to a new cookie cutter life, I didn't buy in, and I watched my simple life wither away. Birthdays were no longer dedicated days but shuffled obligations.

I swallow thickly, stuffing my feelings *down, down down*. No one needs to be witness to those. They're awfully ugly things, twisting my insides until I hardly recognize myself.

"That's really sweet of you guys to include me."

Clara's expression softens. "Of course we would include you."

You know the feeling you get when you're in a moment that you're sure you'll want to remember forever? That is what I feel right now. I feel special and cared for, and *fuck*, it hurts.

"Now I wasn't sure what your favourite flavour was, so I took a stab in the dark and went with chocolate. Everyone loves chocolate," Maggie says.

"You got me a cake?" My voice sounds scratchy even to my own ears, like my words are passing over sandpaper.

"I helped Grammy make it!" Abbie interjects.

"I taste tested the frosting," John adds helpfully.

I *know* that I'm laughing, but I feel like I'm outside my body, experiencing everything through a third-person point of view.

A round cake, iced to perfection, is placed in front of me. Maggie strikes a match and sets the candle—a golden *26*—ablaze. I watch the flame dance. Then Abbie is standing on a chair, belting the birthday song from the top of her little lungs. This whole family is looking at me expectantly. They're looking at me, and it all feels just a little too much.

My lungs expand with the breath that I grapple for. Then I meet Parker's gaze from across the table. His expression is pained, and I hate that this is affecting him, too. I try to wrestle with my emotions, forcing them into submission. They can't explode all over this well-meaning family.

"Help me blow the candle out?" I ask Sophia.

She nods readily and then climbs onto my lap. Together we extinguish the flame. Maggie whisks the cake away to slice it into pieces, conversations converge all around me, and I feel like the room is folding in on itself.

I hastily set Sophia back on her chair before I quietly excuse myself. The front door slams behind me as I rush outside, the house all at once comforting yet stifling. I make it just off the front steps before I bend in half, hands planted on my knees. I take what feels like my first true breath since walking inside the house.

The screen door swings open behind me. I expect to see Clara, or maybe even Maggie, but when I turn around, it's a different Bowman standing on the porch. Luke doesn't say anything. He just grips me with that penetrating stare.

For a moment, I can't bring myself to look away. Even though I visibly have tears in my eyes—even though I hate people seeing me this way—I hold on to his gaze. But soon the embarrassment kicks in and I spin away, severing that connection between us.

I take a moment to carefully swipe under my eyes, and then I move back to the porch. Luke meets me at the bottom of the steps, blocking my path.

"What are you doing?" I ask. My voice comes out shakier than I would like. "I should go back inside."

The last thing I want is for his family to think of me as ungrateful. They threw a whole birthday party for a woman they met a month and a half ago. The least I can do is sit through it, even if guilt and grief threaten to swallow me whole.

"No."

I balk. "Excuse me?"

"No," he repeats. "Not until you forget about what you think you *should* do, and do what you need."

"But your family—"

"My family is fine. Just worried about you."

I try to step around him, but he blocks me again. I frown. "All the more reason for me to go back inside."

Crossing my arms, I stare up at him. He stares right back. The unwavering attention begins to tug at the frayed edges of my emotions until I can't stand it any longer.

"Why do you even care?" I snap.

His laugh is a chill down my spine. "Shutterbug, I have been asking myself that question since you landed on my island in those barely-there denim shorts of yours."

"And?" I ask. "What's the answer?"

He's silent for a moment, like he might not give me one. And then he says, "When I figure it out, I'll let you know."

I scoff. Luke simply leans a shoulder against the column supporting the porch's overhang. He crosses his own arms, putting his strong biceps on display in a way I'm not entirely convinced is accidental.

"If you need a minute, Delilah, then take it. I'll wait."

To his credit, he does. The tears threaten to spill over again and I have to look away. I bite my tongue to give myself something else to focus on. I can feel him watching me, but I surprisingly don't feel rushed under his gaze. Like I truly can take a minute to breathe.

"Our parents died. Nine months ago," I admit quietly.

There isn't a day that goes by where I don't think about that, but I think this is the first time I've ever actually had to say the words aloud. It wasn't as hard as I thought it would be. The admission is freeing, in a way.

When I peek up at Luke, he isn't wearing that pinched expression that everyone else adopts when they find out the reason I have custody of my siblings. Instead he stands just as he has been, waiting like he said he would.

"They were in a car accident at the end of August. It was — It was raining really badly."

I leave out the reason they were even out of the house that day. If it hadn't been for me and the pictures I allowed to be used against me, my parents wouldn't have been on their way to meet with their lawyer. I don't want Luke to look at me differently—the way everyone back home did.

"And this is your first birthday without them," he surmises. His voice has adopted a gentle quality that doesn't right away seem to fit the man in front of me.

I nod, and then I let my head hang. For a moment, I allow myself to be perplexed by his softness. Everything about him before today has been hard edges. But Luke is a fixer—I've witnessed it firsthand. He takes on others' problems like they are his responsibility to manage.

My breath is ripped from my lungs when he suddenly takes hold of my chin. He tilts my face up until my eyes collide with his. "If this is too much, tell me, and I'll shut it down. No mention of birthdays. Just a normal Sunday brunch."

My heart squeezes. Or rather, it feels like something is clutching at the organ. His hand, maybe, trying to steal it right out of my chest.

"It's not too much," I say. I sound out of breath, like I've just finished a hundred metre dash. "Not anymore. It hurts a bit, but it's a good kind of pain."

The bittersweet melancholy of missing someone. The yearning for a past time and place where things were nowhere near as complicated. The kind of pain that affirms you of life.

"You're sure?"

"I'm sure." I worry my lip as I inhale a steadying breath. It's hard when he still holds me so close. "You were right. I just needed a minute."

Luke releases my chin from his firm grasp, and only then does he seem to realize the gravity of that gesture. I can practically see the walls inside him refortifying themselves as we stand here.

"We can go back inside," I say. Despite my wobbly knees, my voice is clear. "I'm okay now. I promise to be less of a mess."

Luke's jaw clenches, and then it's his turn to look away. When he meets my eyes again, they hold. "No one who really gives a damn about you will expect you to be perfect."

"Does that include you?" I ask quietly.

As I wait for his response, my eyes roam, mapping all his features and committing them to memory. The scar almost camouflaged by his left eyebrow, the slight bump on the bridge of his nose, the stubble that covers his jaw.

"Yeah, Shutterbug," he says. "That includes me."

The strange thing is, I think I believe him.

When Luke and I step back inside the house, we find Clara standing in the foyer. She glances between me and her brother, trying to puzzle something out. With a nod in my direction, Luke heads casually for the kitchen, as if the past fifteen minutes hadn't happened at all.

Clara's worried eyes settle on me. "Are you okay?"

I smile, forcing my emotions back into their box. "I'm okay. I promise." I take her arm and loop mine through it. "Let's go eat cake."

"You can tell me if you're not," she says. "I realized after you ran out that maybe we came on a little strong..." Her smile is tinged with sadness. "I just missed having a friend close by and I wanted you to feel special."

Guilt slams into me as my heart squeezes a second, painful time. The last thing I wanted was for the Bowmans to feel like they had done something wrong. It isn't their fault that I can't act normally.

I nudge Clara's side. "Hey, stop that. No one is allowed to be sad on my birthday!"

Not even me.

CHAPTER EIGHTEEN
LUKE

"WHY THE HELL ARE YOU HERE?"

Jodi stands in the doorway to my office, hip cocked as she regards me with a disappointed frown. I'm no stranger to that look. I think this is the fifth time I've seen it this week alone.

"Last I checked," I say, an amused grin stretching my lips, "I work here. I believe I'm your boss actually. Funny how that works."

She waves me off. "Semantics," she argues. "I meant, why are you *still* here? You came in before I finished my shift this morning and here I am, already on another one. Go *home*, Luke."

I rub at my tired eyes as a yawn escapes me. "I'm going, I'm going."

I exit the building to a chorus of *Goodnight, Chief* from the overnight shift. All that does is make me think of Delilah as I get in my truck and peel out of the parking lot. The name Chief will never be the same after her. Hell, I don't think *I'll* be the same when she's through with me. Which is exactly why I set out to steer clear of her. That, so far, has not worked in my favour.

While I cruise through the quiet streets, my mind drifts to yesterday at Haven House. When Delilah ran out of the kitchen, I didn't hesitate to follow her. That alone is worrying. I shouldn't be involved with her. I shouldn't *care* so much. But I do.

Dockside isn't technically on my route home, but I drive by anyway. I always do. Especially around closing, swinging by gives me peace of mind. Tonight, a lone vehicle sits outside. Delilah's. Before I really think about what I'm doing, my blinker is on and I'm turning into the gravel parking lot. The stones crunch beneath my tires as I park beside her car.

By now, the front door is locked, so I make my way around to the back of the restaurant. I let myself in with my key and I'm instantly greeted by the sound of loud music. The volume has been cranked, much higher than what it sits at during operating hours. Out in the dining room, Delilah's hips shimmy to the beat as she wipes down a table with a rag. Instead of her typical shorts, a denim skirt hugs her ass tonight. When she leans over the table, the fabric tightens and I fight the urge to stare.

Once the table is clean, she turns on her heel and instantly shrieks in surprise. A hand clutches her chest.

I arch a brow. "Jumpy?"

She frowns. "What are you doing here? Did Clara send you?"

It wouldn't be out of the realm of possibility for Clara to

do just that. But tonight I came here of my own volition. I can't seem to stay away.

"I saw your car outside. Thought I'd check in." I make a show of looking around the otherwise empty building. "Speaking of, why the hell are you closing by yourself?"

"Jimmy's daughter is sick. He had to go. I told him I'd be alright by myself, and I *am*, so you can leave."

I lean back against the bar, folding my arms over my chest. "No, thanks. I think I'll hang out right here."

She rolls her eyes. "Fine." She tosses the rag at my chest. I catch it before it can hit me. "If you're not gonna leave, then the least you can do is help."

We work in tandem over the next few minutes, and we let the music fill the silence. Every time Delilah leans over a table to clean it, I have to force my eyes away. After the tenth time, I swear she's doing it on purpose to taunt me. When she makes it to the table I stand beside, I know she's teasing me. She presses back slightly, the curve of her ass brushing against my leg, and I can't take it anymore.

"*Delilah.*"

She straightens and then turns to me. "What?"

"You can't ask me to pretend we never kissed and then strut around in a skirt like that."

The look she gives me is puzzled. "We both agreed it shouldn't have happened."

"But it did," I say. I run a hand through my hair in frustration. "And fuck, I don't think I can pretend anymore."

She brushes past me, back toward the bar. "You don't even like me," she says. "I don't see why this is such a problem."

Fuck, this woman still has no idea what she has done to me. What she continues to do to me.

Delilah is quick to set the glasses in the dishwasher and turn it on. I follow her behind the bar. When she turns to look at me, she has to tip her chin upwards to meet my eyes. I love the way she looks in this moment—face set in stubborn determination.

I grip the edge of the bar on either side of her, caging her in. "I like you just fine."

"Yeah?" The word comes out as a challenge. "Prove it."

I press into her space, causing her chin to tip further to keep me in her sights. I bend, hovering my lips over hers. "I think I will."

Her brow arches. "Any day now would be lovely."

I release the counter and let my hands fall to her hips. Then I lift her up and place her on top of the bar in one fell swoop. Much like that day in the walk-in fridge, her legs fall open and I slot myself between them. I can't help but marvel at the way we fit together, like I was always meant to be here doing this.

Delilah's eyes flutter shut, and I close the distance, letting my lips caress hers. This kiss isn't urgent like our first. I take my time settling into it, slowly coaxing her to let me in. I could spend endless moments just like this, getting lost in the feel of her. This should scare me, but I am past the point of caring.

She pulls back, attempting to catch her breath. "Kissing me doesn't prove anything," she insists. "We've already done that, and nothing changed."

That is where she's mistaken. After that kiss, *everything*

changed. I've given in to temptation so wholly, I can't even identify the reasons I was reluctant before. This woman is going to ruin me, and damn it, I'm going to let her.

"What kind of proof do you need, then?"

She hums. The heat in her gaze incinerates me where I stand. "Be extra nice to me and maybe I'll believe you."

The smug look that occupies her face quickly melts away when my hand slips under the hem of her skirt. The skin of her thigh is smooth, but goosebumps begin to prickle her flesh as my fingers trail their path. She widens her legs, giving me easier access. When I reach the apex of her thighs, the pad of my thumb presses against the dampness of her underwear. She bites her lip, stifling the sounds I would give anything to hear in all their glory.

I lean forward, lips brushing the shell of her ear. "Is that nice enough for you, Shutterbug?"

She shakes her head. "You could be nicer."

My lips curve into a grin. "As you wish," I say. "But Delilah?"

"Hmm?"

My teeth graze her earlobe and I can feel her shiver. "I want to hear you."

I toy with the lace of her underwear. She writhes, but stubbornly, her teeth clamp down on her lip, silencing her breathy cries.

With my other hand, I grip her chin, dragging her gaze to mine. "I know you make beautiful sounds when you're turned on. Don't be shy, pretty girl."

Her lips part in surprise at the endearment. Pink spreads

across her cheeks. "I don't want to be too much," she whispers.

The way she says this tells me that she has been made to feel like what she has to give is too over the top. Probably thanks to that same ex boyfriend who keeps texting her, if I had to guess. Well, fuck him. He doesn't know how good he had it.

"I want it all, Delilah. Every cry, every moan. I won't be satisfied until I hear you calling out my name."

I watch her face. She worries her bottom lip for a moment, and then she nods. Finally, I do what I've been dying to since my hand found its way under her skirt. I push her underwear aside, giving myself access to her silky skin. This time, my thumb circles her bare clit, and she lets loose a quiet moan.

"That's it, pretty girl."

My other hand lands on her knee, and I stretch her legs even wider. Her hands tighten where they're looped at the back of my neck, and then she pulls my mouth back down to hers. I keep the pressure on her clit steady as I let my lips claim hers.

"Luke," she says against my lips. "Give me more."

"You are a goddamn temptress," I muse. I draw back. My hand still works beneath her skirt. "But tonight, I want to hear you beg."

Her eyes flash, gunmetal grey clashing with my own. That stubborn streak is back. "*Luke.*"

Another brush of my thumb against her clit has Delilah's lips parting. Her eyes soften, giving way to her pleasure. "You want me to fuck you with my fingers, Delilah, you have to say it."

"*God.*" Her voice is brimming with exasperation. "Yes, *please*. Fuck me with your fingers. I need you."

A warmth floods my chest. *I need you.* Her words come from a place of purely physical want—a desire for me to make good on my promises—but I can't deny the way they spread over me. I ascribe the pounding of my heart in my chest to the anticipation of touching Delilah like this. Of watching her fuck my hand and wishing it was my cock instead.

I make her wait just a moment longer, and then I slide a finger through her entrance. Her whole body shudders when I curl my finger, hitting that spot just right, and return my thumb to her clit. Her hips rotate, trying to create friction. I grab hold of her with my free hand, stopping her movements.

I slowly begin pumping my finger in and out. I set a steady pace, and her head lolls back in pleasure. She grabs my bicep, nails digging into my skin. Branding me. The bite of pain is well worth it.

"One more?" She shakes her head. "You can take it, baby."

Her head tips forward, eyes meeting mine. "*Please,*" she pleads.

I grin. "That's my pretty girl." I add another finger, and her grip tightens on my arm.

God, I want to kiss her again. But I don't want to miss the way her features shift as my fingers move inside her. Delilah Delacroix is breathtaking on a normal day, but when she's on the brink of orgasm? The woman is ethereal. Pink dusts the apples of her cheeks, and strands of hair have slipped from her ponytail, framing her face.

"*Luke*," she rasps.

"That's it, Delilah. Just like that."

And then I can't help myself. I kiss her. I drown in the vibrations of her moan as her pussy clenches around my fingers. Her whole body goes off like a chain reaction, chasing the sensations of her orgasm. As she comes down from her high, I brush my fingers over the blush on her cheeks.

"Do you believe me now, Shutterbug?"

"Yes," she huffs. "I believe you."

After I help Delilah down off the counter, she says she's going to clean herself up in the bathroom, and I set to work fixing the bar. I don't think Clara would appreciate having any evidence of what happened here tonight.

When Delilah emerges, I notice a slight shaking in her hands. I drop the rag I was holding and take her palms in mine, steadying them. "What's wrong?" I ask.

Does she regret what just happened? Because I sure don't.

"It's nothing," she says. She tries to pull away, but I hold on. "I just— I forgot about the cameras."

The thought hadn't even crossed my mind. We generally don't have reason to sift through the camera footage. I can count on one hand the number of times we've had to. But I can see that this is bothering her.

"Consider it taken care of," I assure her. "You finish up. I'll wait for you."

While she sets about finishing the rest of her closing routine, I pull out my phone to text Clara.

> I have a question, but you can't ask any follow ups.

CLAREBEAR
Ominous. What's up?

> How do you access security footage at Dockside?

CLAREBEAR
Why??

> No follow ups, remember?

CLAREBEAR
If you tell me time stamps, I can just do it when I go in tomorrow.

> I would prefer to take care of it myself.

> If you don't tell me how, I'm just going to press a bunch of buttons until something works.

CLAREBEAR
Ugh. You're the worst!

After my nosy sister begrudgingly gives me the instructions, I delete the footage from the moment I walked in through the back door up until Delilah hopped off the bar, clothing back in its proper place. By then, Delilah has already shut off most of the lights and made her way to the break room.

"Ready to go?" I ask.

She slings her bag over her shoulder. "You didn't have to wait for me, you know."

"'Course I did. You never know what kind of trouble could be out there."

She brandishes her keys between her knuckles. "That's why I have these bad boys."

I scowl. "And that's supposed to make me feel *better*?"

Like the gentleman I am, I wait for her to lock the back door and then walk with her across the gravel lot. Her car sits under a flickering light, illuminated like it sits on a stage. Coupled with the moon, it casts an eerie glow over the surrounding areas.

When we round the driver's side of the car, Delilah stops in her tracks. I nearly crash into her back, and the gasp she lets out sets me on edge. I lean around her, and my jaw clenches when I realize the problem.

There, written on the door in vibrant red paint, is the word *slut*.

CHAPTER
NINETEEN
LUKE

THE MORNING after Delilah's car was vandalized, I follow her to the sole auto body shop we have on the island. Since they're the only game in town, they do just about everything when it comes to fixing vehicles. And as it happens, I'm friends with the owner's nephew.

The drive across town isn't long, but it gives me plenty of time to stew about what happened last night. *Slut.* Seeing that one word, etched across Delilah's car like a goddamn scarlet letter, had anger rushing through my veins. When I pulled up to her house a few minutes ago, the anger surged anew.

After Delilah left Dockside, insisting on driving herself home, I went back inside to check the security footage. She told me it wasn't a big deal, but I didn't miss the trembling in her hands that second time. I wasn't about to let some punk get away with fucking up her car. But as I searched the computer for the parking lot footage, I realized that a chunk of time was removed.

I deleted the fucking footage.

Instead of just scrubbing the cameras on the inside, I scrubbed them all. My hands tighten on the steering wheel and my jaw clenches as I pull into the body shop's parking lot. It's my fault that we have no idea who spray painted her car.

I park my truck off to the side, and then I hop out and head toward Delilah's car. When I open the door for her to get out, she gives me a quizzical look. Like she can't believe that I would help her out of her car. Before she can say anything, her phone starts to ring. The distraction saves me from having to explain why opening her door wasn't even a conscious thought.

"It's Sophia's sitter," she says. "Just give me a couple minutes."

I nod. She steps away to take the call, and I head for the building. The smell of motor oil and metal assaults me as I step through the open bay door at O'Donnell's Auto. A familiar voice lets out an equally familiar curse, and then the man in question slides out from under the body of a minivan.

This version of my friend is worlds apart from the scrawny, baby-faced Finn I knew in high school. Back then, he was the happiest of our group, and he did whatever he could to make people laugh. We had no idea what he was dealing with at home. Now this version of Finn is hardened. The years he spent in prison chipped away at him until he was unrecognizable to those who knew him before. He barely smiles, and he only speaks when strictly necessary.

As he approaches, Finn pulls a rag from his back pocket

and wipes his palms. The rag, like his hands, is covered in ink black oil. The colour matches the tattoos that wrap around all his extremities.

"Hey, O'Donnell," I say.

He nods. "Bowman."

I have the urge to reach out a hand for him to shake, but Finn doesn't like to be touched. So I keep my hand to myself. "I brought you another job."

He peers over my shoulder and then raises a brow. "This that car with the busted headlight again?"

"Yeah," I say, "but it's not the headlight this time."

I lead him out to the car and around the driver's side. As Finn studies the paint, he plucks the cigarette from behind his ear and then lights up. He sends a puff of smoke in my direction as he exhales.

"I'm sure the girl would like you just fine if you played nice instead of spending hundreds on car repairs," he says eventually. His lips curve upwards in a wry smirk, the closest thing he can manage to a genuine smile these days.

I roll my eyes. "Fuck off. You know it's not about that."

"And he's not paying," Delilah chimes in. "Hi, I'm Delilah. Are you the guy who fixed my headlight?"

As he takes another drag of his cigarette, he does a once-over of Delilah. His eyes linger a little too long on her legs for my liking. I clear my throat and he straightens, looking smug.

"I am," he says.

Delilah smiles, unfazed by his brusque nature. Then again, she's used to dealing with me. "Thank you! You can't even tell it was damaged. I really appreciate it."

Finn shifts uncomfortably, like the praise makes his skin

physically itch. That, or the lengthy conversation. I decide that now is probably the best time to intervene.

"Do you think you can get this fixed?" It's an unnecessary question. I know he can.

"Leave it. I'll get it done."

He turns on his heel and walks back into the shop without waiting for us, his cigarette still dangling between his fingers. Delilah and I glance at each other, and then we follow. Finn throws his dirty rag onto a workbench in the corner, and then he takes Delilah's keys from her outstretched hand.

He doesn't offer anything else. I don't push. I know better than to expect more of a conversation out of him. Prison changed him irrevocably, and in the years since his release, I've only seen him retreat further into himself.

Delilah, on the other hand, pays no mind to his silent signals for us to leave. "Can I ask when it'll be done?"

Finn's jaw tightens, like it pains him to have to answer. "My uncle's out with a bad back. I'm flying solo, so it's gonna be a few days."

"Oh, that's okay," she says. "I can just bring it back when you have time."

"*No*," I say.

Her sharp gaze lands on me. "Excuse me? Why can't I just keep it until he's not busy?"

"You're not driving that car, Delilah."

She crosses her arms. "What if I need to get somewhere?"

"Then you call me."

She laughs. "Don't you think you're being a little ridiculous?"

"Don't care. It's my fault you have to deal with this in the first place. I'm sure as hell not gonna let you drive around with that word painted on your door for the whole fucking town to see."

Her eyes soften. "Luke, no..."

Now it's Finn's turn to clear his throat. An obvious sign that we have long overstayed our welcome. So we settle up with him, and then Delilah and I make our way to my truck.

"Is all this really necessary?" she asks.

I pull open the passenger door and gesture for her to get in. She places one foot on the running board and then swings up onto the seat.

I place a hand on the frame as I lean in, catching her eye. "Driving you to work the day after your car was vandalized? Yes, I would say it's necessary."

She huffs as she buckles her seatbelt. I shut the door and then round the truck, getting into my own seat. I turn the key, the engine roaring to life.

When I pull into Dockside's parking lot a few minutes later, I expect Delilah to get out of the truck and head straight inside. Instead I watch as she unlatches her seatbelt and then climbs over the centre console, knocking her bag onto the floor in the process. She situates herself on my lap, her legs straddling me.

"Shutterbug," I warn. My hands instinctively find their way to her hips, giving them a light squeeze. "What are you doing?"

She doesn't respond. Not verbally anyway. She twines her fingers in the hair at the nape of my neck and guides my face toward hers. Her lips are soft, coated in that cherry lip balm

I'm afraid I might already be addicted to. As her tongue swirls with mine, her hips rotate, drawing a groan from my throat.

My grip tightens on her hips. As usual, she ignores me. "*Delilah,*" I say against her lips.

She blinks at me, faux innocent. "Yeah?"

"If you don't stop, we are both going to be very late to work."

She grins. "Fine. Thanks for the ride," she says, swivelling her hips to emphasize her words.

"Delilah," I growl.

She has the audacity to laugh. "Bye, Chief."

She leans over and collects her bag from the floor. And then she flings open the door and slides off my lap, leaving me sitting there with pants that are entirely too fucking tight.

I stop at Dockside for lunch. This isn't out of the ordinary for me—it's part of my routine. It definitely has nothing to do with the waitress wearing a skirt almost identical to the one I wanted to rip off of her last night.

As I take a seat on my usual stool at the bar, my eyes search for Delilah without my permission. When they find her, she gives me a knowing smile followed by a wink before she focuses back on her table.

The sound of something hitting the bar top startles me. I turn in my seat to find a plate sitting in front of me. I can't even bring myself to care that it looks like Clara put kale in it. Not when I can still taste Delilah on my lips. As I start to eat,

I can feel my sister's eyes trained on me. I meet her discontent gaze.

"What?"

Clara sighs. "Delilah told me what happened to her car last night. Whatever you're doing with her, you better be careful," she says. "She doesn't need this town talking about her, too."

This grabs my attention. "What is that supposed to mean?"

"It means that everyone on this island thinks the sun shines out of your ass, so you don't exactly fly under the radar. Whatever it is that you're doing—just keep that in mind, okay? I don't want you giving her a reason to leave."

"You make it sound like that's happened before."

My sister looks down, studying her hands. "It's been lonely since Hallie left, and Delilah has been a good friend. A genuinely good friend. I just... I don't want to lose her, too."

Fuck.

I've been so caught up in Delilah—caught up in my attraction for her—that I didn't even stop to think how this would affect anyone else. Clara and Delilah have become fast friends since the Delacroixes moved here. Getting into something with Delilah—something that could only be temporary—would put that at risk.

I set my sandwich back on my plate. "Clarebear, are you okay?"

Gabe's worry from that night on my back porch comes flashing back. The sadness I see in her face tells me that he was right—something is up with her. Something more than just her worry for Delilah. The moment my question registers, her guards slide back into place.

She flashes me a smile, but it's not her usual one. "I'm fine. Just promise me you'll be careful?"

"I'll be careful," I promise. "Are you sure you're okay?"

"I'm sure." She rounds the bar and throws her arms around me, trapping me in a hug. "I've missed you, too, you know."

My brows furrow as I return her embrace. "Missed me? I haven't gone anywhere."

"Physically, yeah." She pulls back. "But you've been gone for a while, Luke. Whatever has changed, I don't care. I'm just happy to be getting my brother back."

The sinking feeling starts low in my stomach, and then it spreads through the rest of my body. The breakdown of my relationship with Kristina happened fast. After what she did, there was no saving it. It's hard to go through with marrying the person that damn near got your niece killed. I knew the situation had changed me, but I hadn't realized just how noticeable it was. Even my sister knows I'm damaged goods.

I can't do this. After what happened with Delilah's car, I don't want this getting any messier. No matter how much I'd love nothing more than a repeat with her, I can't risk ruining her friendship with Clara. I won't.

CHAPTER TWENTY
DELILAH

LUKE IS OFFICIALLY AVOIDING ME. Again.

A month ago that would not have been out of the ordinary. But here I thought that we had turned a corner. That between him kissing me and the moment we shared on the bar at Dockside meant he had decided to stop ignoring that spark between us. That undeniable thread that has been tugging us together since we met.

That first time Luke kissed me, he claimed he couldn't get me out of his head. Well, now I can't get him out of mine. He has had no contact with me since the day we dropped my car off at O'Donnell's Auto a week ago. He's even stopped coming by the restaurant. I thought for sure this would mean that I was on my own to get to work, which is fine, but the frustratingly thoughtful man just had Clara pick me up instead.

Something changed that day. I knew he wasn't happy that my car had been vandalized. I wasn't happy either, and truthfully, it scared me a little. But I didn't expect him to pull away so abruptly.

Now I'm over it.

Today, I plan to get to the bottom of this once and for all. I purposely wore a skirt—the same one I wore that night at Dockside. And when I walk inside the fire station, heads turn. As soon as Gabe spots me, he does a double take, and then a slow grin spreads across his lips. He knows exactly why I'm here. I offer him a wave.

"Give him hell, Delilah!" he calls.

I salute in response, and then I make my way deeper into the building, in the direction I think the chief's office must be. When I make it to some type of reception area, a middle-aged woman with a blonde braid partway down her back steps in my path.

"Hello, there," she says. I notice the name Booth is etched on the sleeve of her shirt. "Can I help you?"

"Is the chief in?" I ask. When she gives me a questioning look, I elaborate. "I'm his..." I shake my head. I'm not *his* anything. "I'm a friend of his sister."

"Delilah?" At my nod, her suspicion melts away and she grins. "Oh, I've heard *so* much about you. You can go on back. Just down that hall, you'll see his office door."

She's heard so much about me? Has Luke been talking to his coworkers about me? Surely that can't be true when the man can't even look me in the face to tell me that he thought we made a mistake. Another mistake.

I thank the woman and then start down the corridor. At the very end, an office looms, a plaque hung on the wall that reads *Chief Lucas Bowman*. For a moment, as my palm rests on the door handle, I second-guess myself. Should I really be doing this? Probably not. But fuck it.

I want to charge in there, guns blazing, but I also don't want to get him in trouble if he's in a meeting or something. I'm actually not entirely sure what it is that fire chiefs do. So I knock, and when he calls out a gruff *come in*, I push through the door. I let it shut behind me, and the lock flips with a resounding click at my back.

"Delilah," he says. I see a faint trace of surprise in his eyes, but the rest of his features remain neutral.

"Oh," I say, voice sickeningly sweet, "you *do* remember me. I was beginning to wonder whether you had developed a case of retrograde amnesia. Glad to see you're feeling well."

He ignores my sarcastic remark. "What are you doing here?"

I fold my arms over my chest, cocking my hip. "You've been avoiding me."

"I haven't—" I cut him off with a sharp look. "I've been busy. Working."

My brow arches. "Really? It has nothing to do with what happened at Dockside the other night?"

"What we did—"

"You mean when you stuck your hand up my skirt and made me come? Don't be shy now, Chief. You can say it."

His jaw tightens. "It can't happen again," he says gruffly.

Maybe it can't. Maybe we should both cut our losses and try to move on. But I want to know *why*. Not whatever flimsy excuse he's telling himself to get by, but the real reason. The pesky voice in the back of my head is telling me it has everything to do with me.

"Was it not good for you?" I ask quietly. Some of the anger has leached from my voice, making way for insecurity.

His eyes soften. "That is not an issue. Don't think that for a second."

I throw my hands in the air, altogether exasperated. "Then what's the problem? If you liked it, then why can't we do it again?"

If I wasn't so mad, the look on his face would give me pause. He looks *defeated*. But I'm angry enough to keep pushing. "You don't want what I have to give," he replies.

At this, I scoff. "Oh, *please*. I thought we were past you making assumptions about me," I say as I take a step toward his desk. "Don't be a martyr, Chief."

The look Luke gives me now is nothing more than a glare. "I'm trying to be smart about this. I can't give you a relationship. I'm not looking for that."

I laugh bitterly. "Guess what? I'm not some naïve little girl who expects to be swept off her feet."

At least not by Luke. He has made it clear that he finds me attractive, but that is where his affections end. He doesn't need to be my Prince Charming. I'm not sure I would want him to be anyway. But he can give me what I crave—a distraction. An outlet to chip away at some of the tension I accumulate throughout the day.

"You didn't even ask me. Ask me what I want, Luke."

His facial expression is nothing short of pained, and I don't care. I want him to *hear* me. I spent way too long with a man that never did. Even if nothing comes of this, I want Luke to know where I stand. I need him to.

Finally, he sighs. "What do you want, Delilah?"

"I want to feel good. You made me feel good. You don't want a relationship? That's fine. I can handle casual." I hazard another step closer. "Can you?"

He leans back in his chair. "Delilah..."

I take this as an invitation to round his desk. "Can you handle that?"

When he doesn't answer, I plant myself on the surface of his desk and loop my feet through the armrests on his chair, bringing him to rest between my legs. My skirt inches up my thighs, exposing more of my skin. A tattoo—floral like my shoulder—peeks out from the hem. It runs from my hip to halfway down my thigh. Almost inadvertently, Luke reaches out and traces the design with his finger. All my nerve endings catch fire, alighting at his mere touch. My body remembers what it's like to have his hands on me, and it wants more. *I* want more.

"I didn't notice this before," he murmurs.

"You had a bit of a one-track mind that night, Chief."

Now he touches the hem of my skirt and a groan slips free. "Did you wear this just to torture me?"

A smirk curves my lips. "You're easy to torture."

As he watches his finger run along my skin, I can almost hear his mind whirring, trying to find a way to say no. I hate that he's thinking so hard—I don't want him to think at all. I want him to throw aside his sense and *live*. I don't want to be alone on this side of mindless pleasure-seeking.

Stupid. My father would say I'm being stupid. After what happened with Mitchell, I could hardly blame him. It wasn't just me that was affected when my pictures got leaked. But I need this. I need something that is mine—something that has nothing to do with my family or the hobby I'm too scared to pick up again.

I glance over my shoulder, ensuring the door is locked, as I left it. Then I turn back to Luke. "Are there any cameras?"

He shakes his head. When he speaks, his voice is strained. "Not in here."

Somehow, I know he's telling the truth. He didn't hesitate to delete the security footage at Dockside that night when he saw how uneasy I was, and he didn't even know the reason why. So I know he wouldn't lie to me about this. Besides, Luke is nothing like Mitchell. I wouldn't be here if he was.

I hook my thumbs into the sides of my panties—a lacy black thong that I mostly wore for me, but also a little bit for him—and tug. I wiggle them down my hips and past my thighs. They hang from an outstretched finger for a moment before they drop to the floor.

His Adam's apple bobs as he watches me. "What are you doing?" he asks.

"We already defiled my workplace," I reply. "I think it's only fair we do the same to yours. I promise I'll be quiet, and no one will even know."

I guide his hand to my waist. His palm moulds to my side, anchoring him. I can see the war he is waging with himself. The ever-responsible Luke Bowman wouldn't dream of fucking a woman at work. But I want him to be a little reckless with me. I want to peel back the layers of propriety and watch him lose some of that control he holds so dear.

"Kiss me," I breathe.

He shakes his head. "I can't."

"No one is stopping you, least of all me. If you want me, Luke, come and get me."

I lean back, my palms braced on his desk. At this angle, my chest strains against my shirt. Luke's eyes darken as he watches my breasts heave with every breath I take. I have all but splayed myself before him, yet he is still trying to resist.

"Goddamn temptress," he murmurs. With reverence. With awe.

He stands abruptly, his desk chair flying backwards and hitting the wall. Then he steps between my parted thighs. I sit up, my chest meeting his abdomen. With the hand not on my waist, he grasps my chin, tilting up until his eyes can search mine.

"Are you sure about this?" he asks. "If you say yes, then you're mine, for however long we decide to do this. I don't share."

"*Yes*." I tip my head back in quiet relief, and then I meet his stare once again. "And for the record, Chief: I don't share either."

His lips curl into a smirk. "Then we have a deal."

And then his mouth descends on mine, capturing my surprise. This is what I asked for, but I'm mildly shocked that he caved. Still, I don't let that stop me from looping my hands around the back of his neck and tugging him closer. Need, pure and heady, washes over me. I want his hands on me; all over me.

Like our first kiss, I feel the energy flowing between us, sending tingles straight up my spine. We fit so well together, Luke's body folding over mine like it was more than pure chance we ended up here. His hand on my waist moves, brushes my thigh, and then it slips beneath the fabric of my skirt. I widen my stance, eager for him to reach my centre again.

Except the phone ringing on his desk pulls me right out of the moment. I narrowly avoid headbutting Luke in the nose as the abrupt sound makes me jump. Judging by the look on his face, reality has come crashing back in and our moment is over.

He clears his throat. "I should probably get that."

As Luke takes a step back, he runs a hand through his hair, fruitlessly trying to tame the strands. I smooth a hand over my ponytail, ensuring it's still in place. Then I slide off the desk and adjust my skirt. The phone rings for another few seconds, though time seems to awkwardly stretch forever as he makes no move to pick it up. Finally, it stops, and the room descends into silence.

I bend at the waist to retrieve my discarded thong. As I stand, I fold it over in my hand before stuffing it into the pocket of Luke's pants. Then I pat his stubbled cheek with a grin.

"See you around, Chief."

CHAPTER
TWENTY-ONE
DELILAH

TRAVELLING the now-familiar road to Haven House, I think about all the ways my life has changed since moving to Kip Island in May. Not only have I found a genuine friend in Clara, but her family has welcomed mine without hesitation. One day I'll pay them back for all the kindness they spent on strangers. I truly don't know where I would be without them.

They make me feel a hell of a lot stronger than I am.

The hulking metal gates are open when I turn into the driveway, and after a moment, Haven House comes into view. It really is beautiful. Once I'm parked between Gabe's truck and Clara's Volkswagen, I hop out of the car and then help Sophia from her seat.

Clara must have heard us pull up because the front door swings open just as we ascend the steps. "No Parker today?" she asks.

I sigh. "Not today."

When I knocked on his door to remind him it was time

to leave, he was conveniently still in bed, pretending to sleep. They say to pick your battles, and I knew that wasn't one I would win. Not that I feel like much of a winner lately anyway.

The three of us head straight for the kitchen. Maggie and John are putting the finishing touches on the food, and Gabe sits at the table, scrolling on his phone. When Clara walks by, she flicks the back of her brother's head.

"What the fu—" He cuts himself off as his eyes land on Sophia, registering her presence. "What was that for?" he amends, glaring at his twin.

She shrugs. "Just because."

"Children," Maggie chides, "behave."

Beside me, Sophia covers her mouth with her hand, hiding her giggles. She always finds it funny when they bicker in front of us. Because my siblings and I are all so far apart in age, we never really had the same type of sibling relationship that the Bowmans do. Clara and Gabe are only three years younger than Luke, so they all grew up together. Sometimes I envy that closeness.

"Can I do anything?" I ask Maggie, just as I always do.

She gives me a stern look. "You can sit your butt at the table and relax. John and I have it under control," she says, just as she always does.

When Gabe sees my sister looking around for his daughter, he gives her an apologetic smile. "Sorry, Soph. Abbie was with her mom last night. She should be here soon."

Sophia nods and quietly climbs into her usual chair. I take my own seat, noting the absence in the spot next to mine. The question is on the tip of my tongue, but I don't want to make it seem like I'm looking forward to seeing Luke. That would be weird. I mean, we agreed to keep hooking up, but we forgot to discuss whether we would hide it from people. Namely, his family.

I don't have much time to ruminate on this before footsteps sound down the hall, and my heart starts to beat in traitorous anticipation. This will be my first time seeing Luke after my visit to the fire station three days ago. As it turns out, finding time to have casual sex is hard when you're the guardian of your two siblings. Who knew?

Luke kisses his mother's cheek and claps his father on the back, and then he takes his seat. For some reason, it feels like he's sitting closer to me than he usually does, like his chair has been moved. I can't say I hate the proximity, but it does wonders to my focus. In that, it totally wrecks it. I'm thankful no one directly addresses me because I find it very hard to follow the conversations taking place around me.

Abbie's mother drops her off shortly after, which brightens Sophia's mood considerably. Then the food is set out and we all fill our plates. After the girls are finished eating, they run off to play, and I'm left alone with the Bowmans.

No one acknowledges it, but everyone at the table notices when Luke's arm casually drapes across the back of my chair partway through a conversation. It's subtle—so much so that I don't catch it at first. But then I see the way Clara's gaze is fixed over my shoulder, studying her brother's actions. I can feel my cheeks heat under the attention.

Why does he have his arm there? And why do I not mind it?

The only logical conclusion I can come up with is that it's some kind of manipulation tactic. Well, two can play at that game. Beneath the table, I set my hand on Luke's knee. He glances at me, confusion in his eyes, but the look quickly morphs into understanding when my hand begins to move. My fingers trail slowly up his thigh, and I revel in the way his muscles tighten from my touch. He goes still and I continue to set a slow pace, exercising every bit of control I have in this moment. Just as the tips of my fingers reach the crotch of his pants, his hand clamps over them, stopping their movement.

"Delilah," he warns beneath his breath.

My lashes flutter as I look up at him, faux innocence in my expression. "Yes, Chief?"

He slowly releases my hand. "Coy doesn't suit you."

"I don't know..." My lips tug into a grin. "I think it suits me pretty well."

My fingers find the zipper on his pants, and I pretend to tug on it. Luke stands abruptly, his leg banging against the table in his haste. The empty dishes rattle. His family stops mid-conversation to look at him in varying degrees of bewilderment. I hold my tongue.

"Are you okay, sweetie?" Maggie asks.

Luke nods jerkily as he white-knuckles the edge of the table. "I'm fine. Delilah just has to show me something on her car," he says. "We'll be back."

"Since when are you a mechanic?" Gabe asks, amusement twinkling in his eyes.

Oh, he definitely knows something is up between us. I want to be embarrassed, but I'm enjoying this too much. Seeing Luke all riled up because of me will never get old.

"Finn has shown me a few things," Luke counters.

"Do you need any help?" John asks, evidently none the wiser to what's really going on. "I know my way around under the hood."

Clara's eyes go impossibly wide, and she has to stifle a giggle behind her hand. She pats her father's arm. "I think Luke has it covered, Dad."

"Alright," John says. "Holler if you need anything."

I have to bite my fist to stop from laughing as Luke grabs my other hand and tugs me behind him. He leads me through the house and right out the front door. When he notices my struggles to keep up with his long strides, he slows his pace.

"What's the rush, Chief?" I ask.

He doesn't respond. We wordlessly pass the cars in the driveway and start down the walkway on the side of the house. A couple of guests staying in the bed and breakfast sit on the back porch, and Luke waves as we walk by. Off to the side of the yard, a wooden shed sits on a concrete foundation. When we reach the door, Luke pulls it open and then gestures for me to walk ahead of him. Inside, the shed smells overwhelmingly like potting soil.

The door closes with a sound of finality. Then Luke's eyes, darker than I've ever seen them, rise to meet mine. I repress the urge to shiver at the intensity.

"On your knees, pretty girl."

My eyes widen in surprise. "You brought me all the way out here to give you head?"

"Don't act shocked, Delilah. You knew exactly what

game you were playing. Now get on your knees and suck my cock like the good girl I know you can be."

In any other context, if a man told me what to do like that, I would gladly tell him where to shove it. After Mitchell, I vowed that I was done being the dutiful little girlfriend. But everything with Luke feels...different. Not like I'm giving up my power, but taking it.

So I drop to my knees. Or I would have if Luke's hand didn't shoot out to stop me. Confused, I look up at him, but he's turned to the side, reaching for something. When he faces me again, I realize it's a small cushion from an outdoor patio set. It looks a little worn, which would explain why it's sitting in the shed. He sets it on the floor at our feet and suddenly, it all makes sense.

Luke Bowman is the embodiment of careful contradictions. He acts like he hates me and then gets coffee delivered when I can't function without it. He seems like he couldn't care less and then he takes my car to get fixed. He mutters filthy words to me and then he gives me something soft to kneel on.

I lower myself to the floor. Even through the cushion, the wood is hard beneath my knees, and I love that Luke anticipated that. I make quick work of his belt and zipper. When his pants and boxers are peeled away, there is nothing standing between me and Luke's cock. I take him in my hand, stroking slowly up and down his shaft. I increase the pressure and he groans, the sound urging me on.

Luke caresses the back of my head. When he winds my hair around his fist and gives an experimental tug, I all but melt. He is the perfect mix of gentle and rough.

"You have no idea," he says, his low voice threaded with desire, "what the sight of you does to me, Delilah. No *goddamn* idea."

An ache spreads through my core. I want him. *God*, I want him. Seeing him now, for the first time, I would love nothing more than for him to be inside me. If he's half as good with his dick as he is with his fingers, I would be seeing stars this afternoon. But he has already been so good to me, so today I'll give him what he wants.

I take the tip of his cock between my lips, swirling my tongue around the head. My hand fists the base, and I can feel him hardening even more beneath my touch. When my mouth opens to take more of him in, he releases a shuddering breath that quickly turns into a loud curse.

I pull him out of my mouth. "I know you like to be loud, Chief," I mock, "but we don't want to alert the guests."

Luke's grip tightens on my ponytail. I'm beginning to wonder if that's his favourite part of me.

His usual brown eyes are dark pools of obsidian. "Work that smart mouth one more time, pretty girl, and see what happens."

I arch a brow. "Is that supposed to be a threat?"

"Part those lips, baby. Let's see how much you like to talk when my cock is stuffed down your throat and I'm fucking your face."

My thighs snap together as I try to relieve the intensifying ache between my legs. I take his cock in my mouth again until he sits halfway down my throat. This apparently isn't good enough for Luke. He thrusts experimentally, and I end up taking him all the way. My eyes water, but that only spurs me on.

Luke, however, pauses. His thumb slides along my cheekbone in an almost tender touch. "Are you good, Delilah?"

I nod as best as I can with my mouth full. Luke takes my permission and runs with it, making good on his threat. The feel of him sliding against my tongue and hitting the back of my throat makes me moan. His thrusts falter as the vibrations make him let out another curse.

"Fuck, Delilah," he rasps. His head tilts back in pleasure. "That's it."

And then I can't handle it anymore. I unhook the button on my shorts and let my hand slip inside my underwear. I circle my clit, working to relieve this pressure that is building inside me.

When Luke notices what I'm doing, he urges me on. "Just like that, pretty girl," he coaxes. "Touch yourself while I fill your sweet mouth."

I take my pleasure as he takes his. It's been a long time since I touched myself. Mitchell didn't like me doing it, especially not when we were together like this. The past few months, I haven't been in the mood. Now, I let myself get lost.

"Can I come in your mouth, pretty girl?" he rasps, struggling to get the words out.

I nod, urging him closer with a hand on his ass. With one final jerk of his hips, he spills down my throat. I swallow as my own climax mounts, and then he slips from my mouth with a prominent *pop*. As Luke takes a step back to catch his breath, I wipe my chin with the back of my hand.

We both spend a few minutes righting our clothing and taming our hair. Still, I know the evidence isn't altogether erased, and I'm not sure how I feel about that.

I clear my throat. "What are the chances your family won't notice?"

He frames my face in his hands and my heart embarrassingly trips over itself. "Do you want the real answer or do you want me to pretend?"

"Pretend, please."

He grins. "You look as perfectly put together as you were when you got here and no one will suspect a thing."

Even though I know it's a lie, I still believe him. Enough to swallow my awkwardness and rejoin the Bowmans in the kitchen like I hadn't just been in their shed getting absolutely debauched. The mimosa Clara slides across the table does little to cool my flaming cheeks, but it does put a damper on the butterflies running rampant in my stomach.

And when Luke's arm returns to the back of my chair, the mimosa goes down like a shot.

CHAPTER
TWENTY-TWO
DELILAH

MITCHELL
You can't ignore me forever, Delilah.

You're dealing with your parents' deaths in a really unhealthy way.

I'm worried about you. Let me help. Running isn't the answer.

Fuck. Off.

MITCHELL
One day you're going to realize I'm not the bad guy here.

IT TAKES great effort to stop myself from throwing my phone at the wall. I was in a good mood this morning, and then he had to go and threaten to ruin it. Instead of wrecking my phone, I stuff it into my back pocket and head out to the floor. When I spot Carole, my new favourite person on Kip Island, talking to Clara, I shove Mitchell and his texts out of my brain. I can worry about him another day.

"Hi, Chickadee," Carole says as she pulls me into a hug. I have yet to figure out why she calls me that, but it's quirky and I love it.

I smile. "Hi, Carole." I hold on just a second longer than I probably should, but I'm in need of a hug right now. She seems to understand as she squeezes me extra tight. "How are you?"

When she pulls back, her gaze is soft. "Oh, just lovely. I actually came by because I wanted to deliver this in person."

"Deliver what?" I ask. I ordered some prints from a local artist whose work had been displayed in the gallery the last time I was there, but I already picked those up yesterday. As far as I know, I haven't ordered anything else.

She grins as she produces a large manilla envelope from her bag and extends it toward me. "Congratulations, Delilah! You won!"

I take the envelope in confusion. "Won what?"

Carole's smile falters. Now *she* is the one who is confused. "The photography contest, Chickadee. You won first place."

Hold on. I *what*?

"But—" My gaze swings from the older woman to Clara and then back again. "But I didn't enter." I push the envelope into Carole's hand. "There must be some mistake."

"It's definitely not a mistake," my best friend interjects. "You deserve this, Dee."

After some mild begging on her part, I caved and showed

Clara some of the pictures I've taken over the years. Now I'm thinking that was a mistake.

I turn suspicious eyes to her. "Did you give Carole my portfolio?"

She holds up her hands. "I swear to God, I didn't. I won't lie—I was thinking about it. But I ultimately decided not to. I figured you would kill me if you found out, and I kind of like being alive."

"Who submitted my work?" I ask Carole. "Because it certainly wasn't me."

"I'm not sure. It was given to one of the panelists anonymously. I can try to find out, but..." She offers me the envelope again. "Clara is right, Delilah. You *do* deserve this. I wasn't on the judging panel, but I have had the privilege of seeing your portfolio and it is breathtaking."

Breathtaking.

Nothing I have ever done has been described as *breathtaking* before. While it may just be a turn of phrase, isn't it every artist's dream to elicit a visceral reaction from their audience? To know that their work wasn't simply admired, but that it resonated deeply with another person? I want my work to matter.

I want to matter.

I swallow the emotion building in my chest as the seams of old wounds start to tear open. I retake the envelope and slide the contents out. All I see are the words *congratulations* and *Delilah* before my eyes blur with tears.

When I was younger, I used to feel so excited sharing my accomplishments with my parents. When I was younger, my accomplishments mattered. When I was younger, I mattered.

As I got older, their attention fractured, and I stopped sharing things with them. It has been years since I felt excited to tell them good news. Still, the impulse never fully went away, no matter how much I learned to downplay my accomplishments. So as I stand here, it is a punch to the gut when I remember that it doesn't matter—I have no one to tell anyway.

Clara's arms come around me, squeezing me tight against her. "I'm so happy for you," she whispers. "And I am so, so proud of you."

I can't help it anymore. Tears fall in rapid succession, wetting Clara's shoulder where my chin rests. Months—years, really—of shame fester and bubble, the emotion both heavy and extremely ugly. I feel so undeserving of her praise, but as I let it wash over me, I don't feel quite as weighed down. As I cry, I let the ugly come out.

"I don't know why I'm crying," I croak. "I'm sorry."

Clara's arms tighten. "I'm not. Sometimes you just need a good cry. It's cathartic."

So much of my life since last August has been numb, but I feel like coming to Kip Island cracked me wide open. Everything that I ignored back in Victoria is finally making its presence known. Perhaps time really does heal. Or maybe I've just found myself in a place, surrounded by good people, that makes me feel safe.

I pull away from Clara's embrace and swipe under my eyes. Tears still cling to my eyelashes, and I thank God that I forewent mascara today. The last thing I need after losing it at work is to look like a raccoon for the rest of my shift.

Carole offers me a sympathetic smile. "We can talk about

all the details another day, Chickadee. For now, just wrap your head around the fact that you won—and that someone saw something in your work that made them enter it on your behalf. Whoever it was, they have great taste."

"Thank you, Carole," I say. "It means a lot. I don't want to seem ungrateful."

She places a comforting hand on my arm. "I know what's in your heart. Don't you worry." She checks the time on her watch. "I'll get out of your hair. Let you get back to work. Congratulations again."

Carole bids us adieu, sweeping out of the restaurant, her flowing skirts trailing in her wake. When she disappears, Clara turns to me and lets out an excited squeal. "This calls for champagne!"

I laugh as I tuck my envelope behind the bar for safe keeping. "Champagne? Since when do you drink champagne?"

"Since my bestie has major news worth celebrating!" She stands on tiptoe and pulls a bottle from the top shelf of liquor. "I hope you don't mind it being room temperature."

She pops the cork out of the bottle, the sound reverberating through the whole room.

"Hey," Gabe calls, "what's the occasion?"

I look over to find both him and Luke standing there, watching as their sister pours bubbly into highball glasses. Apparently we have the champagne, but no flutes.

Clara hands me a half-full glass. "Delilah won the photography contest!"

Gabe's eyes light up. "Oh, no way! Congrats!"

I smile, my cheeks heating. Accepting compliments has

always made me feel uneasy. "Thank you," I say. "It was quite the surprise, seeing as I didn't actually enter."

My eyes, like they always seem to do, find Luke. He tips his chin and accepts the glass of champagne from Clara. The glass he can't drink because he's currently on duty.

"Congratulations," he says.

That one word seems to heat me from the inside out. It's ridiculous. Utterly ridiculous. Still, I can feel my cheeks turning an even deeper shade of pink. Luke's lips quirk slightly as he realizes this. I take a sip of my champagne, letting the bubbles slip over my tongue as I avert my gaze.

It's been twenty-four hours since our tryst in the shed and I haven't been able to convince myself to forget about it.

"To Delilah!" Clara declares, glass raised in the air.

All four of us clink glasses, and then Clara and I both down our drinks before taking the cups from the guys and doing the same.

Luke's brow raises. "Drinking on the job?" he asks. If you didn't know him well, you might mistake that as a judgment. But knowing what I know now, I recognize his tone as one of teasing.

Clara grins. "Unlike you two, we know how to have fun."

Gabe rolls his eyes. "Lunch ready yet?"

She nods. "It is," she says. Then she eyes Luke, who usually isn't present when Gabe or one of the others does the lunch run for the fire station. "Did it really take two of you to pick it up?"

Luke crosses his arms. "There's a lot of food."

"*Right*, that's why," she replies with a laugh. "I'll go let the kitchen know you're here."

Clara disappears and Gabe gets distracted talking to a table of elderly women. Which leaves me and Luke standing there. Alone. He takes a step closer. His familiar scent washes over me, and I instantly wish that we were alone—truly alone. I go to move away, not wanting to make things totally obvious, but he catches my arm.

"You've been crying," he says.

I paste on a smile. "Just happy tears. You know how it is."

He takes another step. I shrug him off, intending on turning away from him. But then, right there, out in the open for everyone to see, he cups my cheeks in his hands. He tilts my head upwards and his eyes roam my face.

"Let's not lie to each other if we can help it, yeah?"

Of course, the one time I want to be all cool and mysterious, I'm dreadfully transparent. Thankfully, the bell above the front door chimes and a group walks in.

"Duty calls," I say, pulling out of his hold.

He reluctantly lets me go.

When I get home from work, I tuck the envelope from Carole under my pillow. I don't want Parker or Sophia to find it. It feels strange, having something to celebrate. I feel like I don't have any right reaching for something like that.

I make a quick dinner for us, and then after Sophia has gone to bed, I wash the day away with a shower. I stand under the spray and let everything out, the water running cold on me, mingling with my tears. Parker is already holed up in his room by the time I get out of the shower, so I head outside alone.

The night air is warm, caressing my skin as I step onto the welcome mat. My new favourite place to sit at the end of the night is the swing hanging at the end of the porch. I take a seat, my legs curled to the side, and then I close my eyes. Mitchell's texts flash behind my eyelids, and before I know it, I'm spiralling into wondering if he's a little bit right.

Was leaving home a mistake? Am I doing this all wrong?

Some time later, the front steps creak and then familiar footsteps sound on the wooden boards. I don't even have to look to know that it's Luke. But when I feel him nudge my shoulder, I finally relent, letting my eyes flutter open. He settles onto the swing beside me and drapes his arm along the back.

"Hi," I say, a little surprised to see him here.

A hint of a smile tilts his lips. "Hi," he replies.

"What are you doing here?"

Luke looks at me, brown eyes meeting grey. He reaches out and takes a strand of my hair, twisting it around his finger. "I was driving past and saw the light on." He gives a slight tug on the strand and then releases it. "Just thought I'd stop."

A teasing smile graces my lips. "Can't resist me, can you?"

He considers a moment. "No," he says. He lets out a low chuckle. "I really can't. I think I've made that pretty obvious."

We settle into the quiet, letting the chirp of crickets and the rustling of the wind in the trees wash over us. Nights on

Kip Island are predictable. Just you and the starry sky, no city noises to be heard. I thought maybe I would miss Victoria after a while. Up until a couple months ago, it was all I had known. But now that this island has become so familiar, I can't imagine being anywhere else.

"Delilah?"

I know that tone. It was wishful thinking that he would forget all about my crying at Dockside earlier. I look down at my lap, finding my hands rather fascinating in this moment. "Yeah?"

"Tell me what's wrong?"

The concern in his voice surprises me. I purse my lips. "Being my therapist wasn't part of our deal."

He frowns. "Believe it or not, I am capable of caring about another person outside of sex."

And now I feel terrible. I hate being vulnerable, especially in front of someone like Luke. But would talking to him be so bad? I feel like we started off on the wrong foot and then jumped into metaphorical bed. Maybe we can genuinely learn to be friends. Friends who fuck—but friends all the same.

I sigh. "I love it here."

"Why does that sound like a bad thing?"

Tears gather in the corners of my eyes. I try to blink them back, but one manages to slip through and slide down my cheek. "Because Parker hates it. Hates *me*. And I can't help but feel guilty for loving something I have solely because my parents are dead."

He's quiet for a moment, and I wonder briefly if I've scared him off. If these thoughts are too big for him. Too much. I was always too much for Mitchell. By the end, he tried to whittle me down so much, I could fit inside the box he had made for me. He almost succeeded.

The release of my pictures was the best and worst thing that has ever happened to me.

"Parker will come around," Luke says. He sounds so steady; so sure. It makes me want to believe him. "As for the rest of it, you can't stop living just because they're gone."

I nod, swiping at the tear on my cheek. "I know. Parker and Sophia need me."

He shakes his head. "Not just them, Shutterbug. You have to think about what you need, too."

I smile sadly. "I don't know what that is anymore."

"Maybe—" He cuts himself off and clears his throat. He almost sounds...nervous? "Maybe winning that photography contest is a start."

"I feel an awful lot like a fraud," I admit. I shift, tucking my knees up to my chest and resting my chin on top of them. "I haven't picked up my camera in a long time."

His smile is soft. "I think you may have found your answer."

Perhaps the reason I feel so adrift is because I haven't done the one thing I love in a really long time. My camera is right inside, sitting on a shelf. It would be so easy to take it from its case and turn it on. Yet the action feels daunting. Maybe that's the perfect reason to go for it.

"Yeah, I think you might be right." I turn my head, catching Luke's eye. "Thank you."

His chin dips as he nods, and then his eyes settle on the

quiet street. The swing starts moving slowly, Luke keeping careful control of the pace. "Anytime, pretty girl."

I let his words settle between us, hoping that he really means them. And then I close my eyes, letting myself be comforted by his presence. I know I shouldn't get used to it, but it might already be too late.

CHAPTER
TWENTY-THREE
LUKE

"IF YOU DON'T STOP CALLING to check in, I'm going to report you for harassment."

I lean back in my seat, frowning as I look out the windshield of my truck. "It's my job to check in."

"No," Jodi says through my phone, "your job is to be the chief. Not to micromanage us to death. On your day off, no less."

"I don't micromanage."

Jodi laughs. "You haven't taken a full day off in the past sixty. I keep a tally. Don't make me sic HR on you."

"You wouldn't."

Lori, the human resources manager, has always scared the shit out of me. Never mind that she's a wisp of a woman, standing at least two feet shorter than me and no more than a hundred pounds soaking wet.

"Don't test me, Bowman!" I can't help but chuckle at this. "The probies have settled in. We'll be fine. If anything major happens, you will be my first call."

I sigh. "If you're sure."

"We've trained them well, Luke. Now trust them to make us proud."

No matter how many times I tell myself that my department knows what it's doing, letting go of the reins doesn't get easier. "Do you ever get tired of being right?"

Jodi snorts. "Never."

We hang up, and then I finally exit my truck. When I woke up this morning, I realized how painfully empty my fridge was. Luckily, Mom is always willing to feed me, so I stopped by Haven House for breakfast.

Breakfast turned into helping Dad tackle the perpetual to-do list Mom keeps. Between hanging shelves, fixing doors and breaking for lunch, I checked in with Jodi more times than was reasonable. In her opinion. Now it's late afternoon and I'm finally getting around to the grocery shopping I made a list for about ten hours ago.

When I step through the doors of Sunnyside Market, I'm greeted with a wall of tourists. Judging by the time, the ferry must have just let out, and weekenders have begun to spill onto our little island paradise. I try not to scowl as I grab my basket and maneuver around people that are paying no attention to their surroundings. Tourism is undoubtedly a big part of what keeps Kip Island's economy going, but that doesn't mean I have to like it.

"You're not going to do *anything*?" a woman cries. The slightly shrill tone of the voice doesn't disguise who it belongs to. I round the corner of an aisle, spotting Gordon in yet another face-off with Delilah. This time, Sophia is nowhere in sight.

Gordon sniffs. "I'm not sure what you would have me do."

"Have a little compassion, for starters," she replies.

The last time Delilah sparred with him, she was pure fire. Today, she's teetering on the edge of desperation. Something isn't right.

"What's going on?" My voice is clipped as I insert myself yet again. But I can't bring myself to care. Especially when Delilah's gaze meets mine, and I stop cold. Her eyes almost cut me down where I stand, the way they bleed with anguish.

"I can't find Sophia," she says, voice wavering. "She's gone."

I take a step closer. "What do you mean, *she's gone*?"

"I— I turned around for one second, and now she's gone. I've looked all over the store. Twice." She shakes her head as she covers her face with her hands. "Oh, God, this can't be happening. This is all my fault."

I drop my basket to the floor and take hold of Delilah's shoulders. I give them a firm, reassuring squeeze. Her body leans toward me, seeking comfort. I gladly give it to her. "Hey," I say softly, "none of that. Let's just focus on finding her, yeah? Do you remember what she's wearing?" I keep my voice calm and steady. The last thing we need is Delilah spiralling when she holds important information.

Delilah exhales a shaky breath. "A pink sundress. She wanted to match her Barbie. And these cute pink jelly sandals." She tries to smile. "She loves pink."

"Do you have a paging system?" I ask Gordon. "Can you get a description to your employees so they can start looking?"

Ever since I put him in his place after the banana incident, I've been on Gordon's shit list. When he doesn't answer immediately, I level him with a hard look. He then stutters, "W-we have walkie talkies."

"Great," I grit out. "Tell them to look for a five-year-old girl with long blonde hair, wearing a pink dress and pink sandals. And don't let anyone leave the damn building."

Gordon begins to march toward the front doors, a walkie talkie pressed close to his mouth.

"What should I do?" Delilah asks.

She looks so small right now—so unmoored. I have the strongest urge to wrap her up in my arms, but I can't do that. For too many reasons to name. "Stay here in case Soph comes looking for you," I reply. "I'll help search."

She nods as worry clouds her gaze. I survey the building, noting that Gordon actually followed through—all employees have seemingly dropped what they were working on and have started walking the store. I join them, looking under displays and on shelving Sophia could have easily climbed on.

I try not to think of the worst case scenario—that one of those tourists decided to grab Sophia and make a run for it. I try to erect my professional detachment. But I fail miserably. Thinking of what I'll say to Delilah if we can't find her sister makes me feel sick. It brings back unwanted memories of Kristina and Abbie and the night that changed everything.

After a few minutes, I come up to an employee-only area. Ignoring the sign, I swing through the door. There are coat racks and small lockers, a few tables and chairs, and a small kitchen setup. Beyond this is a manager's office.

"Sophia?" I call.

I sweep the break room, but I come up empty. Then I move toward the office. The door is ajar, so I tentatively push it all the way open. I glance around, noting that nothing seems to be out of place. Until I notice the pink jelly sandal peeking out from underneath the desk.

I crouch, ducking my head. Sophia is curled into a tight ball under the table, looking terrified. Her eyes are closed, but I can tell she has been crying. The sight nearly breaks me.

"Soph," I say gently.

She startles at my voice, her eyes flying open. When she recognizes me, she relaxes somewhat. "Luke?" she whispers.

I offer her a reassuring smile. "Hey, kid. Your sister has been worried about you. Come on out and I'll take you to her."

Sophia nods and scrambles out of her hiding spot. She covers her face with her curtain of blonde hair, but she loops her arms around my neck, clinging to me. I wrap an arm under her and stand, carrying her out of the office.

"Am I gonna be in trouble?" she whispers, so quiet I almost don't hear.

"'Course not," I reply, hugging her closer. "Let's go find Delilah, okay?"

I head back out to the sales floor. When Delilah sees us, I can see the relief that sweeps through her. She drops to her knees, and I pause, setting Sophia on her feet. She wastes no time barrelling into her big sister's waiting arms. I don't miss the way her tiny shoulders shake as she starts to cry again.

"You're okay," Delilah murmurs, rocking Sophia. "You're okay."

Gordon appears and I give him a nod. He says something into his walkie talkie—likely calling off the search by telling his employees to *get back to work*. I want to lay into him for initially being an unhelpful asshole, but instead I decide to kill him with kindness.

"Thank you for your help," I tell him. "It's much appreciated."

He nods sharply, and then he stalks away.

Delilah pulls back, though her hands stay on Sophia's shoulders, like she's afraid to let go. "Soph," she says, "what happened? Where did you go?"

Sophia sniffles. "The mean man—he yelled. I didn't wanna be in trouble. I tried to go to the quiet, but I got lost."

My anger at Gordon surges anew. What a miserable man.

"Oh, Soph." Delilah runs her fingers through her sister's hair. "I'm sorry he scared you, but you can't run off like that. I was *so* worried about you. It makes me sad when I don't know where you are."

Sophia looks down at her feet. "Sorry, Sissy."

Delilah presses a kiss to the top of her head. "I love you. Next time you're scared, you tell me. It's my job to make you feel safe, but I can't do that if you're gone."

I shouldn't be standing here anymore; my part in this is done. Except I can't quite convince my feet to move. Delilah holds all my attention. Something in me is inexplicably drawn to something in her, and the more I try to fight it, the more I'm beginning to realize that the effort is in vain.

But what we're doing is temporary. We agreed on that. One day, we'll decide we've had our fill—that we've satisfied our cravings. And then it will end. Until then, I'm going to keep losing myself in her.

Delilah stands, meets my gaze, and then she launches herself at me. I'm too stunned to react at first as she wraps her arms around my middle and presses her body into mine. After a second, I regain function and allow myself to touch her, my palm falling to the back of her head and then gliding down her back, her silky hair catching on my fingers. Holding her like this... She fits so perfectly against me, her body moulding to mine.

When she pulls away, I'm reluctant to let her. Her cheeks are stained adorably pink. "Thank you," she says quietly. "Again."

I nod. "Of course."

She lets out an awkward chuckle. "I'm beginning to think this place is cursed. Or maybe I am."

I rub a hand across my jaw. "You've had some bad luck," I agree, "but that has more to do with the *lovely* store manager than it does you."

At the mention of Gordon, her eyes turn hard. "If this wasn't the only grocery store on the island, I sure as hell would not be shopping here."

I chuckle. "You and half the island."

She seems to study me for a moment, but then she shakes herself from it. She curls an arm around Sophia who has latched onto her sister's leg. She does not look prepared to let go anytime soon. Delilah sighs.

"So much for groceries," Delilah mutters. "I think she's going to need three points of contact for the foreseeable future."

I don't think much about what I offer next. In fact, it could be argued that I don't think about it at all. This goes beyond the scope of our agreement, but when I see a need, I fill it. It definitely doesn't have anything to do with the fact that I enjoy spending time with Delilah.

"C'mon," I say. I'm already heading in the direction of the shopping carts. "I have stuff to pick up, too. Read me your list and I'll put things in the cart."

Delilah hesitates. "I don't...have a list."

I stop, my hand hovering over the cart handle. "Then how the hell do you shop?"

She shrugs. "I just walk around and pick up things that look good. I have a mental picture of food we already have at home."

I shake my head as I motion for them to follow me toward the produce. The scene of the banana incident reminds me just how much I'd like to throttle Gordon, but I push that aside. For now.

"You wouldn't survive shopping with my mom. Her list is organized by category and follows the exact route she takes around the store."

Delilah laughs. "God, I *wish* I was that organized."

We walk the produce department, Delilah pointing out what she wants. Before we pass it by, I can't help but lift a bunch of bananas from the display and arch a brow. When Delilah sees them, she rolls her eyes.

We eventually make it to the cereal aisle, and Delilah holds up a hand. "Let me guess," she insists. Her eyes trace me, assessing for hints of my go-to breakfast. "You strike me as a Raisin Bran kind of guy."

I scoff. "*Raisin Bran?*"

She grins. "I'm sure the high fibre content would help dislodge that stick up your ass."

Despite myself, I laugh. "You really think I eat the breakfast of a grandma?"

"I think you eat the breakfast of a serious man with important, serious man things to do." Her voice lowers as she tries—and fails—to imitate me.

My hand settles on her hip as I lean in close, careful not to let Sophia hear. My lips brush Delilah's ear when I say, "Hmm. I can think of something else I'd much rather have for breakfast."

When I pull back, her eyes are already trained on me. They swirl with want, and coupled with her rosy cheeks, I know my words had the intended effect. My lips curve into a smirk.

"Well, that's not fair," she protests.

"When it comes to you, pretty girl, I play to win." These words seem to fluster her. With a chuckle, I change the subject. "I bet you would choose cereal that rots your teeth. Lucky Charms?"

"If you're going to eat cereal, it might as well be fun." She looks down at her sister, still clinging to her side. "Right, Soph?"

We leave that aisle and head into the next. "I am capable of fun, you know," I say. Delilah simply hums as her eyes scan the shelves. "What? I *am*."

She glances at me over her shoulder with a smirk. "The lord doth protest too much, methinks."

I cross my arms. "I'm not sure where everyone is getting this idea."

I know exactly where everyone is getting this idea. Nothing about me screams *fun*. But being around Delilah makes me want to find that part of myself that's been missing for so long. The part that makes smiling a little easier.

"Fine," she concedes, "if you're so fun, then I'm sure you'll have no trouble proving it."

This playful groove we've fallen into is easy. It feels natural. I hold my arms out in a *bring it on* gesture. "I'm ready. What do I have to do?"

Delilah leans down and whispers something in her sister's ear. Sophia still hasn't entirely shaken off the incident from earlier, but her lips still stretch into a smile. She nods emphatically. "Do you wanna see a movie in the backyard with us?" she asks in her small voice.

Any respectable man would have trouble saying no to her. I probably should say no, even though it would kill me. Getting too attached to Delilah's siblings is a recipe for disaster. But those baby blue eyes spear me, and I'm a goner, disaster be damned.

"I would love to."

Delilah's mouth involuntarily pops open in shock. "Really?"

I raise a brow. "Was the offer sincere?"

Slowly, she nods. "It was."

"Then yes, really."

"Alright," she says, turning away and walking further down the aisle. "We're going to need some popcorn and lots of M&Ms."

CHAPTER TWENTY-FOUR
DELILAH

I EXPECTED LUKE TO LEAVE. I didn't expect him to spend his hard-won free time walking around the grocery store with us. Although Sophia calmed considerably after Gordon scared her, she still clung to my side, not wanting to let go. I could hardly blame her. When I turned around and she was gone, it felt like every single one of my worst fears was coming true. Like a nightmare come to life, I was sure she would be taken from me, too.

That's another thing I didn't expect—Luke swooping in and helping. It wasn't his job, but he didn't hesitate to take charge. I don't think I'll ever be able to properly convey how thankful I am that he was there. On any given day, I can hold my own, but for the first time in a long time, I didn't have to. It felt nice to have someone there who had my back.

And now he's coming over to watch a movie. I'm not entirely sure what I was thinking when I suggested it to Sophia. But the way she lit up made me glad that I did. I know she likes him, so I'll just have to put aside my nerves and get through the night.

Backyard movie screenings were a staple of my childhood. One of the houses we used to live in had two big maple trees in the back. They were side by side and an ideal spot to hang a white bedsheet. After dinner, while I hurried to change into my pajamas and brush my teeth, my parents would set up the projector, and gather pillows and blankets. We would make a bed on the grass and spend the next few hours curled together under the stars, watching whatever movie had recently been released on DVD.

It has been years since we last did this. Parker experienced a few summers of backyard screenings, but they fell to the wayside before Sophia came into our lives. I want to give this to her. She only had a handful of years with our parents and it isn't fair. I know I can't replace them, but I want to remind her who they were. I want to give her all my good memories. It's lonely having no one to share them with.

When Parker opens the front door to find both Luke and Riot—who unashamedly bounds inside to seek out Sophia—my brother turns to me with his eyebrows raised. While Sophia is none the wiser to...whatever is going on between me and Luke, I don't think I can say the same for Parker. I've done my best to hide it, but he isn't oblivious.

"It's a long story," I say quietly. Then I clap my hands, addressing the room. "Alright, Soph and I have the popcorn covered. Can you two go hang the sheet in the yard?"

While Parker and Luke head outside, Sophia and I make our way to the kitchen. We set the popcorn to pop in the microwave, and then I help Sophia tear into a bag of M&Ms.

After I pour the fresh popcorn into a bowl, she dumps the bag of chocolate into it.

All the blankets we own are out on the grass. Parker set them out there while Sophia and I were at the store. We settle in, Sophia curling up on my right side. Parker sits as far away from me as possible on the other side of her. Which leaves Luke to settle on my left. Riot curls up by Sophia's feet.

Luke relaxes back with his hands behind his head, face upturned toward the stars. The opening credits of the movie —some Barbie cartoon that Sophia has seen a thousand times —begin to play, but all I can focus on is the heat I can feel coming off of Luke. I have the strangest urge to curl my body against his and rest my head on his chest.

No, I scold myself. *Bad Delilah*.

"Having fun yet?" I whisper.

He turns his head to the side and offers me a smile. "Of course. Sophia's film choice is excellent."

Before I can answer, a piece of popcorn hits my cheek. "Hey!" I whisper-shout.

"Get a room. Some of us are trying to watch a movie here," Parker complains.

I roll my eyes. And then I let out a small squeal as Luke reaches out and pulls me into his side. Part of my upper body rests on his chest and my hand lands just over his heart. I go still, not entirely sure what is happening right now. This is against the rules, right? We shouldn't be doing this.

"*Relax*, Shutterbug," he murmurs in my ear.

While I'm on the verge of freaking out, Luke is as calm as ever. He seems entirely unaffected by our close proximity. I want to find his nonchalance annoying—a dismissal of my feelings—but instead I find it comforting. This doesn't have to be a big deal. It *isn't* a big deal. I release a slow breath, forcing the tension from my body.

"Good girl."

Good girl.

The endearment shouldn't make my insides feel like warm, melted chocolate, but it does. *Bad Delilah*. I want my overwhelming numbness back. It would be much easier to pretend I'm not walking a tightrope and one wrong move will send me careening into something I can't get myself out of. There's no safety net in this scenario.

Later, when the end credits roll on the makeshift screen, I peel myself away from Luke's side. I force myself not to think about the fact that I spent over an hour in his arms.

We're just casual. Everything's *fine*.

At some point, Parker must have retreated back to his room, and Sophia fell asleep about halfway through. Now she's out cold. She has a hard enough time sleeping as it is, so waking her is out of the question. While my sister is on the smaller side, making it up the stairs with her in my arms is going to be a challenge for me and my back. As I unwind the blankets from around her sleeping form, I let out a sigh.

Luke is working on shutting the projector down. He looks over at me. "What's wrong?" he asks.

"I didn't entirely think this through." I gesture to Sophia. "Now I have to carry her to bed."

He crosses to us and then kneels beside me. "Don't worry about it. I've got her."

Before I even have time to respond, Luke is gently scooping her into his arms. My sister looks so small compared to him, and he holds her like she's delicate. Seeing him with her does something to me I don't have the words for.

Regardless of whatever is happening between us, Luke has always shown that he cares about my siblings. Mitchell was never like that. My ex was barely interested in me, let alone Parker and Sophia. He went out of his way to avoid spending time with them. It always bothered me, but I never said anything. I wanted to keep the peace. But peace, as I have come to learn, is only an illusion.

"Lead the way?" he asks.

Right. Because he doesn't know where her bedroom is. Because this is his first time hanging out with us. Because we're *casual*.

Luke follows me through the back door and up the stairs to the second floor. Riot is on our heels, sticking close to his new friend. Parker's bedroom is first and his door is already shut. The small bathroom is next, and then Sophia's bedroom. I'm thankful I had the foresight to request she get ready for bed before we started the movie.

I turn on the nightlight beside her bed and make sure the comforter is turned down. Luke waits until I step out of the way and then he lowers her to the mattress. In her sleep, she clings to his shirt and he has to slide out from under her hand. I hold my breath, waiting to see if she will wake up, but she snuggles into her pillow and continues to dream. With the covers pulled up to her chin and a kiss on her forehead, I tiptoe out of the room, pulling the door shut behind me.

Luke is waiting for me in the hallway, and Riot sits dutifully at his feet. The three of us quietly make our way downstairs. When we reach the landing, Riot runs into the living room and hops up on the couch. He remembers his spot from that evening he stayed with us.

Luke points at him. "He's not allowed on the couch."

I huff, indignant. "At Casa Delacroix, he can do whatever he wants."

"So you're the one spoiling my dog, huh?" Luke advances toward me, a perfectly wicked look on his face. "He came home and decided he didn't need to follow the rules anymore."

I shrug, my lips curving into a grin. "Not his fault your rules are stupid."

I spin away, but he catches me around the waist. I laugh as he turns me to face him. The sound, however, dies almost instantly when his mouth seals over mine.

While we were watching the movie, I took my hair out of its usual ponytail. Now it hangs in curtains over my shoulders and down my back. Luke's fingers tangle in the strands as he cups the back of my head, drawing me closer.

I know this thing between us isn't forever, so some part of me feels like I need to take advantage of every opportunity I have to be with him. When he pulls back, I take my chance.

"It's late," I blurt. *It's not that late.* "Why don't you— Would you want to stay? Just for tonight."

"Alright," he says. He lets me pull him toward my bedroom. "Just for tonight."

Luke fell asleep in my bed. With me. I'm half convinced we both fell victim to some kind of spell that made us make bad decisions. How else can I explain my asking him to stay and Luke accepting the offer?

This morning, however, I'm alone, but muffled voices begin to carry through the air. I untangle myself from the comforter and head for my en suite. Then I pad out of the room, following the giggles that float through the house from the kitchen.

I find Luke, dressed in the same clothes as yesterday, leaning against the island. Sophia sits on one of the tall stools, her legs swinging beneath her as she digs into a bowl of the Lucky Charms we bought yesterday.

"Morning," I say warily. "You guys are up early."

"Morning, Shutterbug." Luke crosses the kitchen and pours a mug of coffee. Then he places it in my hands, wrapping my fingers around it when I'm too stunned to do it myself. "I came out to make you a pot and then Soph decided she was hungry."

His arm loops around my waist, and his fingers dip under my tank top. His hand curls on my hip, squeezing. And then his mouth settles over mine, stealing a kiss from my lips. I pull back, gesturing with my eyes toward my sister.

Luke retracts his hands and settles back against the counter with his own mug. I think we've flown under the radar—Sophia hasn't looked up from her bowl. But then she asks, "Sissy, are you and Luke gonna get married?"

The sip of coffee I just took enters my windpipe as Sophia's question forces me to suck in air. *Lots* of air.

"*What?*"

She looks at me with impossibly big eyes. "Are you gonna get married?"

When I look to Luke for some help, I find him leaning casually, one ankle crossed over the other. Drinking his coffee like my little sister didn't just ask if we were *going to get married*.

I cough awkwardly. "What makes you ask that?"

Sophia shrugs. "You kissed. Mommy and Daddy kissed. They're married."

Those words slam into me with the force of a high-speed train. Luke doesn't look quite as amused anymore. I can feel his eyes tracing me—assessing. I struggle to find the right words. Explaining the nuances of an adult relationship to a five-year-old isn't something I'm prepared to do. It isn't something I should do. Right? Right.

"They did, didn't they?" I offer Sophia a gentle smile. "Soph, sometimes people kiss because they like each other, but that doesn't always mean they get married."

"But are *you* gonna get married?"

I shake my head. "No, Luke and I are not getting married."

"So you like each other?"

Again, I glance at Luke and then back to my sister. "Yes. We...like each other."

She looks a little puzzled, but she shrugs and then digs her spoon back into her cereal. "Okay."

When I turn back to Luke, his eyes are already on me. "Sorry," he says, low enough that Sophia can't hear. "I wasn't thinking. I didn't mean to back you into a corner."

"It's fine. But we probably shouldn't...do this again. I don't want her to get her hopes up. Or get even more confused."

He nods as he sets his empty mug in the sink. "I should go."

"Oh," I say. "I wasn't trying to kick you out. I just…"

He smiles reassuringly. "I know, Delilah. But I should get home to feed Riot."

At the mention of his name, the dog in question hops up from the floor beside Sophia and heads toward us. I narrowly dodge his tongue as I scratch between his ears.

Luke ruffles Sophia's hair. "Bye, kid. Don't give your sister too much trouble, yeah?"

She beams. "Bye, Luke."

I walk him and Riot to the front entrance. Luke hooks the dog's leash onto his collar and then opens the door. I lean against the frame, watching them go.

"Luke?" I call out.

He turns, halfway down the front steps. "Yeah?"

"I was wrong," I admit. "When you really let yourself, you *can* have fun." I shrug. "You should do it more often."

He nods. "See you later, Shutterbug."

I stay there until his truck is backing out of the driveway. And I know it's silly, but it feels a little like he has my heart in his pocket, carrying it with him as he leaves.

CHAPTER
TWENTY-FIVE
LUKE

TWO DAYS after I spent the night at Delilah's, a summer storm rolls in. The rain is relentless as it pounds on the roof of the fire station and trails down the windows in endless rivulets. On a personal level, I don't mind the rain. But when it comes to the job, it makes for a long shift. The amount of car accidents amongst tourists ticks up exponentially and with that comes a steady stream of call outs.

With smaller accidents, I usually don't go to the scene. But today, with how busy we were, I've been out with the crew on and off. Now that I'm back at the station, I have a lot of paperwork to catch up on. If I had known just how much paperwork this job would involve, I'm not entirely sure I would've gone for it.

Then again, it gave me something to focus on after what happened with Kristina. Dealing with the insurance company and the slow rebuild of my house, on top of the guilt I felt for putting Abbie in that situation, left me empty. Having a mountain of paperwork sitting on my desk when I got to work every day gave me purpose. A purpose I had lost that night.

A knock sounds on my door, and then one of the new probationary firefighters sticks his head in. The kid is really green, but he has promise. As the youngest of the bunch, I have no doubt he was voluntold to come to my office to deliver some message.

"Chief," Swain says, "there's a, uh, woman here to see you."

When he doesn't elaborate, I sigh. "Does this woman happen to have a name?"

"Right." He clears his throat as his cheeks pinken. "Said her name was Delilah?" His voice ticks up like he's asking a question.

I don't let my surprise show as I nod. "Send her back."

Swain gives me an awkward and unnecessary salute. "Yes, sir."

When he leaves, I lean back in my chair, forgetting about the files on my computer. Why is Delilah here? The last time she came by the station, it was because I had pissed her off. As far as I know, I haven't done anything in the past two days that would elicit more anger.

While I wait for her, I take the opportunity to look at my phone. I noticed a few texts roll in earlier, but the day has been an utter shitshow, so I haven't had a spare moment to look. I have one message from Clara and another two from my mom. The others are all from Delilah.

> **SHUTTERBUG**
>
> So you probably don't care but I took my camera out this morning.
>
> [photo attachment]
>
> It felt weird, but good.

The rest of the messages came in a couple hours later.

> **SHUTTERBUG**
>
> Wow, it's that bad huh? I know I'm rusty but damn. You can be honest. I'll only be a little offended.
>
> It's raining pretty hard out there... I hope you don't get too many calls.
>
> Luke?
>
> I'm sorry. Ignore me. You're probably really busy.
>
> The rain is getting really bad. Clara said she hasn't heard from you...

After that, she called me twice. My stomach drops. I hear the door to my office open and then Delilah slips in. Her clothes are soaked through from the rain. Even from here, I can see the goosebumps prickling her skin from the chill of the air conditioning.

"What the hell? You're freezing," I say.

She doesn't respond, but her teeth begin to chatter. Rounding my desk, I take a hoodie off the hook on the wall and slip it over her head. She slides her arms through and I adjust the hem. It's long on her, hitting the tops of her thighs, but it looks damn good.

"Not that I'm disappointed to see you, but what are you doing here?" I ask. "And why are you soaked?"

Her head hangs as she tries to avoid my gaze. "I, um, walked here. In the rain."

"Delilah?" When she looks up, there are tears glistening in her eyes. I tense. "What's going on?"

She wipes under her eye, catching a tear that hasn't yet fallen. "It doesn't matter anymore. I'm fine. *You're* fine."

Funnily enough, I don't believe her. I bury my hand in her hair, feeling the raindrops that cling to the strands, and pull her closer. Seeing her upset kills me. What's worse is I know she's trying to hold all this in.

"Tell me anyway."

"I—" She looks away, her cheeks tinged pink with embarrassment. "I know it's stupid, but it's raining a lot and you weren't answering the phone. My mind just started going to the worst places and I couldn't stop thinking…"

The reminder of the accident that caused her parents' deaths hits me—*hard*. She never told me the gory details, but when she told me about the accident, it triggered a memory. A quick search of her last name online brought up the articles I remembered seeing last year when news of Premier Adrien Delacroix's death was sweeping the country.

Her parents were out driving when the rain turned dangerously torrential. They hydroplaned and hit a guardrail. Dead on arrival.

"Baby, that's not stupid," I say. "Shit, Delilah, I'm sorry."

"No, *I'm* sorry. I shouldn't have come." She shakes her

head, trying to pull away from me. "I know that's not what this is."

My brows furrow as I draw her in closer. She's still upset and idiotically, all I want to do is hold her. Comfort her. "What do you mean?"

"This relationship." She places a hand on my chest, trying to push back. I don't let her. "We don't worry about each other like that."

That blow lands like a swift uppercut to the jaw. Because it's not true. No matter how much I tried. No matter how much I wish I didn't, I can't help myself. "Shutterbug, I worry about you all the time."

Her eyes widen. "You do?"

"I do," I reply. My lips quirk up as I try to lighten the mood. "It's become something of a habit. Very inconvenient."

Because I shouldn't want you as much as I do.

She laughs, and the sound is music to my ears. "My bad," she says. She fiddles with the sleeve of the hoodie. "Now that I've properly made a fool of myself, I should go. You probably have a lot of work to do."

"Hold on." Turning back to my desk, I grab my phone and keys. "Where's Sophia right now?"

Delilah looks at me curiously. "She's at Haven House. Abbie begged your mom to let her come over this morning so they could jump in puddles together."

"And Parker?"

"In his room, playing video games. The rain— It doesn't affect him like it does me."

"C'mon." I tug on her hand, pulling her toward my office door.

She follows willingly. "Where are we going?"

"I'm taking you home."

When Jodi spots me with my hand on the small of Delilah's back, she smiles and nods approvingly. I roll my eyes. These days, she never shuts up about Delilah and what a positive influence she's had on me. I can't deny that meeting her has changed my life for the better, but Jodi is living in fairytale land. What Delilah and I are doing is purely casual, and that's how it's going to stay. I care about her. Of course I do. But it can't be more than that. It *isn't* more than that.

The rain has abated some, but Delilah and I still cross the parking lot toward my truck through an onslaught. I tug open the passenger door and shut her inside, and then I round the hood. My shirt is entirely soaked, and the once-dry hoodie that Delilah wears is now damp.

As I pull out onto the road, I remember something. "That picture you sent me," I say. "You took that this morning?"

"Oh." When I glance to the passenger seat, her focus is out the window. She avoids looking at me. "Yeah. It's been a few months since I picked up my camera, so I know it's not that great, but I got out before the storm started. The beach was empty. I was the only one watching the sunrise."

The picture was taken at Anchor's Bay Beach, the one that sits below Dockside, right near the harbour. The water was still, and in the sky, the sun was beginning to rise. The lake looked so clear, like you could almost see to the bottom.

The sky was a canvas of orange and yellow. In short, it was beautiful.

"You have talent, Shutterbug. I wish you wouldn't hide it from the world."

Finally, she turns away from the window and looks at me. "Really?" Her voice is shy, completely unlike the Delilah I know. "You think so?"

"Yes," I reply with a chuckle. "And so does that judging panel for the contest. You knocked it out of the park."

From my peripheral, I can see her chewing on her bottom lip as she agonizes over something in her head. "I don't know if I'm ready for a whole exhibition," she admits. "Maybe I should tell Carole to let the second place winner have my spot."

"You're ready. That, I have no doubts about."

She still doesn't look like she quite believes me, but she smiles anyway. "Thank you."

She spends the rest of the drive in quiet thought. I let her have the time, turning the radio up. It fills the cab with old country music. And then I take her home.

CHAPTER TWENTY-SIX
DELILAH

TURNS OUT, when Luke said he was taking me home, he meant *his* home. He lives on the outskirts of town, surrounded by trees. I watched them go by through the window as I tried to figure out where we were going. As soon as we pulled up to the house, I knew it belonged to him.

By the time we make it inside, we're both soaked through from the rain. I feel chilled down to my bones and shivers rack my body to prove it.

Luke guides me to his en suite bathroom and orders me into the shower. When the door shuts behind him, I strip out of my clothes and step under the hot stream. It steadily washes away the chill. After relishing the warmth for a few minutes, I find some shampoo and body wash on the built-in shelf. As the shampoo slides out onto my palm, I take in the familiar scent. It smells exactly like Luke.

When I get out of the shower, I find a t-shirt and a pair of sweatpants laid out on Luke's bed, waiting for me. I slip the shirt over my head, his clean laundry scent washing over me.

The hem of the shirt hits low enough that I decide not to bother with the sweats.

I leave his bedroom behind and pad down the hallway in search of the man himself. I find him in the kitchen, setting two mugs out on the counter. I'm not sure what he's intending to make, but I don't plan to let him finish.

"You have a really nice house," I say as I lean against the doorframe. "I've grown pretty attached to the pink house, but yours is a close runner-up."

He turns at the sound of my voice. And then he drinks in the sight of my body, from the tips of my toes to the top of my head. He lingers on my exposed legs.

"You're not wearing pants."

"I am not wearing pants," I confirm. "Want to find out what else I'm not wearing?"

His Adam's apple bobs as he visibly swallows. "I didn't bring you here for that."

Why, then? This is what we do, me and him. I want to ask, but I am admittedly a little scared of what he might say, so I bite my tongue. Instead of voicing my thoughts, I cross the room to him.

"I can put pants on, if you really want me to."

His finger brushes the hem of the shirt, running along where it meets the skin of my leg. His jaw works as he decides what to do, but I can tell that his control is slipping. *Yes*, I think. *Let go*.

I only have to wait another second before Luke's hands are on the backs of my thighs, and then I'm lifted into his arms. My legs instinctively wrap themselves around his waist as his palms settle on my ass, holding me up. My fingers tangle in his hair, still damp from his shower in the guest bathroom.

I tilt his face up to mine. The stubble on his cheeks scrapes against my skin and I shiver just imagining what that would feel like on the insides of my thighs. I want to find out for real.

"You are so pretty," I murmur.

He chuckles. "That's my line."

I tug on a strand of his hair. "Guys can be pretty, too."

"Fine," he says. "Then you are a goddamn vision, Delilah."

I lean back. "Even with post-shower, messy hair?"

His eyes shine as he grins. And for a brief moment, I don't breathe. He really is pretty, but that isn't what stands out the most. He spends a lot of time wearing a frown or a neutral expression. Seeing him let go enough to smile is worth whatever I have to do to earn it.

"Especially then."

Feelings I don't want to even begin to name—feelings I'm forbidden from naming—bubble up to the surface. Before I say something I'll regret, I lean back in. My mouth descends on his, and then my tongue traces his lower lip. He obliges, giving me exactly what I want.

Luke moves toward the kitchen island. I draw back, lungs starved for air, and shake my head. "Take me to bed." At his raised brow, I add, "*Please.*"

"Look at you, being such a good girl and asking nicely."

I expect him to set me on my feet, but Luke carries me back down the hallway and into his room. He places me on the mattress and then he stands back, simply taking me in. I squirm under the scrutiny.

"What?" I ask. "What are you looking at?"

He shakes his head. "You. I knew you would look fucking exquisite in my bed, but *fuck*, Delilah, you're better than I could have imagined."

Better than I could have imagined.

Well, shit. If I wasn't already in the mood, I certainly would be now. It's a shame Luke has sworn off relationships because he'd be damn good at one. Even though our arrangement is casual, he has always made me feel comfortable, and he knows the right things to say. He is everything I would want in a person.

But he doesn't want you like that.

I ignore the ache in my chest at that thought. I don't want him either. I just want the *idea* of him; everything he represents. After spending so long with Mitchell, finally being around someone at least halfway decent would feel like I've won the lottery. Luke is on a whole other level.

Ugh, get out of your head. Stop thinking.

Luke touches my ankle. "Delilah," he says, "we don't have to do this."

He mistook my silence for being unsure. But I'm not unsure. In this, I am absolutely certain. I trust Luke implicitly. It's hard to pinpoint exactly when that shift happened—when he went from being a stranger to being someone I need in my life.

"I want to."

"Stay with me, then, yeah?"

I shake off those pesky thoughts trying to ruin this for me and nod. "I'm with you."

His fingers brush against my ankle again, and then they curl around it. With a quick tug, Luke pulls me down the mattress until my ass hangs off the edge. My shirt—his shirt—has ridden up my torso, exposing my underwear. They're plain and not the least bit sexy, given I hadn't anticipated being sprawled across Luke's king-size bed when I got dressed this morning, but the starved look in his eyes indicates that he doesn't mind.

"I've been driving myself crazy, thinking about what you must taste like, pretty girl," he says. "I think I need to find out if I'm right. You gonna let me do that?"

My heart pulses as his words settle around us. *Yes, yes, yes,* my body chants. I offer him another nod, my tongue momentarily frozen by his admission.

"Words, Delilah. I need your words."

"*Yes.*"

I prop myself up on my elbows, watching in rapt fascination as Luke descends to his knees at the foot of the bed. There's something about a man kneeling before me—this man, specifically—that has me aching in sweet anticipation.

Though I can't help the smirk that tugs at my lips. "You look good on your knees, Chief."

His eyes seem to twinkle in this light. "Only for you, pretty girl."

My underwear is quick to disappear, and then Luke settles my legs over his shoulders. He presses a kiss to the inside of my knee that is so gentle, it turns my insides to mush. But as soon as his molten gaze settles on the apex of my thighs, any tenderness is gone and is replaced with pure need. My hands twist the sheets as I wait for him to do something. Anything.

God, I—

"Oh, *fuck*."

Luke presses a second kiss to my clit. It's a split second of relief, followed by an even more intense yearning for more. I tug on his hair, trying to guide his mouth exactly where I want it. He laughs, and the vibrations make me squirm.

"Patience, pretty girl," he says. "I want to take my time with you."

On premise alone, that sounds heavenly. Right now, though? Now it's nothing but torture.

Another kiss, this time to the inner part of my left thigh. He repeats the gesture on the right. I writhe, trying to move my body in the path of his mouth. I gasp when I feel his hand settle on my lower stomach, pressing down and holding me in place against the mattress.

"Luke!"

"Yes?"

"*Please.*"

Finally, he puts me out of my misery. His tongue caresses me, sliding along my slit. My back arches as my hands grapple for purchase. One twists into the bedsheets and the other finds a home at the back of Luke's head.

I can count on one hand the amount of times a guy has gone down on me. The first was a guy I hooked up with before I started dating Mitchell. He meant well, but he wasn't exactly experienced and I didn't know how to tell him what I needed. Mitchell, on the other hand, would gladly receive all the blowjobs in the world. When it came to my turn, he would think of an excuse as to why he couldn't.

But *Luke*... He knows what he's doing, and he seems to be enjoying himself, too.

I can feel my climax building, but something is missing. "I-I need..."

"What do you need, Delilah?"

"*More*."

I gasp when Luke's finger slips inside me. He pumps in and out, and then he curls it, hitting the perfect spot inside. When his mouth returns to my clit and teases it, I know I'm close.

And then I'm tipping over the edge. Luke still has me pinned down and I writhe under his hold, letting the orgasm rush through me. There are no neighbours here to be quiet for, so I don't stop the moan that travels up my vocal chords.

When the last of my orgasm peters out, Luke unhooks my shaking thighs from around his ears. Then he swipes his thumb across his bottom lip. That image alone is lewd enough, but when he licks his lips, I think I almost die.

"What's the verdict?" I manage to ask. "Were you right?"

He shakes his head. "I have a habit of underestimating you," he says. "Every time I think I have you figured out, you surprise me."

"Is that a good thing?"

Luke doesn't seem like the type to enjoy surprises. He's the kind of guy that goes for the predictable.

But in this, he surprises me. "Yeah, Delilah. That's a good thing."

His hand trails along my thigh and then slips beneath my

shirt. His touch skates across my stomach and up my rib cage. Then he palms my breast, squeezing with just the right amount of pressure to earn himself another moan.

"Take the shirt off, Delilah. I want to see you."

Despite the number of times we've gotten each other off, this is the first time I will be fully naked in front of Luke. With the muted light filling the room, there is no hiding here. I sit up and pull the oversized fabric over my head, and then I toss it to the floor in the direction my underwear landed.

"Beautiful," he rasps. "You're beautiful."

He settles over me, his hips rocking gently against mine. He's still wearing his sweatpants, and I find that is entirely too much fabric between us. I want to feel him. All of him.

"Enough teasing," I demand. "And *fuck me*, Luke." His weight disappears as he gets off the bed. The drawer of his nightstand opens and shuts, and then a condom is tossed on the surface. "Now take the pants off, Luke. I want to see you."

He does so with a grin. Once his sweats and boxers join the pile of clothes on the floor, I can see every inch of his body. My thighs clamp shut as I desperately try to relieve the ache building there. The anticipation damn near does me in.

He *tsks*. "Spread your legs for me, pretty girl."

I melt into the bed and my thighs fall open. Luke's gaze settles on my pussy as he wraps a hand around his cock, fisting it. He pumps it a couple times, his eyes never leaving me. Then I watch as he rolls the condom on.

"So goddamn beautiful, laid out just for me," he muses

as he approaches. "How does my pretty girl want to be fucked? Soft and slow? Or hard and fast?"

I can feel my cheeks heating. "Hard."

When Luke settles his weight over me, I tangle my fingers in the hair at the nape of his neck, tugging slightly at the strands. He leans down, capturing my lips with his. At the same time, I feel his cock nudging against my entrance. My teeth clamp down on Luke's lower lip and his hips jut forward, his length entering me part of the way. We both groan.

"That feels so…" I murmur.

"*Fuck*, Delilah."

"Yes, please do."

He shakes his head. "You and that goddamn smart mouth."

Luke slams the rest of the way inside. My eyes flutter shut at the sensation. Luke gives me a moment to adjust to him, and then he starts to move. He draws back, pulling most of the way out, before he thrusts into me again. My head presses into the pillow as my back arches. When Luke thrusts, he hits a spot I didn't even know I had.

He grabs me by the back of one knee and tugs it over his hip, opening me wider. My hands drift from his hair to his back. My nails dig into the strong muscles of his shoulders. Luke's hand snakes between us, and then his thumb is circling my clit. My mouth falls open as the pleasure mounts.

"Luke, *yes*."

His thrusts continue. The snap of his hips mixed with the pressure on that sensitive bundle are enough to get me there. I tip over the edge, hurtling toward oblivion.

"That's it, pretty girl. Come for me."

My pussy tightens around his cock. His thrusts intensify as I ride out my orgasm. Then he explodes. My chest heaves as I grapple for air. I can't even form words, my mind is so fried. I knew he would be good, but *damn*.

Luke slowly pulls out, and then he heads to the bathroom to dispose of the condom. I swipe the shirt I was wearing off the floor and slip it back over my head, and then I trade places with Luke. When I come out of the bathroom, Luke is sitting on the bed in his boxers.

"When do you have to leave?" he asks.

I glance at the clock on his nightstand. "I have a couple hours."

He holds out a hand. "C'mere. Stay with me for a bit?"

I should say no. I should put my clothes back on—*my* clothes, not the borrowed ones of his—and ask him to drive me home. I should, but I don't. Instead I take his hand and let him pull me into bed with him. And I definitely don't fall asleep tucked against his side.

Definitely not.

CHAPTER TWENTY-SEVEN
LUKE

"WE'RE RESPONDING *to a call at 148 Pine Street. Structure fire. Possible residents trapped inside.*"

In a place the size of Kip Island, save for the tourists, you know pretty much everyone. There is a good chance that any given call will hit a little too close to home for comfort. But hearing those words out of my captain's mouth, I know that no call I have taken before could have prepared me for this.

My house is on fire, and my fiancée and niece might be inside.

"Shit," Jodi curses. "That's Luke's house."

The panic threatens to rush in, but I tamp it down. Gabe, however, is unable to do the same. The pure fear in his eyes when he turns to me is almost enough to wash away the numbness I've managed to erect. Seeing that look on my brother's face kills me.

"Abbie," he says.

That's all he has to say. I understand. The whole crew understands. Abbie has been a staple at the station since birth.

Everyone starts moving faster, donning our gear and loading into the fire engine. My hands shake as I struggle to latch my seatbelt.

The drive across town feels short and long all at once. The sound of the siren above us is drowned out by the pounding of my heart. A million thoughts race through my mind. How did this happen? Did they make it out? Are they hurt?

The second we pull to a stop, I'm out of the vehicle. My head whips from left to right as I assess the scene. A group of people have spilled out onto the grass from the front of the house. All of them are strangers. I don't have the time or the wherewithal to question why they're here. When I finally spot Kristina, I don't hesitate. I race across the yard and pull her into my arms.

"Oh, thank God," I mutter, running a hand over her hair. The short blonde strands slip through my fingers. "You're okay."

After a moment much too short, I pull back to inspect her. She seems unharmed, though I find myself supporting most of her weight. What the hell? When I loosen my grip, she starts to sway.

"Kristina," I say. Her eyes are hazy. It seems as if she's looking straight through me. "Where's Abbie?"

She doesn't answer, and I can feel Gabe's panic as if it was my own. Abbie has to be out here. Because if she's not...

"Please," my brother pleads, his voice cracking. "Where is she?"

Still, Kristina doesn't answer. It's like she doesn't even know we're here. Is she drunk? High? She was supposed to be watching Abbie tonight. I trusted her with that.

I grasp her shoulders, fighting the urge to shake her. "Where is she, Kristina?"

My fiancée finally blinks up at me, seeing me for the first time since I got here. "Oh, Luke," she says, a loopy smile stretching her lips. "You made it!"

Frustration and anger grip me by the throat. All the chaos in the world couldn't compare to the tumult swirling inside me.

"Kristina. Where the fuck *is my niece?"*

When I wake, my heart is racing. I haven't had that particular dream in a long time. Or rather, that memory. It comes to me in bits and pieces every so often, but almost never as clearly as this. Tonight, the whole ordeal played out in my head like a movie, each minute detail accounted for. The endless drive from the station, Kristina's zoned out state, the panic when I didn't know where Abbie was.

The late afternoon sun, now done hiding behind storm clouds, filters into my bedroom through the open curtains. I sit up, bracing my forearms on bent knees as I try to catch my breath. My pulse thunders in my ears. I hadn't intended to fall asleep. These nightmares are unpredictable, and I never wanted to subject Delilah to that.

Delilah.

I feel her hand as it hesitantly rests on my shoulder. I expect it to make me feel itchy—being touched after these nightmares always feels a little like sand beneath my flesh—but her cool skin is a soothing balm to the burning of mine.

"Are you alright?"

My ability to form words escapes me. *Am I alright?* The right answer is no, probably not. The safe answer is yes. I settle for something in the middle.

"Fine," I say with a jerky nod. "Just a nightmare."

Silence stretches between us then. If I didn't know any better, I would assume Delilah had fallen back asleep. But the sheets ruffle as she sits up against the headboard, crossing her legs. I figured she would be out the door by now. After all, she didn't sign up for this.

"Was she your ex?" she asks. "Kristina?"

My lips roll inwards as I nod. I can't bring myself to look at her, so I stare at the calluses on my palms instead. Above all else, I feel ashamed. I hate that I have these nightmares, but I hate even more that Delilah has witnessed me like this. I feel like I've lost all sense of control and I don't know how to get it back. Maybe I can't.

"Do you want to talk about it?"

My gut instinct is to say no. Whenever Gabe or Clara or my parents ask me that, I immediately shut them down. They don't need to hear me feeling sorry for myself. Not when they almost lost someone they love because of me. Because I had the stupid sense to fall into bed with an irresponsible woman and think that things would be different. That I would be enough for her.

But some part of me wants Delilah to know. Maybe because I want her to truly understand why we can never be anything more than this. If, after I tell her, she wants to walk away, I'll understand.

"Two years ago," I say. "I wasn't chief yet, but I wanted to be. It was well-known that the chief at the time would be retiring in a matter of months and I was eager to prove myself. That night, Gabe was on shift. Mom and Dad were out of town. Clara was busy manning Dockside and Haven

House. I was off, so I told Gabe that I would take Abbie." My hands clench into fists. "But then a call for overtime came in."

I pinch my eyes shut, trying to escape the memory. If I can just outrun it, I won't have to see the flames dance as I run into the house, not knowing what I'll find.

"Kristina never really took to Abbie. Looking back, that should have been reason enough to end things. When I got the call, I begged her to watch Abbie while I went in to work. We were *engaged*. I thought—" My voice trips. "I thought she could be trusted."

I thought, I thought, I thought. But I didn't *know*. The months after were spent going over every moment, from the day we met to the day it all came crashing down. I spent many nights agonizing over what I could have done differently.

"What happened?" Delilah's voice is nothing but a whisper.

The laugh that leaves me is raw. "She held a fucking party. Kristina could befriend anyone, and that week, she met a bunch of college kids up from the States. They were renting a cottage on the lake and they invited her to hang out. Thank God she told them she couldn't come over, but she had no trouble inviting them to our house."

Delilah waits patiently as I collect my thoughts. She doesn't rush me. Really, she doesn't ask anything of me. I always felt like I was trying to keep up with Kristina. Like I was never quite good enough for her. There was one thing or another she kept wanting me to change. But never Delilah.

"They got wasted and high while Abbie was asleep

upstairs. Everything was fine until someone lit a candle that inevitably got tipped over. When they started to smell the smoke, they freaked out and ran outside. And they—" My voice falters. "They left Abbie inside alone."

Delilah doesn't gasp or make any sound that would indicate she heard me. But I watch her hand settle over my palm, her fingers fitting into the spaces between mine. Her grip is steady, serving as a grounding point when it feels like the memories might drag me straight into the undertow.

"I found her hiding under a bed," I spit out. "She was so scared."

When I look at her, Delilah's eyes are full of tears. "I'm so glad she was okay."

And I have to believe that she truly means it. Because if she doesn't, then that just proves how much of a fool I am—letting myself become attached in all the wrong ways, not once, but twice. I have to look away.

"I broke up with Kristina a week later. I—" I shake my head. "I couldn't look at her without being reminded of all my mistakes. Being reminded that it was my fault."

"Luke, it wasn't—"

"*It was.*"

My tone brooks no argument. Delilah clamps her mouth shut. I know she doesn't agree with me, but I can't hear her say it. My family has tried, over and over. Their words don't erase what happened. Nothing can. Nothing can take back the emotional trauma that Abbie went through that night because I had to be the fucking hero. Helping is as innate as breathing to me. But that impulse almost cost me everything.

We sit in silence for a few long moments. I can feel her

watching me. Waiting to see if I'll say more. But I've already wrung myself dry.

Eventually, Delilah releases a small sigh. "I should get going," she says quietly. She gives my hand a squeeze, and then she slowly pulls hers from mine. My jaw clenches. "Your mom is probably ready to hand Sophia off."

I try to shake the anger and the guilt, and I let out a chuckle. It comes out a little flat. "Mom would keep her forever if she could."

The smile she gives me is sad. Full of pity. *Fuck*, I hate that.

Delilah and I dress in silence. The clothes she was wearing earlier have dried some, so she slips them back on. I notice that she doesn't bother returning my hoodie, though. Instead, she tugs it over her head and lets the sleeves cover her hands. I have to hide my small grin.

The drive from my house to hers is silent, too. My memories have me in a chokehold, and I think she's trying to give me space. The problem, I have come to realize, is that I don't want space. Not from her. And that is the most dangerous feeling of all.

Something about Delilah makes me want to tell her everything. Lay it all bare. But the risk, if it all went south, is too great. I don't think I would survive a second time.

When I pull into her driveway behind her car, she shoves open the door and hops out before I can even think of doing it for her. She thanks me for the ride and then goes to shut the door. But she pauses, looks up at me, and says, "I hope you realize one day that you are deserving of love. The right kind of love. One without conditions." She smiles softly. "That's my wish for you, Luke."

Then she's gone. I wait to pull away until I see her unlock her front door and step inside. And then I wait a minute longer just in case.

In another life, I could see myself falling for Delilah. She is undoubtedly a beautiful woman, but that isn't the only reason why. She shines brighter than everyone else in the room. Every single thing I've come to know about her—her sense of humour, her passion, the way she loves her siblings—is another reason why. Another reason why I can't.

In another life, maybe I could freely admit that I was well and truly *fucked*.

CHAPTER TWENTY-EIGHT
LUKE

JULY HAS COME AND GONE, and with it went any remaining hope I had of keeping Delilah at arm's length. I would say that she's a friend, but she knows me more intimately than any other friend I've ever had. I also don't make a habit of fucking my friends. No, Delilah defies all descriptions. She's just...Delilah.

Lines are beginning to blur—if they were even clear-cut to begin with—and I'm not sure I can stop it.

When I enter the kitchen at Haven House for yet another Sunday brunch, I'm surprised to find Delilah at the counter with my parents. Somehow, she has managed to convince Mom to let her help with the food preparation. I place a hand on Delilah's hip and give it a squeeze in greeting, and then I kiss my mom on the cheek before heading for the table.

Parker is already there, his nose buried in his phone. When I sit down, he doesn't so much as spare me a glance.

He wears his distaste on his sleeve. He isn't outright rude, but you can tell that he would rather be anywhere else.

When Delilah takes her usual seat beside me, I'm struck with how different this feels than it did that very first Sunday. Back then, I wanted nothing to do with her. Simply because I knew we'd end up here, toeing the line between stable ground and the free fall.

I reach out and grab the corner of her chair, tugging her closer. "Morning, Shutterbug."

Today, her eyes are more blue than grey. Her irises are ever changing, and this soft hue reflects the happiness she wears on her face. "Morning, Chief," she replies, a smile in her voice.

I lean back, making a show of inspecting her. "Good day?" I ask.

She grins, though it's tinged with a bit of shyness. "Carole and I were just talking about the ideas I have for my exhibition next month. I wasn't sure about them, but she's totally on board. So I guess you could say it's been a good day."

As much as she tries, Delilah can't keep her emotions from displaying themselves in her expression. Beneath her nerves is a steady thrum of excitement, and fuck, if it isn't infectious. A feeling both foreign and familiar slithers through my veins, sending a bolt of fear running through me. It threatens to drown out the pride I feel for Delilah. It threatens to send me over the edge of a reckoning I'm not ready to have.

I smile through the feeling. "That sounds great, Shutterbug. I'm proud of you."

This seems to knock the breath right out of her. She inhales sharply, her eyes searching mine. "You are?"

"'Course I am. I know how apprehensive you are about the exhibition, but you're doing it anyway. I admire that."

I admire you.

Her eyes shine with an emotion I refuse to name. Naming it makes it real. Her lips part, ready to respond, but then her sister comes up beside her. Sophia whispers something in her ear, and Delilah's expression softens into one reserved solely for her siblings.

"Okay," she says, "go ahead."

Sophia rounds behind our chairs and then comes up on my other side, peering shyly up at me.

"Hey, Soph," I say. "What's up?"

Eventually, she brings her hand out from behind her back. A bracelet—one of the ones she was making with Abbie—is clasped in her hand. A few different colours of string are braided together and tied off at the end.

She holds the bracelet out to me. "I made you this."

"Thank you." I take it from her, turning it over in my palm. "What's it for?"

She looks down at her feet and mumbles, "A friendship bracelet."

Fuck, these Delacroix girls are certainly good at bringing me to my knees. The way she looks so unsure about herself damn near kills me. I want to erase all her insecurities. Her sister's, too.

I tip her chin up until she meets my gaze. My other hand, still holding the bracelet, rests over my heart. "I love it, Soph. Thank you."

She shows me her own wrist. "It matches me."

"Even better. Do you want to do the honours?" I hold my wrist out, and she eagerly fastens the string. It sits a little loose, but I smile encouragingly. "Perfect fit."

I watch her as she runs off giggling to herself. Then my eyes land on Delilah and I really wish they hadn't. The soft expression she wears is full of affection. Not the kind you have for the friend you happen to be fucking. I swallow.

Delilah gestures to my wrist. "Here, let me fix that."

The bracelet has already started to come undone, so I hold out my arm. I watch intently as Delilah leans closer, her fingers brushing against my skin. She tightens the bracelet until it fits snugly around my wrist and then she ties it in place. When she sits up, her gaze meets mine again, and I get lost in the depths.

Thankfully, my parents start to set the food on the table before I truly get swept away. I volunteer to grab the girls from the living room, and then I send Sophia and Abbie out ahead of me so I can have a second to myself. A second to get my shit together. Then I haul my ass back to the table and pretend like nothing is wrong. Like I'm not slowly losing a battle of my own making.

"So, Parker," Mom begins as she cuts into a waffle, "are you excited to start school in the fall?"

I'm not sure why that's every middle-aged adult's go-to question whenever a teenager enters a room. I used to get it all the time when I was Parker's age, and the answer is always *no*.

He shrugs. "Yeah, I guess."

"It'll be a lot smaller than your old school," Dad chimes

in. "I'm sure you won't have any trouble making friends though."

There is a moment of silence as Dad's words settle over the table. Parker shifts in his seat uncomfortably. "I don't need to make friends," he says. Then his expression hardens as he looks at Delilah. "I already *had* friends."

Before I can blink, he stands from his seat and storms out of the room. We all watch him go. Dad offers Delilah an apologetic smile, but she just shakes her head.

"I'm so sorry," she says. "Um, excuse us. I'm just gonna go…"

She goes to stand, but I place a hand on her arm. "Can I?"

At this point, I would do anything to take that defeated look off her face. Though she seems reluctant, she eventually nods and slowly lowers back into her chair. I waste no time following Parker out of the room. I find him outside, sitting on the front steps. Taking a seat beside him, I brace my forearms on my thighs.

Parker's jaw works as he watches me get settled. "I came out here to be alone."

"See, I don't buy that," I say. "I think you came out here, hoping someone would follow."

"And like the knight in shining armour you are, you had to come to her rescue," he says bitterly.

I shake my head. "I came out here for you, Parker. Not for her."

The kid is angry, that much is obvious. What I want to know is why. His relationship with his older sister has been strained for as long as I've known them. I know it hurts Delilah. I think it hurts Parker, too.

He scoffs. "Right."

Parker turns away from me, and I let silence settle in. He isn't going to believe me if I tell him that people here actually care what he has to say. So I wait. Eventually, the silence becomes too loud. He crosses his arms, refusing to look my way.

"All of this is her fault anyway," he mutters.

"Damn."

His head swings sharply in my direction. "What?" he snaps.

"I didn't know your sister had that much sway with the universe," I reply. "I'm going to need her to give me the winning jackpot numbers next."

To this, Parker rolls his eyes. "If you have a hard-on for my sister, just say it. You don't have to walk around, kissing her ass."

I choose to ignore his jab as I stand from my spot on the steps. "C'mon."

Warily, he stands, too. "Where are we going?"

"You'll see."

I descend the steps and then take a hard right, setting a path across my parents' lawn. Parker hurries to keep up. He wants to act disinterested, but he's still following me willingly. Progress. A little more of this and we'll be better off than when we started.

Parker quickens his pace to match my stride. "Trying to bond with me won't help you get in my sister's pants, you know," he says casually.

Looking over my shoulder at him, I arch a brow. "You seem awfully concerned with my being into your sister for someone who hates her."

His steps falter. "I don't hate her."

I shrug. "Could've fooled me."

He glares, stopping short. "I *don't* hate her."

I stop a few paces ahead. "Well, there's obviously something eating you up inside." He glances away, telling me everything I need to know. "You don't have to tell me, Parker, but I'm here if you want to."

We walk the rest of the way to the pond in silence. Growing up, some kids had pools—I had a pond. Clara, Gabe and I spent countless summer days swimming in the backyard. And when the weather turned, we used to skip rocks. Along one edge of the pond, on either side of the small wooden dock, Mom keeps a rock garden. She was always after us to stay out of it, but we couldn't help stealing some of the smooth, flat stones for skipping.

I take a couple stones from the pile, and then with a flick of my wrist, I send the first one sailing across the surface of the water. It skips twice before promptly sinking.

Parker sends me a skeptical look. "This is what you want to do right now?"

"This is what I want to do right now. Feel free to join me."

He picks up a rock, then hesitates. "And you aren't going to ask me a million stupid questions?" At my questioning look, he sighs. "Delilah made me see a shrink after Mom and Dad...you know. She asked me all these questions I didn't know the answers to and it made everything worse."

I hold up my hands in surrender. "No questions."

He studies me for a moment, trying to decide if he believes me. I pick up another stone and cast it over the water. After a minute, he follows suit. His first couple attempts skip once and then drop. By the third, he grows agitated. He lets the rock fly and it immediately begins to sink. A noise of frustration falls from his mouth.

"She always treats me like a fucking child. She didn't even ask me what I thought about moving or selling the house. She just went and did it."

He picks up another rock and throws it. It sails halfway across the pond before hitting the surface. I don't say anything, letting him have his moment. It seems like he needs it.

"She walks on eggshells, trying not to talk about them. We don't *talk about them*." His voice breaks with emotion. "I miss them."

The last part is little more than a whisper, but I hear him loud and clear. "She misses them, too," I say, because I'm sure of it. Because I see the grief that clouds her expression when she thinks no one is looking.

He lets out a humourless chuckle. "She has a funny way of showing it," he says. "Some people said our dad crashed on purpose, you know. They speculated and made jokes that it was suicide."

This stops me in my tracks. *What the hell?* As far as I know, it was an accident. Their car hydroplaned and that was it. The articles didn't say anything about foul play or suspicious circumstances.

"Why would they say that?"

"Because of her."

What is that supposed to mean? I want to ask, but I don't get the chance. Parker drops the stone, stuffs his hands into the pockets of his hoodie and then charges back toward the house. Instead of going inside, he heads toward Delilah's car and gets in the passenger seat.

I scrub a hand down my face. *Fuck.* I hope I didn't just make everything worse for Delilah. But I have a feeling that's exactly what I did. When I make it back, Parker is still sitting in the car. Delilah steps out of the house and meets me on the porch.

"What happened?" she asks. "Parker texted me and said he needs to go home."

"I'm sorry." I run a hand through my hair, frustrated with myself. Sometimes I truly can't leave well enough alone. "I thought I was helping, giving him a place to vent. Things were going okay, and then he shut down."

She shakes her head. "I appreciate the concern, but it's not your job, Luke. He's my responsibility."

"I know. But it's not fair that you have to do it alone."

Her smile is sad. "He should get to grow up with his parents. That's what isn't fair."

She leaves me on the porch as she jogs down the steps and gets in the car. Parker doesn't look at her; he just stares out the passenger window. And as I watch them leave, I'm reminded once again how much of an idiot I've been.

CHAPTER TWENTY-NINE
DELILAH

SATURDAYS AT DOCKSIDE only seem to get busier as the summer progresses.

Earlier today, my section was full and the restaurant itself had a waitlist a mile long. Now the lunchtime rush has petered out, leaving just a few patrons enjoying a late afternoon meal. I stuff my most recent tip into my pocket as I take advantage of the lull and pour myself a glass of water. When it touches my lips, I realize just how dehydrated I am. I don't usually mind the busy shifts, but not being able to stop for hours on end takes its toll.

When the bell above the door sounds, I set my glass aside with a sigh. *Showtime.*

"Hey, Chief Bowman!" someone across the room calls.

Luke waves to the overly friendly townie as he makes his way toward me.

"Hey," I say. "Fancy seeing you here."

I'm still not used to Luke's smile. He doesn't give it to

everyone—and he certainly didn't give it to me in the beginning—but that just makes it all the more special. It softens his otherwise serious exterior and makes my insides feel like the middle of a warm cookie right out of the oven.

"Hey, Shutterbug," he says.

"Do you want your usual?" I hook a thumb over my shoulder. "I can put the order in."

He shakes his head. "Just here to see Clara about something. She in her office?"

I laugh. "It's schedule day. She's been holed up since six." I grab the sandwich that just came out of the kitchen. "I was just about to bring this to her, but now you can have the honours."

He takes the plate from my hands and then brushes a kiss to my cheek on his way past. I can still feel exactly where his lips touched even though he is long gone. I resist the urge to put my hand there.

The bell above the door jingles again and this time, instead of a handsome fire chief, a group of four guys come in. They all could be stand-ins for Ken dolls with their nearly identical short-sleeve button-ups and chino shorts. They have varying shades of blonde hair and overly cocky smirks. I roll my eyes heavenward when I see the way they jostle one another, clearly intoxicated, as the host leads them to a table. In my section, of course.

I preemptively grab four glasses of water and carry them over to the table with me. "Hi, guys," I say in my perky customer service voice. "I'm Delilah. I'll be taking care of you today."

Ken One does an exaggerated perusal of my body. "I know how you can take care of me, sweetheart."

Ken Two nudges Ken One with his elbow. They share a look and then dissolve into laughter. I grit my teeth, sure that my smile is hanging on by a thread.

"I brought you all some water. I'll give you a minute to look over the menu, unless you'd like to order something else to drink."

"Beer!" Ken Three shouts. "A Canadian."

"How about we stick to the nonalcoholic side of things for now?" Each of them has more than a buzz going. I'm not going to be responsible for their alcohol poisoning. "I'll be back to take your food orders."

"Man, the service here fucking sucks," one of them complains to my back.

I refill another table's water and help bus another table that just cleared out. Then I make my way back over and manage to get orders for appetizers out of the rowdy group.

Just as I move to step away, a familiar hand settles on my hip, giving it a squeeze. Suddenly, the group of guys in front of me looks *very* interested in their drinks, and their obnoxious chatter has completely died out.

"Can I help you?" I ask, sparing him a glance over my shoulder. "Or are you just here to glower at my customers?"

"I don't glower," Luke insists. "And they were being little assholes."

I head for the bar. His hand falls from my side, but he trails after me like a stupidly handsome shadow. "I won't argue with that, but I can handle myself."

He crosses his arms. "I know you can. Doesn't mean I have to like it."

I grin. "Jealous, Chief?" I tease. "Scared one of them might charm me into ditching you tonight?"

This is fun, poking at things that annoy Luke. I have no intention of spending any amount of time with the quartet of barely-legal business-major bros, let alone one-on-one, but the spark of irritation in Luke's brown eyes is worth a little bit of deception.

I can feel the heat of his body as his chest presses against my back. He places both hands on the edge of the bar, caging me in. I glance left and right, making sure that no one is watching us. Satisfied, I relax back into him. When he leans forward and his lips brush the shell of my ear, I shiver.

"Oh, I'm not jealous, Shutterbug. Only one of us has had his hand up your skirt while your perfect ass was planted on this very bar and it wasn't any of them." And then, just to show that he can, he nudges my feet further apart with his boot. "And only one of us has been inside that perfect pussy. So, no, pretty girl. I'm not jealous. I have no reason to be."

My knees feel a little weak. If most of my weight wasn't being supported by Luke right now, I am fairly confident I would be a puddle on the floor. I thought I had the upper hand, but he bested me at my own game.

"Alright," I concede, "you're not jealous."

I can feel the curve of his smirk where his lips now rest against the skin behind my ear. I tip my head to the side, giving him better access. He peppers kisses there.

"I should get back to work," I say. My voice comes out a little breathless.

"You should."

I don't move and neither does he. I want to ask what game this is we're playing, but I'm enjoying myself too much to risk it ending. One wrong move could have this whole thing blowing up in my face.

When I tilt my head again, my eyes catch on a multi-coloured string, twisted under the watch band on his left wrist. Without thinking, I grab his arm and pull it closer to my face, as if that will change what I'm seeing. I thought it looked familiar before, but up close I know without a doubt that the braided strings in alternating hues of pink, blue and green are courtesy of my sister.

I drop his arm and spin around, my back pressing into the counter. Instead of his one hand returning to the bar, he places it on the curve of my waist. His thumb fiddles with the tied string of my apron as he looks at me, waiting for an explanation.

This feels so natural, being in his arms like this. I wish we were alone instead of in a restaurant full of people. I... *I wish things were different.*

"You're still wearing Sophia's friendship bracelet," I say softly. I hold my own wrist, adorned with beaded and string bracelets alike, up for emphasis.

Luke gives me a confused look. "Yeah... Was I not supposed to?"

"Yes." He quirks a brow. "No. No, I mean— It's fine. It's *great*. I'm just...pleasantly surprised."

More like so blown away, I struggle to find words. Mitchell would never be caught dead wearing a bracelet made for him by my sister, and he was my actual boyfriend.

Luke has no reservations about rocking that bracelet. And that means...*everything*. It's a simple gesture, but it's one I would have never expected from my— What the hell do you call the guy who's not your boyfriend, but you can't stop thinking about?

Dangerous, my brain supplies.

Dangerous because my heart is recklessly beating to a new tune. Dangerous because I shouldn't be enjoying our close proximity like this. Dangerous because I can't have him —not forever. I'm not sure when I started even entertaining the thought of forever, but having these ideas ping-ponging around in my head is not what I need right now.

The sound of glass shattering brings me back to life. *Real* life. A life where Luke is only touching me to get those guys to back off.

"I have to go back over there eventually." I glance toward the group to find an appetizer plate on the floor beside their table, splintered from the fall. "Preferably before someone needs a first aid kit."

He reluctantly lets me go so I can retrieve a broom. As I sweep up the mess, I can feel his eyes on my back. When I glance over, Luke is leaning against the bar, his arms crossed over his chest. I roll my eyes, and he grins. And it's pretty. Stupidly pretty. It transforms his face and makes me want to be the reason he smiles every single day.

"We're having an open house at the station on Sunday afternoon. Showing kids around the equipment and talking about what we do," he says when I return to his side. "You should bring Sophia."

I know I shouldn't read into it, but this is the first time

he has invited me to something. Well, me *and* Sophia, but still.

I nod. "Sounds like fun. I work in the morning, but we can stop by when I get off."

My phone begins to vibrate in my back pocket, signalling a call. I pull it out, thinking it might be Sophia's sitter. Wishful thinking, I guess. Mitchell's name flashes across the screen, and I wonder for the millionth time why I haven't blocked his number yet.

"Your ex is still harassing you?" I don't realize Luke is looking over my shoulder until I glance up to see his raised brow.

I nibble on my lower lip, impatiently waiting for the call to go to voicemail. "He doesn't text me that much now," I say with forced levity.

"Phone," Luke says, holding his hand out.

"What?"

"Let me see your phone. If he doesn't take the hint from you, maybe he'll take it from your boyfriend."

Hold on.

Time stops and I freeze. *Am I having a heart attack right now?* It's highly possible. My grip on my phone loosens, and he plucks it out of my hand, answering it. My jaw is firmly on the floor as I watch Luke listen to whatever shit Mitchell is spewing on the other line.

"Delilah is no longer your concern," he says. "She's moved on, and I suggest you do the same."

She's moved on. I certainly have, and I'm beginning to realize I've reached the point of no return. I am firmly going down with this ship.

Luke's jaw tightens as Mitchell says something. I want to tell him not to bother—to hang up the phone and forget about it all. My ex is relentless and doesn't take kindly to suggestions.

"I'm only going to say this once," he then says, his voice low. "You better lose this fucking number. Stop texting and calling my girl. She's with me now, and you need to accept that."

His *what*? My eyes remain saucers as Luke hangs up the phone. He fiddles around on the screen and then tries to hand it back to me. I don't take it. My whole body feels like Jell-O.

When he realizes that I'm a little stupefied, he takes it upon himself to slide my phone into my back pocket. "I blocked his number. Let's hope he's not desperate enough to get another one."

"What, um—" I swallow, my mouth suddenly dry. "What just happened?"

And why did I like it so much? I haven't ever been anyone's girl, but it hits me now—I like the thought of being his. I think I want to be his.

"A little lie to get him off your back."

I can't help the disappointment that slams into me. *Of course*. My foolish heart ran away with my brain. He didn't mean it. Empty words meant to throw Mitchell off. Just a *little lie*. But I was unprepared. I didn't think it would hurt this much.

I swallow, trying to rid myself of the emotion beginning to bubble up. "Well, thanks for trying."

He frowns. "Is something wrong?"

I shake my head. "No, it's— I'm fine. I have to get back to work."

Slowly, he nods. "Alright. I'll see you later?"

"Yeah," I say with a placating smile.

But as he reaches for me, I slip away.

CHAPTER THIRTY

LUKE

"WHERE DO YOU WANT THIS, CHIEF?" Connor asks, holding up a poster reminding people to change their smoke detector batteries.

Along with all the goddamned paperwork, a good portion of my job consists of overseeing the department's public education programs. When one of the summer camps on the island reached out to book a station tour, we decided that an open house would be more beneficial. Now anyone in the community can stop in and learn more about what we do besides put out fires. About half our volunteers are on deck today to assist with the activities. Hopefully, there won't be any call outs while all the kids are here.

"Over there is fine," I reply, pointing across the room.

Jodi sidles up beside me, nudging my shoulder. "Lookin' good, Chief."

I arch a brow. "Me or the station?"

She rolls her eyes and I chuckle. "Is Mayor Otis coming today?" she asks, ignoring my question.

I nod. "Unfortunately. I'm sure I'll be getting an earful about one thing or another."

She shakes her head. "Honestly, that woman can kiss my—"

"Luke," Gabe calls, cutting her off. "Have you seen Forrester and Greenaway? They said they were coming to help me, but that was a long fucking time ago."

I sigh. "I'll go find them."

Kevin Forrester and Mike Greenaway are two of our newest volunteer recruits, both still in their probationary period. So far, I'm not sure how I feel about them. On paper, they're the perfect candidates and look like great additions to the crew. But there's something about them—something I can't exactly put my finger on—that throws me off.

After searching damn near the entire building, I finally find them in the kitchen, sitting at the table. They have their heads bent over a phone, totally oblivious to my presence. I'm already a little pissed that they're shrugging off their duties when they are supposed to be downstairs helping, but what happens next just adds to my anger.

"*Damn*," Greenaway says. Forrester whistles.

As I walk up behind them, ready to hand them their asses, I catch a flash of dark hair on the phone's screen. I stop in my tracks. Something about it seems familiar. I inch closer, taking in the familiar sight. Forrester must sense me behind him because he tries to tuck his phone away, but I snatch it from his hand.

Shock holds me captive. A picture of Delilah stares back at me. It's not simply a picture of her that has me seeing red —it's the fact that in it, she's completely topless. She looks nervous, like she isn't sure about taking the picture. The floral tattoo on her shoulder is missing, which means that the picture has to be from sometime before she moved here. But it's her.

"Hey! That's my phone!" Forrester turns in his chair, glaring at me. Wrong fucking move.

I haul him out of his seat by the collar of his shirt and shove him against the nearest wall. I don't tend to lose my temper this way, but like hell am I going to let Delilah be disrespected in my house.

"Chief, what the hell?" Greenaway shouts.

I ignore him. "Why do you have a picture of my—" I cut myself off. She isn't *mine*, in any sense of the word, and that's no one's fault but my own. "Where the fuck did you get this?" I demand instead, shoving the phone in Forrester's face.

"It's all over the internet," he says with a shrug. He is much too nonchalant for someone who is seconds away from being punched in the face. "She seemed familiar when she first moved here. Couldn't remember where I'd seen her. When I Googled her name, it all popped up. There's articles about the leak."

The prospect of these pictures being accessible with a single search has dread pooling in my gut.

"Delete it."

"Man, I—"

"If you know what's good for you, you'll do as you're told. And then I never want to see this shit in my house again. That picture clearly wasn't meant for you, so keep your goddamn eyes to yourself."

"*Yes, sir*," he mocks.

"What was that? I couldn't hear you."

His eyes harden. "Yes, sir."

I release him and hand his phone back. I cross my arms, waiting as he removes the picture from his camera roll. "Now get out of my sight," I command.

Forrester adjusts the collar of his shirt, and then he and Greenaway slink out of the kitchen. When I'm sure they're gone, I release a frustrated breath as I run a hand through my hair. I feel like punching something. It isn't like I have any kind of claim over Delilah, so why am I this angry? The way that I'm feeling goes beyond a general distaste for Forrester and Greenaway's actions.

One thing I know for sure is that I need to talk to Delilah.

I watch the clock while the open house carries on around me. I go through the motions of answering questions and being the dutiful fire chief I'm expected to be, but all the while, I'm waiting for that beautiful brunette to walk through the door. When Gabe notices how antsy I am, all he does is shake his head in quiet pity. I'm not the one he should be pitying. I haven't been in love with my sister's childhood best friend for the better part of my life.

When Delilah finally walks into the station with Sophia and my sister, I head right for them. After seeing that picture, all I could think about was talking to her. To reassure myself that she's okay.

"Hey," Delilah says. The smile on her face falls when she takes note of my expression. "What's up?"

"I need to talk to you," I say.

She glances down at Sophia. "Can it wait?"

I shake my head. "I'd rather not."

Clara glances between us, worried. I think she can tell that whatever is going on is serious because she takes Sophia by the hand. "C'mon, let's go find Abbs," Clara says to her. "I think my brother brought her today."

I watch my sister lead Sophia into the crowd. When they meet up with Abbie and Gabe on the other side, I pull Delilah down the hall toward my office. On our way, we bypass the mayor. She looks like she wants to talk to me, but I just keep moving. I'll deal with her later. I've already spent enough time catering to her today—I have more important things to worry about right now.

When I shut us inside my office, it becomes apparent just how small the space truly is. With a wary glance my way, Delilah perches on the edge of my desk. I continue to walk the length of the room, too keyed up to stand still.

"If you brought me back here to get lucky, I'm sorry to inform you that you can't. I'm on my period and—"

"I didn't bring you back here for that," I interject.

Delilah's frown of confusion deepens. "Then what are we here for?"

For the first time since I saw the picture, I stop and think. How am I even supposed to broach this subject? What if she has no idea her picture is out there? What if she does and I just jumped the gun? There is no easy way, so I go for the full truth.

"I found a couple of my guys looking at a...picture today," I say. "Delilah, it... It was yours."

I stop in front of her and study her face. Her already pale skin goes impossibly whiter as she registers my words. Reads between the lines. She swallows thickly. "Oh."

She doesn't seem surprised. I feel somewhat better knowing that at least I wasn't the one to break the news to her, but at the same time I hate that she already looks so defeated. I would do anything to take that look off her face.

I take a step closer and find her hand again. I give it a gentle squeeze. "What happened?"

She offers me a self-deprecating smile. "I was young and stupid."

"Hey." My thumb begins to move in slow circles across the back of her hand. "The last thing you'll ever be is stupid."

She sighs. "I met Mitchell in high school. He was one of the first guys to ever give me attention. I didn't know any better. We were together for *seven years*. I didn't see it then, but he was just using me to make himself look good. I gave him friends in high school, and he piggybacked off my father's reputation after graduation. Last summer, I found out he had been cheating on me. I broke up with him after that," she says.

I nod in approval. "That's my girl."

She offers me a small smile. "After a few days of not responding to his texts or calls, I got the news that my picture was spreading across the internet. It was from shortly after I turned eighteen." Her hand tightens on mine as she swallows. "It would be bad enough for anyone, but it didn't just affect me. It affected my dad's job, too."

Her dad, the premier. No wonder the picture spread as widely as it did. If her last name was attached to it in any way, of course it would get picked up by the media and anyone who had a bone to pick with her father.

"This Mitchell guy—he's the one that shared it?"

She nods. "He would never admit it, but I know it was him. He's the only person I've ever sent pictures like that." Her cheeks flush in embarrassment and I hate that this is making her uncomfortable. "I guess it was some kind of power trip to try to make me come back."

Anger surges through me. What a pathetic man. To have someone as remarkable as Delilah and then to fail to cherish her... It's unthinkable. She deserves much better than her shitty excuse of an ex.

"My dad had to pay to have the pictures removed." A guilty look crosses her features at this. "But by then, it was too late. Everyone knew, and they couldn't scrub all of them."

Suddenly, it all makes sense. The way she worried about the cameras; how she seemed so desensitized when her car was vandalized. She's probably had that word, and worse, hurled at her already.

"I'm sorry. You didn't deserve that, Delilah."

Surprise paints her pretty features. "It's o—"

"Don't you dare say it's okay." With my free hand, I cup her jaw, tilting her head. I need her to see me. I need her to hear my next words. To know that I mean them. "Nothing about what he did is okay. It was a blatant violation of your trust and privacy."

She looks at me for a long moment. Her eyes begin to

well before a single tear slides down her face. I sweep it away with the pad of my thumb, then continue stroking the soft skin over her cheekbone. She leans into my touch.

"*Thank you*," she whispers. And with those two words, the tension in her shoulders melts, replaced with overwhelming relief.

"He hasn't reached out again, has he?" I ask.

If he has, I'll have to think of a better way to see to it he stops bothering her. I'm sure Finn wouldn't mind helping. He, more than anyone, hates when a woman is taken advantage of. And despite it being hard to tell, I think he took a liking to Delilah the day they met at his shop.

Thankfully, she shakes her head. "Blocking him seems to have worked. It's stupid—I should have done that months ago."

"Let's not focus on the past, yeah? Let's just focus on the fact that fucker is out of your life for good."

She laughs. "I'll drink to that," she says with a smile, her tears now dry.

There she is.

"Are you alright to head back out there?" With her hand still in mine, I tug her off my desk. "I think the mayor is probably ready to mount my head on a stick after I ignored her earlier."

This causes another laugh to escape her. "I don't think it's wise to make an enemy of your boss, you know. Why didn't you just talk to me later? This could have waited."

To this, I shake my head. "It couldn't wait," I insist. And I mean it. "I had to assure myself that you're okay. I know you are, but I had to see it for myself."

Her eyes soften on me. "I'm okay, Luke. I've been through worse."

She's been through a lot and that damn near destroys me. I'd take it all away if I could—all the reasons in this world she has to hurt. I never want to see that light in her eyes dimmed by anyone. She deserves to shine.

I squeeze her hand before letting it go. Reluctantly, but it's for the best.

"Let's go find Soph," she suggests, pulling me out of my thoughts.

I nod, and then I follow her lead. I couldn't stop following her even if I wanted to.

CHAPTER THIRTY-ONE
DELILAH

"HOW'S YOUR PIZZA, SOPH?" I ask.

"'S good," she says around her current slice.

I turn to Parker. When he catches my eye, he nods. "Fine," he mumbles.

"And how is my favourite family doing tonight?" Clara asks as she sidles up to our table at Dockside. I wasn't in the mood to cook tonight, so when Clara reminded me about the specials at the restaurant, I took full advantage.

Sophia beams, her mouth covered in tomato sauce. "Good!"

I snatch a napkin off the table and wipe at her cheeks. She squirms, trying to pull away. "Soph, you have to stay still. Just let me—"

"*Holy shit*. Isn't that your ex boyfriend?"

I let go of Sophia and look up at Clara quizzically. She resembles an unsuspecting deer caught in someone's headlights. Her eyes, blown wide, are pointed at the door. I follow her gaze and instantly wish that I was anywhere else but here.

Mitchell Seegars looms in front of the host stand, adjusting the cuffs of his button-down as he scans the restaurant. His blonde hair is neatly tamed and his pants are expertly pressed, as if he had a dry cleaner on standby after the car and ferry rides to get here.

The Mitchell I knew, especially dressed like that, would not have been caught dead in a restaurant like Dockside. Hell, he wouldn't have even set foot on Kip Island. His family is old money—he alone has a higher net worth than my parents ever did—and they tend to frequent places that have a much more established dress code.

For many reasons, breaking up with Mitchell was a gift. It made me realize that I wanted no part in his stuffy world.

I turn back to Clara. "How do you know what he looks like?"

Her wide-eyed expression turns sheepish. "I may have done some light social media stalking. I had to know who I was dealing with, in case something like *this*—" She waves a hand, wildly gesturing in the air. "—ever happened."

I want to laugh, but worry has firmly lodged itself in my chest. "Can I borrow your office?"

Her jaw drops. "You're actually going to *talk to him*? No!"

I push back my chair and stand. "If I don't, he isn't going to leave. He's here because Luke blocked his number on my phone. He'll want answers."

The surprise in her expression turns to concern. "You sure? Because I can go kick his ass right now."

And that is exactly why I love my best friend.

It's not like I want to be anywhere near him. I don't even

want to let him into the restaurant any further. But if I drag him outside, half of Kip Island will know all my secrets by morning. I like my clean slate here. I don't want to mess that up.

I offer her a grateful smile. "Tempting, but I think it's safer if I take care of it."

"I'll stay here," she offers. She pulls out the unused chair beside my sister. "Miss Soph can share her pizza with me."

I can feel Parker's eyes on me as I make my way toward my ex boyfriend. I offer my brother a reassuring smile over my shoulder before turning back to the front. Then my mouth settles into an unimpressed line. Mitchell's perusal of the room finally ends when his eyes land on me. He looks taken aback. Perhaps because I am nothing like the woman I was when he saw me last.

Once upon a time, I thought I loved him. I thought he loved me. But love isn't supposed to hurt—not like that.

"Delilah?"

I cross my arms. "Mitchell."

His eyes rake over me, though they don't manage to set my blood alight like Luke's gaze does. I know I shouldn't even compare them. But I can't help it. What I have with Luke—however fleeting and temporary—has shown me that I don't have to settle for terrible sex and an even shittier relationship. That it's not wrong to want things.

"You look...good," Mitchell says. Then his gaze narrows on my shoulder. "You got a tattoo."

Ah, yes. How could I forget? I mentioned wanting a tattoo once when we first started dating and he was quick to point out how trashy I would look. The first thing I did post-breakup was book an appointment with a local tattoo artist.

"I assume you aren't here just to scrutinize my appearance."

His eyes finally find my face. "I want to talk."

What about what I want? He never cared about that before, so I shouldn't be surprised that he doesn't care now.

I sigh. "Fine. But we aren't doing it out here."

I turn swiftly on my heel and walk toward the back of the building. Mitchell's loafers slap on the floor as he follows after me. Everyone in the kitchen gives me a strange look when we walk past and I herd him into Clara's small, boxy office. I close the door behind us and then lean on the edge of the desk, trying to look unbothered. The exact opposite of how I feel.

I've tried my best not to think about Mitchell since moving to Kip Island. When I met Luke, my ex simply didn't matter anymore. What he did to me didn't matter anymore. Him showing up here after I have carved out a place for myself feels worse than him leaking my pictures. It's hard to move on when the past keeps getting thrown in my face.

"You wanted to talk," I say. "So talk."

His eyes flash with annoyance. "I don't want to talk *at* you. I want to have a *discussion*."

"Discussions are two-sided. I don't have anything to say. I'm offering to hear you out, but then you have to go." More than he deserves, but I'm feeling generous. And I'm not in the mood to deal with his temper tantrum if he doesn't get his way.

"You need to come home," he demands, finally cutting to

the chase. "This little game you're playing isn't funny anymore."

"I'm not playing any kind of game, Mitchell. This is my home now. Even if it wasn't, you have no right to tell me what to do."

His eyes flash with annoyance, the *real* Mitchell finally coming out to play. "What would your parents think?"

It's a low blow and he knows it. I was always concerned about what my parents would think. But something inside of me broke the day they died. I still ask myself that question every day, but I've had to learn to navigate life in spite of their disappointment. It's freeing, in a way.

I shake my head, choosing to ignore his question. "How did you even know where to find me?"

I know that our move wasn't top secret information, but I'm curious to know how he found us. Found *me*. Did he hire a private investigator? Hack my credit card statements?

"Parker messaged me."

I can feel all the blood draining from my face. "He *what*?"

I don't even have time for the betrayal to set in because the door to the office suddenly swings open. I jump at the intrusion. Luke is standing in the doorway and he looks *pissed*.

"I'm sorry!" Clara yells from the hallway, blocked by her brother's broad frame. "I tried to stop him!"

"It's fine!" I call back, even though it's anything but. I place a hand on my temple, trying to rub away the headache that has begun to form. "Can you take Sophia and Parker home? I'll meet you there after I deal with this."

"Sure. I'll bring the wine!"

Another reason I love my best friend. I look forward to nothing more than getting rid of Mitchell—and now, dealing with Luke—so I can curl up on my couch with Clara and a full glass of pinot. I even think a sleepover is in order. The kind where we stay up late and fall asleep in the living room, a movie forgotten on the TV because we spent the whole time talking.

No one says anything. Even the kitchen has gone quiet as my coworkers unashamedly watch everything unfold. With a roll of my eyes, I close the office door. I already know I'm going to be the topic of conversation during smoke breaks for the foreseeable future—I don't need to add fuel to their fire.

Mitchell boldly breaks the silence. "Who the hell is *he*?" The look he shoots Luke can only be described as pure disdain. While my ex is everything prim and proper, Luke is the opposite. He looks as if he just got off work.

Luke crosses his arms. "You don't know me, but I know *exactly* who you are. And I know that you shouldn't be on my island, let alone anywhere near Delilah after what you did."

Mitchell scoffs. "What I did? I haven't done *anything* except try to keep our relationship intact."

I roll my eyes. "It's been a year, Mitch. You can drop the fucking charade."

His eyes harden at my tone. I haven't used that one on him before. "Little Miss Perfect has learned to talk back, huh?" he sneers.

Luke starts forward, but I place a hand on his chest. "*Don't*," I say firmly. "I can handle this on my own."

He looks as if he plans to protest. I press my hand harder into his chest, begging him to meet my gaze. When he does, I plead with him to drop it. His shoulders drop as he takes a step back, but he still recrosses his arms and glares at Mitchell.

I whirl on my ex. "You need to go," I tell him. "I'm not entirely sure what kind of fantasy you've cooked up in your head, but I don't respond kindly to insults. Never mind the revenge porn. We are *over*. We have been for a year. Go back to Victoria and never contact me again."

I'm done with this conversation. It's only going to end up in circles. I spin on my heel, more than ready to get out of this office, but Mitchell has another idea.

He grabs hold of my wrist. I try to twist free, but his grip is strong. This time, I don't have any hope of stopping Luke. I'm not sure I even want to. He takes hold of my ex boyfriend's shirt collar and shoves him backward. The shock has Mitchell dropping my wrist. Then he hits a filing cabinet with a bang.

"Del—"

"You're done," Luke cuts in. His voice is darker than I have ever heard it. "The second you put your hand on her, you lost the privilege to speak to her. Far as I'm concerned, you should've lost it a long time ago, but she's a better person than I am." Mitchell struggles against him and Luke pushes him harder against the cabinet. "Here's what's going to happen. You're going to go outside, get in whatever fancy ass car you rented at the airport, and then you're going to get the fuck off my island. You aren't going to see or hear or speak to Delilah ever again. Do you understand?"

Mitchell scoffs. "You can't—"

"Do. You. *Understand*?"

"He does," I say. My voice is strong, though it threatens to waver. "He understands."

Mitchell looks over Luke's shoulder at me. "I don't even recognize you anymore," he spits.

I smile, sickeningly sweet. "And thank fuck for that."

A lot of dominoes had to fall for me to wind up where I am. It sure as hell wasn't the smoothest course, but it's mine.

Luke reluctantly lets him go. Mitchell smooths out the front of his shirt indignantly while glaring at Luke. We both watch as my ex throws the door open with enough force for it to slam against the wall. He throws me one last look over his shoulder, but Luke steps in his path, effectively blocking his view. And then he's gone. If that is the last time I see him, it will be too soon.

When Luke is confident that my ex isn't coming back, he turns. His expression, once hard as he stared Mitchell down, is now soft when it settles on me. He takes careful hold of my arm and inspects it, and my lips tip down in confusion. Then I realize that I have subconsciously been rubbing the spot where Mitchell grabbed me.

"Delilah," he murmurs, "talk to me."

"I'm okay," I say, taking my arm back. "It was just a shock more than anything."

That isn't a lie. Mitchell has been known to throw fits, but he has never been physical like that with me before. Frankly, I didn't think he would have the audacity to try, especially with Luke standing there. Just goes to show what desperation can do to a person.

"What is he even doing here?" he asks. "Why were you talking to him? *Alone*?"

"Parker told him where we live." I shake my head. "God, does my brother really hate me that much?"

I'm not sure what kind of expression crosses my face, but I do know it's enough for Luke to draw me into his arms. I go willingly, letting him pull me flush against his body. My ear rests over his heart, and I can hear the steady beats. I feel his chin settle on top of my head. And in this moment, I feel safe. Like nothing can hurt me. I know that when I look up, things won't be that simple, so I relish the feeling while I can.

"He doesn't hate you," Luke murmurs. "That, I can promise you."

I hold on to this promise because in the morning, Parker and I are going to have to talk. He's been avoiding it, but now, his time is up.

CHAPTER THIRTY-TWO
DELILAH

THE NEXT MORNING, I hug Clara hard before she leaves to get ready for work. After my epic showdown at Dockside, she met me at my front door with the promised wine and an armful of chocolate she somehow managed to procure. Over our drinks and snacks, I gave her a detailed play-by-play, pausing for her to gasp at the appropriate times. And then we put on a movie that we never watched.

I'm not sure I'll ever be able to describe how much Clara's friendship has meant to me. When I was stranded, afloat at sea, she pulled me in to shore. She has welcomed me and my siblings into her life as if we were always meant to be there. And in a way, I think we were.

Clara rests her hand on the driver's side door. "Call me later after you talk to Parker."

My phone buzzes in my hand, and I look down to see Luke's contact flash across the screen.

> **CHIEF**
> Has Mitchell tried to contact you since last night?

> No, I think he got the message.

> **CHIEF**
> Good.
>
> Let me know if you need me.

"Who's that?" Clara asks, clearly fishing.

I roll my eyes at her. "Just Luke checking in after last night."

"You know," she begins. "My brother cares about everything more than he probably should, but he's never been like this. Not until you."

Not until you.

Butterflies swoop low in my belly, set on a path of migration right to my heart. Hope like this is dangerous. I can't entertain ideas of being special. I'll only end up disappointed.

"Get out of here!" I say, obviously eager to change the subject. "Go get ready for work."

She shakes her head at me, but she obliges. As she drives off, she sticks her hand out the window to wave. When I get back inside, Maggie calls me to ask if Sophia would want to go to the park with her and Abbie. After getting my sister ready and then saying goodbye when they come to pick her up, I know that this moment is the perfect time to talk to Parker. I'm not looking forward to it, but it has to be done.

When he eventually makes his way down the stairs, he slows when he spots me sitting at the kitchen island.

"We need to talk," I say, not in the mood to beat around the bush.

He avoids my eye as he grabs the orange juice from the fridge. "Fine."

"You told Mitchell where to find me. Why?"

Parker shrugs. "He asked."

The nonchalance cuts like a knife. "But you know we're broken up." *You know what he did.* "What is going on with you? Talk to me, Parker. Please."

The carton of juice slams on the counter and I jump in surprise. He turns to me with a glare. "You want *me* to talk?" he spits. "That's rich coming from you. We don't even talk about them. Why don't we talk about them?"

Our parents.

"I—" This feels utterly pathetic, what I'm about to admit. "I can't."

"Why not?" he demands.

Why, why, why? Because I'll break. And broken people are hard to put back together. The pieces never fit exactly right, and the glue holding them doesn't always stick. The tears I tried desperately to keep at bay are streaming down my face now.

"I'm trying to be strong," I whisper. "For you."

"I don't want you to be strong!" he shouts, a plea in his voice. "I just want you to be *my sister*!"

He abandons his juice and storms back up the stairs. I rest my head in my hands, letting the tears fall freely. God, what has happened to us? They say grief changes you, but I didn't expect it to irrevocably tear us apart until we're unrecognizable to our past selves.

I'm not sure I fully think it through when I pull out my phone. All I know is that I need something to get rid of this ache in my chest and there's only one person who can help me with that.

> I need you.

I messed up.

When I woke up in Luke's arms, I knew. I fucked up—bad. This thing between us wasn't meant to come with any strings, but now I have nothing but strings and they all tie back to Luke. Which means that I need to get out of here before I do something stupid like confess everything I've been feeling.

I always knew this thing between us had an expiration date. I just didn't expect it to come so soon. But this is my fault. It's all my fault.

"Ow, *fuck*."

While my focus is on my throbbing big toe—the one I just stubbed rather brutally on Luke's bed frame—a pair of arms wind around my waist. I land on the corner of the mattress, wedged between two muscular thighs and trapped with my back to a hard chest.

"Where are you running off to, Shutterbug?"

God, his sleepy voice. I was hoping to avoid that—slip out while he was still sleeping. Then I wouldn't have to try to conjure the willpower to leave him behind.

"I wasn't *running*," I argue. "I was just...quietly going home."

"Okay," Luke says. His barely-contained amusement rumbles in his chest. The asshole is actually *laughing* at me. "Why were you *quietly going home*?"

I sigh. "Because I fell asleep."

"You're gonna have to spell it out for me, baby, because I'm not following."

When I push to stand, he releases his hold, but he doesn't let me go far. He moves to the edge of the mattress, his feet planted flat on the floor, and I stand between his legs. One of his hands curves around the back of my knee, like it's pure instinct for him to be touching me somehow. That makes my chest ache.

I shouldn't tell him. I shouldn't because everything will come crashing down around me and I don't know if I can take that right now. But I can't lie. I don't have it in me anymore.

"I told myself I wasn't going to fall asleep here. Because I knew that if I did—" I cross my arms over my chest as I look everywhere but at Luke. The man with the most endearing case of bedhead I've ever seen. "I knew that if I did, I wouldn't be able to walk away after and still pretend I don't want more."

Luke freezes, and then his hand slowly falls away, leaving me feeling cold. "Delilah..."

I chew on my lower lip. "I know, *I know*. That's not part of the agreement. I'm just gonna... I'm gonna go."

I take a step backwards, out of his personal space.

"Delilah, wait," he says, reaching for me. "Can we just stop and think for a second?"

I shake my head, still refusing to be caught. "No, I can't. Nothing has changed for you." I allow myself to meet his eyes, even though it hurts. "Tell me I'm wrong."

The wait is absolutely devastating. His eyes hold a torrent of emotions, all unreadable. "I can't," he admits.

I nod, biting my tongue so I can focus on that pain instead of the pain lancing through my heart. I refuse to cry in front of him—not when I knew what I was getting into from the start. Not when I promised him I could handle our arrangement. Goaded him even. The sting of heartache is amplified by the embarrassment I feel. I was so stupid to think that this wouldn't end in disaster.

"Goodbye, Luke."

"So that's it?"

"That's it." Based on the frustrated look on his face, I can tell he doesn't like this. "I'm not sure what you want from me when you're not giving me a reason to stay. And I get it. God, I get it, more than you know. But I have to go."

The silence is agonizing as I finish gathering my things. He still sits on the bed, running a hand through his hair. He has a couple false starts, opening his mouth and shutting it again. I stupidly want him to say something—say anything. But he never does.

When I get in my car, the tears finally fall. I swipe at them, frustrated that they exist at all. After I pull myself together enough to drive, I back out of Luke's driveway and head toward home. *Home.* Everything right now feels so far away—so ridiculously not part of my plan. Falling for Luke certainly wasn't part of my plan.

But it doesn't matter. *It does not matter.* Because he doesn't want me. Not like that.

And you know what, I don't want him either. I want someone to wade in the mess with me. I want someone to love me through my faults. I want someone to *want* me. Not just for a week or a month. I'm not naïve enough to ask for forever, but I deserve someone who wants it anyway, even if it's futile.

Clara picks up the phone on the first ring. "Hey, how did things go with Parker?"

I sniffle. "Um, not good. Do you think maybe... Can I come over?"

I can almost feel her gaze, weighed down with pity, through the line. "I'll see you soon. And Delilah?"

I chew on my lower lip as I turn down her street. "Hm?"

"You're going to be okay."

Am I? I don't think so. Not this time.

CHAPTER
THIRTY-THREE
LUKE

NOT EVEN COFFEE has been able to salvage my mood today. It's been a week since Delilah walked out of my bedroom. My house. My life. I want to say that I haven't noticed; that my routine has reverted back to the way it was before she arrived on Kip Island. But I would be lying.

I lean back in my chair with a sigh, rolling my neck. I've been cooped up in my office all day and I need to get out, even if it's just for a pointless drive around town. I grab my truck keys from my desk drawer and make my way outside. The midafternoon August sun beats down on the asphalt, adding to the heat in the air. I twirl my keychain around my finger as I head around the side of the building to the back of the lot.

When I round the corner, I stop short. Three figures, dressed in all black from head to toe like classic TV criminals, are standing along the edge of the station. Cans of spray paint fill their hands, and I watch as streaks of blue and red mar the brick. They don't appear to have noticed me, so I make a concerted effort to stay silent as I come up to them.

"What the hell do you think you're doing?" I ask when I'm right behind them.

The figures all jump in surprise, and then they spring into action. The two furthest from me grab their backpacks from the ground and take off, sprinting around the other side of the building, out of sight. The third tries to do the same, but I grab hold of the shoulder of their hoodie and stop them dead in their tracks. I pull back their hood and almost do a double take.

"Parker?"

Delilah's brother stands before me, a cross between embarrassment and annoyance painting his features. The incriminating can of spray paint is still clutched in his hand. Neither one of us says anything for a minute.

Eventually, I clear my throat. "Hand it over," I say, palm outstretched. "And I think you know I have to call your sister now."

Parker sets the can of paint in my hand and then kicks at the asphalt with the toe of his Vans. "I figured."

We walk side by side into the building. He keeps his head down and stuffs his hands in his pockets. My firefighters send us curious looks, but I ignore them. I'm not about to embarrass the kid any further. That isn't my goal.

When we make it to my office, I let Parker go inside first, and then I shut the door tightly behind us. He slumps in the chair across from my desk, looking down at his feet. I sigh as I lean against the edge of my desk and pick up the corded phone. I don't use my cell because I suspect Delilah is screening my calls. Not that I blame her.

"Hello?" she says warily.

"Delilah," I say, and then I rush to continue before she hangs up. "I have Parker here at the station. I hate to do this, but... We have to talk. I can bring him to you—"

"No, thank you. I'll come there." The formality in her tone is like a stab to the chest. All gentleness I've come to know is nowhere to be found. "I just have to let Clara know I'm leaving and then I'll be over."

This time, I let her hang up. I set the phone back in the dock, and then we wait. About ten minutes later, there's a knock on my office door. Delilah sticks her head in before slipping inside. I don't miss the fortifying breath she takes before she lifts her head to face me.

It's only been a few days. There shouldn't be this gigantic shift in the way she looks at me, but there is. I can feel it.

Her eyes are only on me for a brief moment before they slide to her brother. "What's going on?"

I scratch the back of my neck, feeling awkward that this has to be done. "Do you want to tell her?" I ask Parker. He keeps his head down, and then slowly, he shakes it. I nod and then meet Delilah's worried gaze. "I found your brother and his friends spray painting the side of the building."

She gasps. "What?" She whirls on him, crossing her arms. "Seriously, what is going on? This isn't you, Parker."

"Maybe you don't know me as well as you think," he snips. Then he stands abruptly and heads for the door. She calls out to him, but he doesn't respond. He doesn't even turn back.

Delilah swipes at her cheeks, ridding them of tears that haven't yet fallen. "I'm sorry," she says, "for the damage he caused. He'll clean it up."

"Shutter—" She seems to flinch at the nickname, so I backtrack. "Delilah, that's not why I called you. I don't care about the paint. I'm worried about him, and I just want to help."

Because now I have a sneaking suspicion that what happened to Delilah's car a couple months back was not a coincidence.

She nods as her jaw locks. "I appreciate your concern, but I have it handled. He'll clean up the paint because that's the consequence our parents would have given. Now if you'll excuse me, I have to go find my brother and then get back to work."

Delilah leaves my office in a hurry, not unlike how she left my house a week ago. I run a hand through my hair as I let out a frustrated breath.

Fuck.

I've been avoiding my family.

It's no easy feat when I work with my brother, my sister runs the restaurant where I eat a lot of my meals, and my parents have a knack for showing up at unexpected times. It's not easy, but I've managed. Until now.

Clara comes to stand behind the bar opposite my stool and Gabe slides into the seat directly beside me. I expect

Mom and Dad to arrive next, but it seems it's only my siblings ambushing me at Dockside today.

I raise a brow. "Can I help you?"

"No," Clara replies, tugging the glass out of my hands. "But we can help you."

I snort. "And what exactly do you think I need help with?"

Both Clara and Gabe share a look. They've always done that—*it's a twin thing*, they say. It has never annoyed me as much as it does in this moment. I hate the fact that they've clearly been talking about me. Wondering why I've gone radio silent, no doubt. They'll be disappointed to know that I don't have an answer.

"Delilah told me you guys broke up," Clara says gently.

I try to take my glass back, but my sister has a strong grip. "Hard to break up when we weren't together."

Clara waves me off. "Tomato, *tomahto*. Point is, she said that you're no longer seeing each other. We wanna know why."

I can't explain it, but the next thing I know, I'm telling them everything that happened. From Delilah confessing that she wanted more to me not wanting her to leave. I even tell them what happened today. I haven't been this open with my family in a long time. Not because they didn't want me to be—I decided I was better off pushing them away.

"You're an idiot," Gabe says when I'm finished.

I glower, already rethinking my choice to share. "Thanks, brother."

He shrugs. "Just thought you should know."

"Our parents didn't raise hypocrites, so unless you've got

something to say about you and Hallie, I don't want to fucking hear it."

Gabe's jaw tightens. He stands, nodding at our sister. "See you later, Clara."

He leaves without a backward glance, and Clara takes his place on the stool beside me. She shakes her head. "You really had to drop the H word, huh? Low blow."

"He started it," I say, well aware that I sound every bit the petulant child.

Clara rolls her eyes. "You're *both* idiots. There. Are you happy now?" When I don't answer, she does it for me. "No, you're not. Because you're letting what happened with Kristina fuck up what you could have with Delilah."

"I can't have Delilah."

"Can't? Or won't?"

I take a healthy sip of my drink—beer, not water like usual. It was already shaping up to be a long day at work before I caught Parker with the paint. Having to call Delilah and tell her that her brother was committing vandalism was just the cherry on top of a shit pie.

Clara sighs. "I'm not sure what to say to convince you that this is different. That it *could* be different. I just want you to know that it sucks watching you deny yourself something—*someone*—you clearly want."

It's the wanting that scares me.

That night, I found out just how little my fiancée truly cared about me. I don't want to be in that position again—meaning less to someone than they mean to me. I gave Kristina everything and I got nothing in return. I want to believe that Delilah isn't like her, but every time I try to think about the future, my chest tightens with something I can only describe as anxiety.

I finish off my drink and slide the empty glass toward my sister. Then I slip off my stool. "Night, Clarebear," I say with a nod.

I can feel her worried eyes on me as I head out the door. The air has cooled off some from this afternoon, but the heat is still palpable. When I get to my truck, I roll the windows down, and then I just sit there as the small breeze filters through the cab.

Delilah deserves the world. She deserves someone who can give her everything she needs. Someone who isn't me.

CHAPTER THIRTY-FOUR

DELILAH

THINGS between me and Parker have been even more strained than usual since Luke called me to the station the other day. My brother spent all day yesterday cleaning the paint off the building, and he's been holed up in his bedroom since he got back.

I can't help feeling defeated. I don't know what to do anymore. Right after our parents died, everything was hard. But then my relationship with Parker deteriorated so fast, I blinked and it was gone. I don't know where I went wrong.

It doesn't help that today marks one year since they died. Parker decided to keep to himself this morning, but I spent the time with Sophia. We made cookies and ate them for breakfast, and then we binged all her favourite Barbie movies. Clara called to check in at one point and I almost broke, but I managed to keep it all together.

Now I'm on the edge of losing it all over again. I feel bad leaving my siblings at home, but I need a minute to breathe.

> Just got to the gallery. I'll pick something up for dinner later.

Not my finest moment as a guardian, serving takeout two nights in a row, but it's all I can do to keep myself afloat.

Parker sends me a simple thumbs up. Even though his response isn't atypical, I can still feel the chill of our disagreement. I've been at odds with my brother countless times over the years, but never to this degree. Something is wrong, and once we have each had some time to breathe, I'm going to get to the bottom of it. He can't dance around it forever.

Carole greets me at the gallery's door. Today she wears a long sleeve tunic dress in an earthy brown colour. Her necklace hangs from her neck, a big owl with bright feathers on the end resting on her chest. An outfit repeater, she is not.

"Hi, Chickadee," she says with a bright smile. "What brings you in?"

Despite my rotten mood, I still manage to return her smile. "I was hoping to get a head start on organizing my photographs for the exhibition."

Her smile falters. "Gosh, I'm sorry. I have an appointment to get to. I'm closing early today."

"Oh." I try not to let my disappointment show. "That's alright. I'll come back another time."

She thinks for a moment. "Tell you what. I'll shut everything down, but you can stick around and do your thing. So long as you lock up and set the alarm before you skedaddle."

"Are you sure?"

Her smile returns as she pulls a chain from around her neck. It was hidden by the giant owl, but on the end hangs a key. She hands it to me without hesitation. "I'm sure," she says. Her eyes gain a little twinkle. "That Lucas is a lucky, lucky boy."

I falter, almost dropping the key. Luke and I were never actually together, but that apparently doesn't stop Maggie's friends from talking. I nod stiffly. "Thanks again, Carole. I'm just going to grab some stuff from my car. I'll be sure to take care of everything before I go."

When I turn to head back outside, she stops me with a hand on my arm. "Are you doing alright, Chickadee?"

The concern in her voice and on her face nearly makes me crack. Coupled with Parker's distance, I've been feeling rather fragile the past few days. The first anniversary came up faster than I was expecting and I'm not sure how to feel. I don't *want* to feel.

I try to smile reassuringly. "I'm fine! Just a little tired."

She doesn't look like she totally believes me, but she lets me go nonetheless. I take the chance I'm given and head out to my car. From the trunk, I grab my camera bag and the box of picture frames I picked up from the thrift store on the mainland.

Once I get set up inside, Carole sticks her head into the room, waving goodbye. And then I'm alone. Just me and my thoughts. I haven't truly been alone in a long time. If I'm not with my siblings, I'm at work. The odd time I haven't been, I've been with Luke. Other than quiet moments as I try to fall asleep or the brief stretches where I'm in the shower, I'm never by myself.

Without my permission, my thoughts drift to Luke again. Perhaps it has to do with the photo of him that peeks out from beneath the pile of others. Will he still come to the exhibition? The thought of him not being there, even though it would be my own doing, is a sucker punch to the gut. He's the one that pushed me to get back into photography, and I want him to be proud of me. I want someone I care about to see my accomplishments.

I've done this—put my work on display for others to see—once before. When I was in grade twelve, my high school had a winter open house. My photography teacher encouraged me to submit my portfolio to be exhibited in the gymnasium with the other students' artwork and photographs. I was excited. At seventeen, that was the highest compliment I had been paid. My work was good enough to show off.

I invited my parents to the open house. I wrote it into their calendars, circled and underlined. I was giddy with the knowledge that I had done something impressive. Not every student had their portfolio on display. I was one of the chosen ones.

After the first half hour, I was confused. An hour in, I realized they weren't coming. My photography teacher reiterated how proud she was, but it felt hollow. Not the same when my parents weren't there to share her pride. Apparently, they had forgotten about my open house when they agreed to attend a function that same night. A dinner with the Minister of Something for one cause or another. I hadn't known what it was like to resent my father's profession before that night, but I knew then. The hate grew steadily until I wished that everyone in the province would forget his goddamn name.

Just for one night, I wanted him to belong to me again. Too much to wish for, evidently. The memory alone leaves a bitter taste in my mouth, followed by the foul tang of guilt. It was almost nine years ago, and he's dead—I need to get over it.

Thoughts of my parents inevitably morph into thoughts of Parker. Back then, he was seven years old and he looked at me like I was his favourite person in the world. I didn't expect to live on that pedestal forever, but being knocked off so abruptly is jarring.

When the thoughts get too loud, I silence them. I stick my earbuds in and turn my music up to a decibel that is sure to cause some kind of hearing damage. And then I really get to work. As I mouth the words to that one Carrie Underwood song, I lose track of time.

When I eventually resurface and reality slams back into me, it's hours later. I check my messages and realize that Parker has sent some, each getting increasingly worried.

"Shit," I mutter. I didn't mean to cause him any anxiety. I may not exactly be happy with him right now, but I would never be that cruel on purpose.

I open my thread with Parker and begin to type. *Sorry, lost track of time. I'm okay. Going to ge—* At the same time, I grab my camera bag and sling it over my shoulder. My eyes are on my phone, so I don't realize I've knocked anything over until I hear the shattering of glass.

The broken frame doesn't mean all that much on its own, but the picture it houses sends a shot of grief straight to my heart. It wasn't supposed to be in this pile. Somehow it got mixed in with the pictures I plan to share in the exhibition.

My back hits the wall and I slide down. The strap of my bag slips off my shoulder, and the bag falls to the floor the same moment I do.

And then I lose it.

CHAPTER THIRTY-FIVE
LUKE

I HAVE CONTEMPLATED REACHING out to Delilah about a hundred times. I find myself reaching for my phone, only to remember that she doesn't want to hear from me. So when said phone begins to vibrate with an incoming call, my traitorous heart thinks for a moment that it will be her. The second I think it, I know it's not true. If anyone has to cave on this one, it's me. And fuck, I am damn near close.

The number is one I don't recognize, but that's par for the course. Half the island has my personal cell number and isn't afraid to hand it out to whomever they deem in need of it. The 236 area code, however—the same as Delilah's—has me picking up without hesitation.

"Hello?"

"Luke? It's, uh— It's Parker."

"Parker." I relax back in my chair. We haven't spoken since that day in my office, so I'm surprised he's calling me now. "What's up?"

The first time I tried to talk to him—get him to open up

—didn't exactly end well. Maybe after the spray paint incident, he's ready to give it a go. Even though I've made a mess of things with his sister, if Parker wants to talk, I'm not going to deny him that.

"It's probably nothing, but..." He trails off. "Have you seen Delilah recently?"

I haven't seen her since she rushed out of the station after him, not even sparing me a glance. Not looking at me when all I could do was look at her. "Not since you were here the other day."

"Oh."

The worried tinge of that one word has me sitting straight in my chair again. "Why?"

"I know it's probably fine. But she hasn't checked in in a few hours, and ever since our parents... We just always check in, even if we're mad at each other, and she's not responding and I don't know what to do."

"Okay, Parker, just take a breath." He says he knows it's most likely nothing, but the way he's speaking a mile a minute tells me he doesn't *feel* like it's nothing. "Do you know where she went?"

"She said she was heading to the gallery. That was about three hours ago."

"Have you heard from her since?"

"She texted me when she first got there." His breath hitches. "Her phone is probably just dead, but I don't know... I feel like something might be wrong. It's, um... It's the anniversary."

Fuck. Of course, the one year anniversary of your parents' deaths isn't going to be an easy thing to handle on your own. Knowing Delilah, though, that's exactly what she's trying to do. She is religious about checking in on her siblings. Especially Parker, who, more often than not, is doing his own thing. For her to go an unusual amount of hours without responding to him is worrying, to say the least.

"Are you at home?" I ask.

"Yeah, I am. I've got Soph."

"Okay, sit tight, Parker. I'm going to head to the gallery and see if she's there."

"What if she's not?" His voice has grown quiet.

"Let's take this one step at a time. I'll call you when I find her, yeah?"

He reluctantly agrees, and after I promise again to keep him updated, I hang up. Then I try Delilah's number. It rings through until I get to her voicemail. I hang up and dial again, getting the same result. Deep down, I know it's futile, but I try texting her anyway.

> I know you're upset with me, but I just need to know that you're okay.
>
> Please.

Minutes tick by without a response. I don't bother waiting any longer. I pocket my phone and grab my keys. I try not to rush out of the station—try not to make a scene—but Jodi sees right through me. She falls into step with me as I head for the front of the building.

"What's wrong?" she asks.

I tighten my palm around my car keys. "Parker hasn't

heard from Delilah in a few hours. Could be nothing. Dead phone battery."

Jodi's eyes sweep my face. "But you don't think it's nothing."

There's no use lying to the woman. "No, I don't."

Jodi claps me on the back. "Let's go."

I scowl. "You're supposed to be going home."

"I was, but my favourite boss just extended my shift. Approved the overtime and everything. Real nice guy, that one."

I shake my head. "Vera isn't going to think so when you're late again."

"I'll make it up to her, don't you worry. Now let's go find your girl."

The gallery is dark when we arrive. The front door is locked up tight, but the one in the back is still unlocked. That alone has alarm bells ringing in my head. Although Carole isn't always the most organized, she would never be so careless as to leave the place only half secured.

Jodi and I make our way through the back rooms. There aren't very many windows in this part of the building, making it hard to see. Jodi manages to find a light switch on one of the walls, and the overhead bulbs flicker on. I scan the room, looking for any sign of Delilah. Sitting on the ground, a pile of shattered glass around it, is a picture frame.

And then I see her. She's on the floor, her knees tucked up to her chest. Her back is against the wall, as if she slid down it when she couldn't hold herself up anymore. Her eyes are closed, but I can see the evidence of tears still on her ashen cheeks.

"Delilah," I say gently, not wanting to startle her. She doesn't look up.

Jodi clears her throat. "I'll give you two some space," she says. "And I'll let Parker know what's going on so he doesn't keep worrying."

I nod my thanks, and she slips out of the room. After she's gone, I don't hesitate to lower myself to the floor and take Delilah into my arms. She pushes at my chest, trying to resist.

"Delilah," I plead, "let me hold you. Please."

Her body goes slack and she slumps against me, burying her face in my chest. Her fist bunches the back of my shirt, and it isn't long before I hear the sound of her sobs. My heart breaks then, even worse than the day she walked out on me.

"Shutterbug," I croak, "look at me." She shakes her head. "C'mon, baby. Let me see those pretty blue eyes."

This is a blatant attempt to provoke her. Delilah was insistent that her eyes are grey when I mentioned them being blue one time. She doesn't see what I see. When I piss her off, they're a steely grey. But when she looks at me like maybe I'm somewhat worthwhile, all I see is blue.

I want her amused gaze on me. I want to see the ocean in her eyes. I want her to know that she isn't alone, even though she convinces herself she is. Maybe I can't be exactly what she wants me to be, but that doesn't mean I don't care about her. That I don't want her in my life.

Slowly, she pulls back. She isn't touching me anymore, and I instantly miss her body close to mine.

"Tell me what's wrong."

Tell me what's wrong so I can help.

She offers me a watery smile. "You can't fix this one, Luke."

"I can try."

She shakes her head. "I just found a picture of my parents when I was getting ready for the exhibition. I accidentally knocked it over and…" Her hand extends, gesturing toward the mess of glass on the floor. "But I'm fine."

The words leave her lips, but I am entirely unconvinced. The pain in her eyes is palpable. She told me once that she didn't owe me her pain. That's true, she doesn't. But I think Delilah deserves to have someone listen anyway, and I don't think she realizes that I'm willing. She rarely talks about her parents and maybe that's by design, but I've seen the way that bottling it up hurts her.

"I know it's the anniversary."

She looks away, and fuck, I hate that I'm causing her any pain at all. But she's lying to me and she's lying to herself, and I can't watch her do it anymore.

I reach out and extract the frame from the pile of glass. I shake it off, expelling the extra shards, and then turn it over. A younger version of Delilah stares back at me. She couldn't be more than eight or nine. Her hair is the same dark colour, and her eyes are a perfect mix of baby blue and stormy grey. On either side of her, a man and woman stand, their arms over her shoulders. They wear proud smiles.

"Tell me something good," I say. Tears still cling to

Delilah's lashes. She swipes at her eyes as she turns away from me. I take her chin and turn her back to face me. "Don't hide from me. Please."

Reluctantly, she nods. "Something good?" she reiterates.

"About your parents. Where were you when this picture was taken?"

She takes the frame from me and stares at it for a moment. A trembling finger reaches out and brushes over her mother's smile. Delilah's lip quivers. "The library was holding a contest for kids to enter their art," she says. "I really wasn't any good at art or photography or anything." She lets out a quiet laugh. "Actually, I was really bad. I didn't place in any of the categories I entered. But they were proud of me."

I stay silent, just letting her say whatever comes to mind. I want to hear it all.

"Some days I don't know if they would still be proud of me," she continues. "They would probably see my relationship with Parker and be so disappointed with how I've handled it."

"I disagree." She looks at me sharply. I point to the photo in her hands. "Those two people don't look like the kind of parents that would hold something like that against you. You're doing your best, and they know that."

"And it's still not enough."

"You are more than enough, Delilah."

I see the question in her eyes. The pain, too. *Enough, but not enough for you*, they say. She looks away. This time, I let her hide. Because I am a coward who doesn't have a good response to that.

We sit in silence, letting it settle over us. She studies the picture in the frame. The more she looks, the more her breathing evens out. Her eyes don't well with tears and her hands don't shake. A soft smile even plays on her lips.

"What are you doing here?" she eventually asks.

I brush a strand of hair behind her ear. "Parker was worried when he hadn't heard from you. He called me."

Delilah gasps. "Oh my God." She breaks free of me, rising quickly to her feet. "I can't believe I let that happen. I-I have to go."

I take her elbow, stopping her from flying out of here. "Slow down. You're in no state to get behind the wheel. Let me drive you."

She shifts, her arm falling from my grasp. "I'm fine."

My jaw clenches. "Try a different lie. That one doesn't work on me."

Her eyes harden. "You know what? I don't really give a damn what works on you. We've already had this discussion. I'm not yours to be concerned about."

You'll always be mine. Now that I've started, I don't think I can ever stop concerning myself with her. Not completely.

"It's my job to be concerned about the people of this island, Delilah. You and your siblings are no different."

Delilah's head shakes in astonishment. "Wow. The depths of your saviour complex really are astounding, Chief. Truly."

"Fuck," I curse. I run a hand through my hair in frustration. "That's not what I meant."

She throws her hands out between us, as if to create a

barrier to prevent me from coming any closer. "It doesn't matter. I'm going home and I'm driving myself."

She takes a step back. I hate seeing her pull away, but I can't stop her. She moves toward a closet across the room and pulls out a broom to sweep up the broken glass. She declines my offers to help and soon after, she collects her things in a hurry. I hover, afraid that if I let her be, she might fall apart again. I want to be there to help her collect all her pieces. She locks the backdoor behind us and then doesn't spare me a glance as she heads toward her car.

And for the third time, I let her walk away.

CHAPTER THIRTY-SIX
LUKE

IT'S STILL EARLY when I knock on the Booths' front door. I don't even fully know why I came here. Jodi is always complaining that I never come visit her, but today of all days? Must be something in the air.

The door swings open and Vera greets me with a smile. "Morning, Luke."

I consider myself a morning person, but Vera is a *morning person*. When I roll out of bed, it takes me a while to be suitable for human interaction, but she doesn't require any extra time before her smile graces her face. Already dressed for the day, she sports a red plaid flannel, jeans and a pair of black rubber boots. Her black hair hangs in a braid down her back.

"Hey." I tuck my hands into my pockets, feeling like I want to turn around and head home. But now that Vera has seen me, chickening out is not an option. Her wife would never let me live it down. "Is Jodi around?"

"She's still sleeping," she replies. "She figured you would be by one of these mornings. Come. Walk with me."

Vera doesn't wait for a refusal—doesn't give me space for one. She simply steps outside and pulls the front door closed behind her. Sitting on the bistro table on the front porch is a wicker basket, and she loops it over her arm before taking off. I have no idea where we're headed, but I'm in no position to argue. I feel a little lost right now—some direction would be welcome.

We don't talk as I follow her across the property. Jodi and Vera's little farm is situated far away from the ferry port and all the shops that make up the downtown. If you keep driving down the road, you hit the western edge of Kip Island, where tourists—and Clara—like to hike up to the top of the bluffs. This side of the island is shrouded in trees hundreds of years old.

At the bottom of a slight hill behind the house, a small red chicken coop comes into view. Vera cuts a path straight for it. Inside the coop, she hands me the basket. She begins sifting through straw nests, searching for the eggs that have been laid. I stand in silence, dutifully keeping to my task as she reaches underneath the remaining hens and then sets the pilfered eggs inside the basket.

"Jodi told me you met a woman."

Well, *fuck*. She certainly doesn't pull any punches. "Your wife is a gossip," I gripe.

She grins at me over her shoulder. "Maybe. But isn't this what you came here this morning to talk about?" She cocks her head. "Unless you just came by to stand in chicken shit with me."

I scowl when I note that I am, indeed, standing in chicken shit. I shuffle a little to the side, though that does nothing but prolong my response. I'm the older brother; the person my siblings come to for advice. I don't know how to ask for help. Even if it's something I desperately need.

When I look up, Vera has a brow raised, waiting on me. I sigh and relent. "I met a woman."

"*But?*"

"But it's over."

"Because she ended it? Or you?"

"She did."

She did and I let her. If it was up to me, I would have kept us both in suspended animation. I didn't want things to change. But seeing the look on Delilah's face that day was more than enough for me to understand that wasn't fair to her.

Vera nods like those two words have told her everything she needs to know. She deposits three more eggs in my basket and then begins to pour feed for the hens. They cluck excitedly, surrounding her on all sides. There is something comforting about the monotony of their routine that lulls me into my thoughts. But then the silence, save for the birds at our feet, stretches. When I deem it too long to be bearable, I speak.

"She wanted more, and I..."

"Couldn't give it to her?" she guesses.

Either Jodi truly is a gossip or I am much easier to read than I thought. Probably a bit of both.

"I knew it was a bad idea, getting involved with her. But I couldn't help myself."

"I said the same thing about Jodi." She offers me a grin. "I was freshly divorced and had just moved here. I wasn't looking to start anything, but some things are beyond our control."

Control.

Everything about Delilah made me feel out of control. From the moment she walked into my life, I haven't been the same. I tried so hard to resist her pull—the hold she so effortlessly had on me. *Has* on me. I thought putting an end to our arrangement and letting her go would free me from her, but I am more tangled up in her now than I ever was before.

"That's an awful lot of thinking you're doing over there. Care to share?"

Words creep to the tip of my tongue, but I can't bring myself to voice them. Vera regards my internal struggle. When I don't say anything, she checks her watch. "Jodi is probably up now," she says. "Let's head back."

When we arrive at the house, Jodi is in the kitchen, chopping vegetables. Like they've done this a million times, Vera takes the basket of fresh eggs from my hand and begins washing them in the sink. Most of them will be sold at the local farmers' market later in the week, but a few will be used for our breakfast this morning.

For a moment, I simply watch them. They dance around each other the way my parents do—with expert precision from years of doing life together.

When I was younger, I didn't put much stock in what my future would look like. I knew that I wanted to carve out a place for myself at the firehouse, but everything else was a little fuzzy. Once I found my footing with my career, I started to feel like something was missing. When Kristina came along, I thought I had found it. I was wrong.

How can you be that *wrong* about a person? I read fires for a living, yet they seem to be more reliable than Kristina ever was.

"Well, don't just stand there," Jodi scolds. When she turns to me over her shoulder, there is an unmistakable twinkle in her eyes. "Set the table for us."

I chuckle, but do as I'm told. I pull three plates down from the cupboard and find the cutlery in one of the drawers. As Vera tends to the omelettes now cooking on the stove, Jodi pulls a jug of orange juice from the fridge and pours three glasses.

"Did Vera manage to knock some sense into you?" Jodi asks. "Or do I have to do it?"

Her wife tuts. "Let the poor man eat his breakfast first, love."

Jodi rolls her eyes. "He has had more than enough time to come to his senses. These are desperate times."

"Damn, I thought you were on my side," I say with a laugh.

Her lips purse. "I am on your side, Luke, but that doesn't mean I'm going to sit idly by while you act like an idiot."

We sit down to breakfast in silence. Jodi and Vera talk amongst themselves, but I hardly hear them. I'm too stuck in my thoughts. After a while, Jodi sets her knife and fork on her plate with a loud clank. Vera and I both look at her in surprise.

"You wanna know what I think?" she asks.

I set my own cutlery aside as I face her. "I'm sure you're going to tell me anyway."

A wry smile stretches her lips. "I think it was your pride that got hurt, not your heart." I open my mouth to protest, but she cuts me a look that has my jaw snapping shut. I may be in charge at work, but this is Jodi's house and here, she makes the rules. "You have had people looking up to you for practically your whole life. You've always been steady—sure in everything you do. But Kristina threw you for a loop. Made you question your judgment. But I don't think you were in love with Kristina any more than she was in love with you."

I lean back in my seat, stunned. I can't say that's something I've heard before.

Vera sets a hand on my arm. "Think about how you feel with Delilah. How she makes you feel. It's different, right?"

Different is an understatement. Even my best days with Kristina pale in comparison to a regular day with Delilah. This realization hits me hard. Have I really been holding on to all this shit with Kristina for no reason?

Jodi turns to Vera with a soft smile. "Love is taking a leap of faith, falling and hoping they will be there to catch you, and all the million other clichés. But most of all, love is knowing that you won't always get it right and trying anyway."

"It's ultimately your decision," Vera says.

"But you would be a damn fool not to listen," Jodi adds.

Thinking about giving Delilah more is scary as hell. With all the good comes all the worries about how it will inevitably go wrong. It's fucking terrifying, and I hate that. But...I hate not having her even more.

I truly had no idea what I was missing until she walked into my life. I didn't want to see it, but I do now. This clarity is refreshing, though it also means that I now have something I need to do.

My chair scrapes on the floor as I stand from the table. "Thanks for breakfast," I say. "I have to go."

Jodi grins. "I knew you weren't a total idiot."

CHAPTER THIRTY-SEVEN
DELILAH

"ARE you going to tell me what we're doing?"

Clara grins as she steers my car down Hawberry Lane, away from the pink house and my sanctuary for the past week. It's safe to say I have been wallowing just a bit, contemplating how ridiculous it would be to pack up and move again.

The answer: absolutely ridiculous. I know that, and I don't actually mean it. Kip Island has more than grown on me in the past few months. Victoria was stifling—all the unsolicited opinions and unwanted looks. This island feels *right*. Not to mention, Clara would kill me if I decided to leave her.

But I severely underestimated how hard it would be seeing Luke everywhere. Though I only have myself to blame —he made it clear from the very beginning that he wasn't interested in anything more. I'm the one that got overconfident, and it backfired. Big time. Now I have to suck it up and hide behind grocery store displays when he walks by. One day

I'll be able to watch him walk away without my heart threatening to follow. Maybe.

"What do you think, Soph?" Clara's eyes flick to the reflection of my sister in the rear view mirror. "Should we tell her?"

Sophia giggles as she shakes her head. "No! It's a *secret*!"

When Clara burst through our front door and demanded I exchange my pajamas for the black cocktail dress she had draped over her arm, I flat out refused. But when Sophia skipped into the living room wearing a pink dress and matching Mary Janes, and Parker joined her wearing a button-up instead of a t-shirt, I reluctantly agreed. If only to see what was important enough for Parker to agree to come along.

I look over my shoulder to Parker in the back seat. "You gonna take pity on me?" I ask.

"Not a chance," he says, forced levity in his voice.

Sophia bounces in her seat as she looks out the window. "You have to close your eyes now, Sissy!" she squeals. I shake my head, but comply. "No peeking!"

"No peeking," I promise.

The rest of the drive is spent in stilted silence. Eventually, I can feel the vehicle pull to a stop. Doors open and shut, but I remain in my seat as instructed. Clara comes around to the passenger side to help me while Parker wrangles Sophia from her car seat.

"Am I going to hate you for this?" I ask Clara.

She laughs. "You might a little at first, but I'm confident you'll come around." She takes hold of my hands and begins leading me. We walk up a short set of stairs, and then we stop. "Alright, go ahead and open your eyes."

When I do, I find myself standing on the front porch at Haven House. It's been a while since I've stood in this spot. I'm not proud of it, but I've been doing my best to avoid the rest of the Bowmans. Although Luke and I were never in an actual relationship, his family knew there was something going on between us. I couldn't handle the looks they would surely send me.

I turn to Clara in confusion. "What are we doing here? Dressed like this?"

She grins, her eyes twinkling. "Go inside and see."

When I walk through the door, my heart stutters in my chest. People—*so many* people. And there, in the middle of them all, stands Luke. He looks soul-shatteringly handsome tonight.

Am I breathing? I feel like I'm not breathing.

He takes a step forward and I take a step back. I don't mean to, but the hurt that flashes across his face kills me all the same. I feel like a deer caught in a hunter's crosshairs. And I do hate Clara just a little for subjecting me to this torture. I want to hate him, too. *God*, I want to. But the only crime he has committed is not falling in love with me. I can't exactly fault him for that.

"Why am I here?" I ask. "What's going on?"

Luke steps toward me again. This time, I don't allow myself to falter. I let him eat up the rest of the distance until he is right in front of me.

"We're all here for you," he says.

I look around, eyes wide in disbelief. "Why?"

"The gallery is a little too small for the turnout you deserve, so we brought the exhibition here." He reaches out, tentative. When I don't pull away, he tucks a strand of hair behind my ear. "Tonight everyone will finally have the privilege of seeing your art."

"You did this for me?"

"With a *lot* of help," Clara interjects.

And then a million hands are pulling me in different directions. Clara draws me into a hug, followed not long after by Maggie. Soon after, I'm whisked away into the crowd.

I look back at Luke, needing to know what this all means. *Does* it mean anything? Or is he just being a good friend? The thought of the latter makes me feel sick, but so does the former. Both options leave a nasty bubble of anxiety in the pit of my stomach. But I can't focus on that right now.

It's a good turnout at Haven House tonight. Somehow Carole managed to spread the word through town without me finding out. No easy feat, but if anyone could pull it off, it is evidently her.

"Oh, *good*," Carole says, releasing a relieved breath when she manages to catch up with me. "You're here! I've already fielded five different offers to purchase some of your prints, but I wasn't sure what you wanted to charge. Do you have a price point in mind?"

I hardly register her question. I'm having a hard enough time wrapping my head around the fact that people actually like my photography enough to pay for it. It's at this point that I truly get swept away, losing track of Clara or any of the Bowmans.

Sometime later, as a couple of Dockside regulars bid me a

good night, Clara sidles up beside me. "Dee, there's someone here I want you to meet," she says.

When I turn, I come face to face with a familiar blonde woman. Familiar not because I know her, but because Clara has talked about her so extensively, I feel like I do. Hallie smiles shyly as she tucks her long hair behind her ear. I hope my answering grin is at least somewhat reassuring.

"Hi, I'm Delilah," I say.

"Hallie," she replies. Her eyes do a quick once-over of the crowd at my back before returning to me. "I really love your work. I was—"

She cuts herself off as she gasps quietly, her gaze locked on something across the room. In the next second, I watch her duck behind Clara and maneuver our friend to keep herself hidden. I look over my shoulder, but I don't notice anything altogether alarming.

"Hallie," Clara calls.

The woman in question ducks her head further. "Yeah?"

"What are you doing?"

"Nothing." She peeks out around Clara and again looks across the room. "I'm just gonna...go to the bathroom."

Then she all but sprints out of the room. Clara and I share a look, and then I turn around to see what has Hallie so spooked. The only person standing in that corner is...Gabe.

"Is something..." I trail off. "Do Gabe and Hallie have a *thing*?"

Clara's laugh is deep. "They definitely have a *thing* and they're the only two people on the planet who don't know it."

"You mean they've never—?"

She smiles sadly. "Hallie's been my best friend since kindergarten. When high school hit, we were all sure they would get their heads out of their asses, but then she left for university in Toronto. She hasn't really been home since."

"But she's here now."

She nods. "She is. She hasn't told me why yet, but I'm just happy to have her back."

I eye Gabe across the room. "I bet your brother is happy she's back, too."

"Oh, he will be. But good luck getting him to admit it."

I grin. *Challenge accepted.*

The first moment I can get Gabe alone, I pounce. Call me nosy, but I want to know what's going on between him and Hallie. I find him in that same corner he's been keeping company all night. And though he may be standing with me, all his attention is focused across the room. Specifically, on a certain blonde standing with his sister.

"Hallie's back," I say, mostly just to get some kind of a reaction out of him.

The mention of her name brings his focus back to me. "Huh?"

I chuckle. "I said that Hallie is back."

"You know Hallie?"

My shoulders tip up in a shrug. "We met a couple hours ago. I like her." When he doesn't say anything, I add, "So... she's back."

"So she is."

My voice is gentle when I ask, "What happened, Gabe?" Because you don't look at your sister's best friend like *that* if something hadn't happened.

Gabe looks across the room again. His jaw clenches, and then he shakes his head. "Nothing that matters," he replies. "Not anymore."

I wince, but thankfully, he doesn't notice. His eyes are still trained on Hallie. "Gabe..."

He nods, as if he has made a decision about something. "I'm going to find Abbs. Make sure she isn't getting Sophia into trouble." He slips away, but tension still coils in his shoulders. And when I look back across the room, I find Hallie watching Gabe as he weaves through the crowd.

I'm still paying attention to them, so I don't notice anyone coming up behind me until I hear his voice. "Delilah," he says.

I turn, face to face with Luke for the first time since the beginning of the evening. I offer him a smile, even though nerves dance in my stomach like I've downed a whole bottle of something fizzy. "Hey."

He tucks his hands into his pockets. I don't think I've ever seen Luke sheepish, but right now, that's exactly how he looks. "Are you having a good time?"

I look around at all the people—this town I've come to love—then back to him. "This is amazing," I say. "Thank you, Luke."

"It's nothing," he insists. "You deserve all of this and more."

My hand instinctively reaches out, landing on his arm. "It's *not* nothing. It means a lot." I swallow, working up the courage to voice my next question. "But I have to ask... Why did you do it?"

Why are you making it that much harder to move on?

He removes his hands from his pockets and reaches to take mine. He meets my gaze and then holds it, for a moment that feels infinite. "Because I miss you, pretty girl, and I'm hoping you miss me, too."

My heart stutters. I'm tempted to pinch myself to make sure this is real. Luke squeezes my hands, and God, yes, this is really real. My brain tries to form words, but my tongue won't move. *Say something, Delilah. Anything.*

Before I can, I notice someone pushing through a group of people out of the corner of my eye. When I turn, I realize that it's Parker. From the expression on his face, I can tell that he's upset. He slips around the crowd and rushes out the front door.

"I'm sorry," I say to Luke. My hands slowly slip out of his as I begin walking backwards toward the door. "I have to go find Parker."

And then I turn around and run after my brother.

CHAPTER
THIRTY-EIGHT
DELILAH

I FIND Parker on the far side of the Bowmans' property, sitting on a bench that faces their small pond. The sun is making its final descent, and it casts shadows across my brother's already haunted face. I feel guilty for leaving Luke behind, but my siblings have always taken priority. Whatever he was about to say will just have to wait.

I sit on the opposite side of the bench, giving Parker space, but making it known that I'm there. We sit in silence for a few moments, simply watching as the wind ripples the surface of the pond.

"What are you doing out here?" he eventually asks. "You can't miss your party."

"I don't care about the party, Parker. You and Soph are my priorities."

His voice is quiet—so much so that I almost don't hear it. "Are we?"

The pain starts in my chest and spreads through my whole body. I choke on a sob that barrels up my throat. Did I really get it that wrong? Have I really been naïve enough to think that I wasn't causing that much damage?

"The fact that you don't know that, I— I'm sorry," I whisper. "I'm sorry they went out that day because of me. I'm sorry my careless decisions wrecked our family. I'm *sorry*. If I had known how little time we had left with them, I would've... God, Parker, *I'm so sorry*."

"You didn't wreck us, Delilah," he says. "I'm not...*mad* about that."

I nod, chewing on my bottom lip. "Still. I'm sorry you're stuck with me."

"I'm not. I would be in a group home if it wasn't for you." He looks down at his hands. "I've been really shitty at showing it, but I'm glad you took us. You're, um... You're doing a good job."

I choke on a laugh. "You don't have to lie to me, Parker."

His brow furrows. "I'm not lying."

"I took you away from your friends on a whim. I've been letting you down for months."

"I know things weren't easy with Dad at the end, so you might not believe me, but what you did is a big deal. You stayed for us when you didn't have to." He clears his throat. "That's a big fucking deal."

"Anyone would."

"No, they wouldn't," he insists. "I won't lie, I was angry at you. For taking me away from our home, from my friends. I was focusing on everything I was losing and not what I would gain. Because you're happier here." His eyes flick to the house. "So is Sophia. And I think... I think maybe I could be, too."

I shake my head. "That's not how this works. *I'm* supposed to look out for *you*."

"Why? Because you're older?" he counters. "That's bullshit. You didn't ask for this any more than we did. We're family, so we take care of each other the best we can. The way I see it, you've spent a long time taking care of me and Soph. It's about time someone took care of you."

"Parker," I whisper.

"I can deal. I can learn to call this place home, so long as I get to stay with you and Soph," he says. "That's all I want."

"Always," I promise. "I'm not going anywhere. But we need to talk. The graffiti. What's going on with you? I know things have been shit lately, but you're not that kid."

He presses the heels of his hands into his eyes. "I *know*."

"I want to hear it, Parker." I place a hand on his shoulder and give it a squeeze. "All of it. I haven't been great at this, but I'm listening now."

"I—" His voice breaks, and so does my fragile heart. Suddenly, he looks every bit the sixteen-year-old boy that he is. "Deedee, I messed up."

I wait for him to get his thoughts together. He looks so defeated, I struggle to stop myself from smothering him in a hug.

"A couple days after we moved, you and I had a fight. I— I just had to get out of the house, so I went to the skate park. These guys were there, smoking a joint. They offered it to me and I took it. And then I just told them *everything*."

"What do you mean by everything?"

Parker looks down, an angry blush coating his cheeks. "How angry I was at Mom and Dad for dying. How mad I was at you for not caring—not talking about them. How I hated this island. How I felt out of control of everything in my life."

I swallow, trying not to let my emotions show on my face. He doesn't need to worry about how I'm feeling right now. But I guess I don't do a good enough job because he rushes to reassure me.

"I'm not saying this to make you feel bad, I swear." He swallows. "But that's what I told them. At first, they were being supportive. I thought maybe I had found some friends here. But then they started getting weird ideas in their heads about getting back at you. I told them not to, but they called me a pussy and said they'd take care of it themselves. I didn't think they'd actually—"

His voice drops off, but I don't need him to continue. I understand. "My car?" I ask.

He nods. "I met up with them again the other day. They had the spray paint, and I knew it was bad, but I just wanted to feel something else for a while. Then Luke found us, and Caleb and Markus took off."

"And left you to take the fall," I add.

His head hangs. "Yeah."

I scoot closer on the bench and wrap my arm around his shoulders. He leans into me. We sit like that for a minute, watching the water in the pond move with the breeze.

"I'm proud of you."

He scoffs. "You shouldn't be."

"It's not easy owning up to your mistakes. But you did, and I'm proud of you for that." I squeeze him tighter. "Everything is going to be okay, Parker."

He turns to look at me. "How do you know?"

I give him a soft smile. "Because if we could get through the past year, then we can get through anything. But we have to be a team from now on."

Slowly, he nods. "That means you have to talk to me, too."

It goes against every one of my impulses, but he's right. I can't expect him to trust me with his feelings if I don't trust him with mine. "Agreed," I say. "I didn't want to talk about them because I didn't want to fall apart. I didn't realize how much that hurt you. But I promise I'm going to try. You and Soph deserve that."

Before Parker can respond, the sound of grass crunching comes from behind us. Parker and I pull apart, looking over our shoulders to find Luke. His face is full of worry as he looks between us.

"Sorry to interrupt. I just wanted to make sure everything was okay," he says. "Tell me to go and I will."

Parker clears his throat, standing from the bench. He jerks a thumb toward the house. "It's fine. I'm gonna head back inside."

I stand, feeling too restless to stay seated. My brother nods at Luke on his way by, and then he continues on toward the house. I round the bench, coming face to face with Luke. I have him right in front of me, but suddenly, everything I wanted to say earlier seems to fall out of my head.

I tilt my chin up, meeting his gaze. "Chief?"

His lips quirk slightly at the familiarity of the nickname. "Yeah, Shutterbug?"

"I miss you, too."

CHAPTER THIRTY-NINE
LUKE

NOW THAT I'M standing in front of Delilah, my tongue is tied. And then she tells me she misses me, too, and I swear I've never felt more alive. I take another step until the tips of my shoes touch the tips of hers. The heels she has on tonight offer her extra inches, but she still has to tip her chin upwards to meet my gaze. I have to wait for it, but eventually I get to see her grey-blue irises, shining in the waning sun.

She is as breathtaking as ever in her black cocktail dress. I itch to pull her into my arms, where she should have been all along. But I'm done ignoring what's been right in front of me.

"I miss you," she continues with a sad smile, "but it's too hard to be around you. Maybe one day we can start over—be friends. It's just a little too much right now."

Friends? Fuck being friends. I want it all with her. I want to marry her; make a family with her. I want to watch her gather the courage to start her photography business. I want to be there to see Sophia grow up and to watch Parker grow into himself. I want her to wear my ring and call herself my wife. I want her to be the mother of my children.

Everything meant nothing until I met her.

"No."

Her shoulders fall. Just a little, but I catch it. "Then I don't know what you want from me, Luke, but I can't keep doing this."

She steps backwards and turns toward the house. But I've already had to endure watching her walk away more than once—I'm not doing it again. I grab her hand and spin her around. She hits my chest with a gasp, and I keep her in place by curving one hand over her waist and letting the other get tangled in the fall of her dark hair.

"I figured it out."

Her eyes search mine. "Figured what out?"

"You asked me once why I cared that you were upset." Being in her orbit is dangerous—always has been—but I'm not scared. Not anymore. "I didn't have an answer then. But I have one now."

Her lips part, perhaps in disbelief. "You remember that?"

"I remember everything when it comes to you. You're impossible to forget." My fingers slip from her hair and settle at her neck. My thumb brushes her pulse, both erratic and strong. "I care, Delilah, because I have unknowingly been waiting for you my whole damn life."

"Luke..."

"You have the power to ruin me," I say. "You already have. I am utterly wrecked for anyone else. Hell, there is no one else. It's you for me, pretty girl. Only you. I'm sorry it took me so long to realize that."

Her eyes—glittering and blue like the lake on a midsummer's day—shift as she assesses me. "What changed?"

"Nothing. *Everything*. I was scared before. After Kristina, it was hard for me to trust anyone. I guess somewhere along the way, I forgot how. But not having you isn't an option, Delilah. You are worth every bit of fear."

"What are you saying?" she whispers.

"I'm saying that I want you to be mine, and I want everyone to know it."

As she takes in my words, she nods. "I'll be yours if you'll be mine," she says.

I don't even have to consider my answer. My lips stretch into a grin. "I've been yours for a long time now. I just didn't want to admit it."

She pushes up onto the tips of her toes and throws her arms around the back of my neck. When our lips meet, it feels distinctly like coming home after a long month away. I wrap myself around her, wholly content with never letting her go.

Eventually, we're forced to pull apart. Delilah's eyes shine as she looks at me. "There's one thing I have to ask you."

I nod. "Anything."

"Were you the one who gave Carole my portfolio?"

I rub the back of my neck with my hand, somewhat sheepish. "Will you be mad if I say yes?"

She shakes her head. "How did you even get it?"

"That day we took your car to Finn's shop, your bag tipped over on the floor of my truck. You didn't realize, but your camera card fell out." I tighten my arm around her waist. "I'll admit, I was curious. After I saw what was on it, I figured the committee deserved to see it."

This causes her to laugh. "I want to be mad at you, but I'm finding it very difficult at the moment."

I grin. "You can be mad at me later. Right now, I just want to hold you."

She leans closer, but then her eyes narrow. "Wait a second. What about when you got my headlight fixed? How did you get my keys?"

"That one was Parker. I came by that morning to try to reason with you—" Delilah rolls her eyes, and I give her waist a playful squeeze. "And he was sitting out on the porch. He gave them to me."

Her eyes soften as she takes this in. I can see her mind trying to put the pieces together; to reconcile that action with the brother she thought hated her. But he never hated her—not truly.

"Any other pressing questions?" I tease.

She laughs. "No, I think that's it." She glances quickly toward the house and then back to me. "We should probably head inside or someone is going to come looking for us."

I cup her face in my hands, still in disbelief that this woman is mine. "Let them look, pretty girl," I reply. "We can put on a hell of a show."

The smile she gives me then could outshine the sun. In this moment, Delilah is radiance personified, and I want to bask in her glow for the rest of my goddamn life.

Four days after the exhibition, I park my truck in Delilah's driveway at the end of another work day. I let myself inside, and Riot bounds toward the front door, his favourite ball stuffed in his mouth. I kick off my shoes and then kneel to greet him properly, my fingers sinking into the fur around his collar.

My dog has been having the time of his life hanging out at Delilah's. The backyard is nowhere near the size of mine, but the extra attention from Sophia and the extra treats from Delilah more than make up for it. Even Parker has taken a shine to him.

When I walk into the kitchen, I find Delilah hunched over the island, half-heartedly chewing on a slice of pizza. "Hey, Shutterbug," I say.

Delilah blinks. Then she abandons her pizza and falls into my open arms. "Welcome home," she says. "We have cold pizza and even colder beer."

The way my chest tightens as her lips form the word *home* would have frightened me a few months ago. Now I can't imagine finding my home anywhere but with her.

I chuckle. "Sounds perfect."

She presses a kiss to my chest, right over the heart that beats solely for her, and then she draws back. My hand sweeps through her hair, brushing the strands back from her face. "How was work?" she asks.

"It was a nice, slow day," I say. "How was the first day of school? How's Parker?"

"*Parker* doesn't want to be talked about like he's not here."

At his voice, Delilah and I pull apart. Her brother stands

in the threshold looking decidedly less nauseated than he did this morning. Today was Sophia's first day of senior kindergarten and Parker's first day of grade eleven. While Sophia was cautiously optimistic, Parker looked as if he could hurl at any moment.

"Fair enough," I say. "How did it go?"

He shrugs. "Alright, I guess."

"C'mon," I coax, reaching for a slice of pizza. "You've gotta give me more than that."

He rolls his eyes. "My first period teacher is an asshole. My second period teacher doesn't know what the hell he's talking about. I'm surprised she even made it past teacher's college. My third period is English, so that's gonna be a cake walk. And fourth period—" He cuts himself off and averts his eyes. "It's alright."

I grin. "What's her name?"

His eyes snap up to me. "What?"

"I asked what her name is. The girl that's in your fourth period. You've got that look on your face. So what's her name?"

At first, I don't think he's going to answer. Then he eventually says, "Jenna." I nod, self-satisfied that I managed to read him like that. He shakes his head, an amused smile on his lips. "You know, you're not half-bad, old man."

Delilah's giggle fills the room as my jaw drops. "Did you hear that?" I ask her, pointing toward her brother.

Her lips roll into her mouth as she tries to stifle her laughter. "I believe he called you old, Chief." She shrugs. "He's not wrong."

As I set my slice of pizza down, I attempt a glower, but it

appears I've grown rusty because all she does is giggle again. She tries to make a run for it, the traitor that she is, but my finger catches in her belt loop and I draw her back into my chest.

"Hey! *He* started it!" she complains.

I plant my hands on her hips and spin her around to face me. "Yes, he did," I acknowledge. "And now I'm using you as payback." Hands caressing her face, I draw her lips toward mine. She melts into me, fisting my shirt.

"Aw, *c'mon*, man! I thought we were cool." Parker pretends to gag. "Alright, truce! White flag! I surrender!"

We both start laughing too much to continue with our kiss, but I refuse to let her go. With one arm still wrapped around her, I pick up my pizza again and listen as Parker properly recounts his day. Sophia comes down from her bedroom and insists we watch a movie—as a family. We all settle on the couch, Riot included. He curls himself up at Sophia's side.

Delilah gets comfortable beside me, her legs draped over my lap. When she turns to me, her eyes soften. "I'm sure this isn't how you pictured spending your evenings," she whispers.

"No," I reply with a shake of my head. "This is so much better."

CHAPTER FORTY
DELILAH

NOVEMBER HAS ARRIVED on the island with a vengeance. Gone are the sunny summer days I've come to love, and in their place is a cold front that is bound to turn into snow any day now. Winter back home in Victoria is usually on the milder side, so I'm not sure what to expect out of my first Ontario winter.

Strong arms wrap around me from behind, pulling me back into a hard chest. Luke bends and places a kiss to my shoulder. "What are you up to?" he asks. I can feel the reverberations of his voice against my back.

I shrug. "Just thinking."

"Hm," he hums. "How dangerous."

I pinch his forearm, and then I spin in his embrace. In response, he pins me against the bathroom counter and steals my breath with a kiss.

These past couple months with Luke have been everything. Getting to experience his love for myself is a precious gift, but I don't think I will ever get over how he loves my siblings, too. He knows just how messy my life is, but he wants to lie in the dirt with me anyway.

"I love you," I say.

He grins. "And I love you, Shutterbug," he replies. "But we're going to be late if you don't hurry up."

With a roll of my eyes, I turn back toward the mirror to finish my makeup. I'm rewarded with a swift smack on my ass. I'm tempted to take my time just for that, but we have an appointment to make.

A little while later, as we head across town to get in line for the ferry, a flurry of activity in Dockside's parking lot grabs my attention. "What's all that about?" I wonder.

Luke glances out my window. "The town council approved some movie to shoot on the island," he says. "The crew is renting Dockside's parking lot for a couple weeks. Clara isn't happy about it, but our parents didn't want to turn down the amount of money they offered."

I grin. "So what you're saying is a bunch of good-looking actors will be hanging around my workplace for the next couple weeks?" I laugh when Luke's gaze cuts to mine. The look swirling in his irises tells me that I'm going to be paying for that comment later. "Who is it?"

"I heard it was Hudson LeFort," Parker interjects, leaning forward between the seats.

"*What*?" I shriek.

"Who the hell is Hudson LeFort?" Luke asks.

"Some guy that Delilah has been obsessed with for years."

Luke shoots me another look. I roll my eyes. "I'm not *obsessed* with him. He played my favourite character on this vampire show I used to watch in high school. Looking back, the show was pretty terrible, but I wasn't necessarily watching it for the plot..."

Luke's hand on my thigh tightens in response. Now I'm *really* going to pay later. I can't wait.

While Sophia's reward for her therapy session was playing mindless games on my phone and Parker's was picking what we have for dinner, my reward was time at the beach to take pictures. We made it there just before sunset, and I got to watch the late autumn sun descend from its spot in the sky.

It was way too cold for swimming—not that Sophia didn't try, puppy dog eyes and all—so Luke taught her how to skip rocks. My photos started as landscape portraits of the setting sun, but they quickly morphed into snapshots of my boyfriend and my little sister together. Parker begrudgingly joined them.

"Get any good ones?"

My feet are propped on my coffee table and my laptop rests on my thighs, camera card inserted in the slot. A gallery of the photos I shot today is splayed across the screen— varying shades of oranges and reds, and then the three loves of my life.

Luke settles on the couch beside me, draping an arm across the back behind my shoulders. I angle myself against his side, adjusting my laptop, so he can see the screen.

"These ones need some editing," I say, pointing to the sunsets. Then I click on my favourite shot of Luke, Sophia and Parker. "But I think I'm a little biased because I find I'm partial to these three."

In the photo, Luke is holding Sophia upside down as she shrieks in delight. She had just finished splashing him with the freezing lake water and as retribution, he picked her up and flipped her over. Parker stands by, a smile on his face. I managed to catch him mid-laugh.

"You're amazing," Luke says. I squirm at the compliment. "I mean it, Shutterbug."

I shake my head. "You love me. You have to say that."

He grins. "I *do* love you, but that's not why I'm saying it."

I click out of the photo and close my laptop, setting it aside. "It's just a hobby." Besides the contract with the BIA, I have no plans to pursue photography.

His arm drops to my shoulders, tugging me further into his side. "But what if it wasn't?"

A long-forgotten dream latches on to Luke's words. But the fear of the unknown and the worry that no one will truly care still hold me back.

"I don't know," I say. "What about Dockside? Clara would be devastated if I quit. Besides, I need to make money. I can't just gamble it all on something that—"

"Delilah."

"Yeah?"

"I understand some of your reservations," he says, "but don't hold yourself back because of them. You know Clara would understand. She'd be pissed if she was the reason you didn't follow your passion."

That much is true. If Clara so much as caught a whiff of

these ideas, she would do everything in her power to make it possible for me to succeed.

"It's scary," I admit. I can't look at him, so I stare at the fire crackling in the hearth. "Thinking of doing something for myself."

"I know, but you're not alone. I've got you." Luke presses a kiss to the crown of my head. "It's high time you go after what *you* want."

I hum. "You know what I want right now?"

"What's that?"

I twist in his hold, throwing a leg over his lap until I'm straddling him. "You."

His irises swirl, a heady mix of love and want. "You have me. In this lifetime and the next."

Footsteps sound on the stairs, and then Parker comes into the room with a hand covering his eyes. "Just because I'm cool with you guys being in love or whatever doesn't mean I should be forced to see this couple shit all the time."

I laugh as I slide off of Luke's lap. "Okay, you're clear."

Parker slowly uncovers his eyes. When he sees that we are no longer touching, he holds an envelope out to me. "This is for you."

"What is it?"

Parker shrugs as he heads for the door. "Don't know. It was in the mailbox."

The envelope looks as if it has seen better days. Wherever it came from, it must have been on quite the journey to me. I hook a nail under the flap and tear into it. On top of a folded piece of paper is a pink sticky note. *I hope this brings you peace*, it reads. It's signed by someone named Tanya.

I suck in a sharp breath. Reading that name brings me back to the day I received her call. It was months ago now. I completely forgot about this letter—so much has happened since then.

"What is it?" Luke asks, peering over my shoulder.

I swallow. "A letter from my father."

Luke's hand settles on my thigh in a comforting gesture. "Do you want me to stay while you read it?"

"Yes, please." My voice comes out small.

With shaking hands, I unfold the paper. I expect to find a typed document with my father's signature letterhead, but I'm met with a sea of black ink, smudged by his left-handed strokes. It isn't some carefully-worded memo with his signature hastily scrawled on the bottom. He actually *wrote* me something.

> Delilah,
>
> Words have never been my strong suit, at least not when it comes to you and your siblings, but I'm going to try.
>
> At the end of the month, I will be announcing my resignation. It has taken me far too long to see that I have been neglecting my family in favour of my work. That stops today. When I look back at my life, I want to be proud of the man that I was. And I haven't been proud of myself in a long time.
>
> I'm sorry for the way that I acted. You

should have felt safe coming to me, and instead, I let you down. I want you to know that none of this is your fault. I hope you'll let me make this up to you.

Love, Dad

Tears cascade down my cheeks in unending streams. I knew this would hurt, but I didn't know just how much

"Delilah," Luke says, pained.

"He loved me," I whisper.

Luke turns my face toward him, swiping at the tears staining my face. "'Course he did, pretty girl." He tips his forehead to mine. "How could he not?"

My lashes flutter against my damp cheeks as I close my eyes. "He was going to resign. He was going to quit for me, Luke."

I pull back and bury my face in my hands as my lips begin to tremble. A sob works loose, wrenching itself from my chest. My father's words pour into me as the tears pour out. I feel Luke's arms wrapping around me, and then he cradles me on his lap. His lips press gentle kisses to my temple as I cry.

When I moved to Kip Island in May, I felt like I was numb. A shell of a person, only halfway existing, and all of it was for those around me. I thought I needed the lighthouse to pull me out of the fog, but the lighthouse simply brought me here. This island—these people—were the ones to strip me bare and rebuild me, piece by piece. They gave me space to feel after I had spent so long trying not to.

Loving Luke brought me back to life. Denying my feelings would be to deny all that I feel for him, and he makes that impossible. With every gesture—fixing my headlight, entering me into the photography contest when he knew I was too scared to—he cleared away some of the fog. He didn't set out to rescue me, and he hasn't. He simply shone a light so I could see in the dark. So I could find my own way. And I think I'm getting there.

"Photography has been my dream for as long as I can remember." My voice is raw, still clogged with emotion. Luke holds me, listening intently. "Somewhere along the way, I got so caught up in not being a disappointment that I lost sight of who I truly am. I want to find her again."

"You will," Luke says. He sounds so sure, I have no choice but to believe him.

"I want to go back to Victoria," I say eventually.

He nods, taking in the information. "Alright. I'm sure they could use another fire chief out there."

I pull back from his chest. "What are you talking about?" I ask with a laugh.

His brows draw together. "What are *you* talking about?"

"I want to go back to Victoria to visit my parents. Just for a weekend."

His head tips back against the couch as he chuckles. "I thought you meant that you wanted to move back."

I shake my head. "Victoria will always be home, but it's not *my* home. Not anymore." I search his face, wondering how I managed to get so lucky. "You really would have moved there? Just like that?"

"Just like that, Shutterbug." He cups my face in his palms. "Don't you know that I would follow you anywhere?"

Yes, I think as I draw him in for a kiss. *I know.*

EPILOGUE
DELILAH

"WHAT ARE YOU DOING?"

I raise a brow as I turn to Clara. "Uh, my job?"

One of them, at least. A year ago, after gentle encouragement from Luke, I cut back my hours at Dockside so I could start taking on more photography clients. As it turns out, the demand on the island was pretty high and there was no one to fill it. My schedule has been booked solid for months.

Clara takes the cloth from my hand and starts to push me toward the break room. "You were supposed to leave twenty minutes ago!"

"It's no big deal." I shrug. "I told Luke I would be late."

She tries to fight a grin, but fails. "Trust me, Dee. You wanna go home. Now get your cute butt in your car."

I unlock my locker and retrieve my bag. My eyes narrow as I take in her odd expression. "What is going on with you?"

She waves me off. "Nothing. Get out of here or I'll have to fire you!"

Considering Clara has threatened to fire me no less than

a hundred times in the last two years, I struggle to believe her. Still, I say goodbye and head out to the parking lot. The sky is a beautiful mix of red and orange as the summer sun continues to sink lower. When I pull out of the lot, I roll my windows down, letting the breeze flow through my car.

My drive home isn't as short as it used to be. A few months ago, a house that is almost identical to Haven House came on the market. Luke and I had been talking about moving in together—it only made sense considering how little time we spent apart—and the house coming available seemed like the perfect opportunity. Luke's house sold quickly and we moved into the new one shortly after. It sits on the outskirts of town on the same stretch of road his parents live on.

Eventually, I pull into the driveway, and I park between Luke's truck and my brother's new car. Parker bought it a couple weeks ago with the money he had saved working part-time on the weekends. And in a few short weeks, he'll be packing it up and heading out west to start university.

When he started grade eleven the year that we moved to the island, I wasn't sure what to expect. The previous school year had been rocky after our parents' deaths, and he had just barely scraped by with his marks. That fall, I had low expectations. I didn't want to put more pressure on him when he was already starting at a new school. I knew that wasn't going to be easy.

I didn't need to worry, though. That year, Parker thrived. Attending a small public school instead of his previous private one definitely had a steep learning curve, but having the chance to reinvent himself in a place where no one had any preconceived notions about him was the fresh start he had needed. He made friends almost immediately; began acing his classes again. He even got himself a girlfriend.

When I heard that he had been named valedictorian of his graduating class—in part because of his exceptional grades, but also because his classmates voted him in—I cried. I've done a lot of that over the past two years, making up for those nine months when I hardly felt anything at all. But these days, most of the tears that I shed are happy.

I barely have time to make it up the porch before Sophia flings open the front door and grabs my hand. While Parker heads off to university, Sophia will be starting grade two at the island's only elementary school. It feels like she grows up more every day. I swear I'm going to blink and accidentally miss something.

"C'mon, Sissy," she says. "We have to be fast!"

"Fast?" I ask. "Doing what?"

"Getting ready!"

Turns out, getting ready involves showering off my day at work, blow drying and curling my hair, and slipping into a blue floral sundress that Sophia picked from my closet. I don't usually wear dresses, but it was one of the options I bought for Gabe's wedding last summer. Every time I try to ask my sister what I'm getting dressed up for, she hides her giggle behind her hand and then encourages me to move faster.

Once Sophia is satisfied with my appearance, she makes me close my eyes and then leads me down the stairs. We move through the house and out the back door, and then she finally tells me I can open my eyes.

When I do, my mouth pops open in shock. On the grass, all the blankets and pillows that we own are spread out. The projector rests back on a small table, and Parker sits beside it. But none of that is what truly catches my attention. Strung between the two big trees in our backyard—a major selling point for me, to be honest—is a giant white sheet. And at the centre of it all is four words that make me fall in love all over again.

Will you marry me?

Luke stands beneath the screen, watching me as I assess the scene. He isn't dressed in his usual t-shirt tonight. Instead he wears a button up shirt with the sleeves rolled to his elbows. Based on the smirk that graces his lips when he catches me admiring his forearms, I'm confident that was done on purpose.

"Come here, Shutterbug," he beckons. "I have a question I want to ask you."

I swallow the emotion threatening to knock me over and descend the back steps. I look over to Sophia and Parker for reassurance. They both grin at me, and then my sister makes a shooing motion with her hands. I roll my eyes before turning back to Luke.

"Hi," I say when I reach him.

He smiles. "Hi, pretty girl."

My lips stretch into an answering grin. "I think you have a question for me?"

He nods. He reaches into his pocket and pulls something out, and then I hold my breath as he lowers himself to one knee. My heart beats steadily in anticipation.

"When I first met you, I was adamant that I didn't want

you like this. That I couldn't want you like this," he says. He raises his hand, and a glistening ring catches the fading light. "But I realized rather quickly that I do want you. Forever, in fact. So, Delilah Delacroix, will you give me a shot at forever?"

I nod as I pull Luke to his feet. "Yes," I say, looping my arms around the back of his neck. "Let's do forever."

His hands settle on my waist, and he ducks down to capture my lips. I let him steal my breath for a moment, his arms tightening around me as he claims me. We almost get carried away, but a rather loud throat-clearing, courtesy of Parker, pulls us back to reality. Luke and I pull apart, and then he takes my hand, sliding the ring onto my finger.

A set of small arms slide around my waist and squeeze. Sophia practically vibrates with joy as she hugs me. When I look to Parker, he gives me a warm, encouraging smile.

"So," I say, trying to bring myself down from the delirious high, "what movie are we watching?"

Luke scratches the back of his neck. "Actually..."

"*Congratulations!*"

Abbie comes running out of the house, followed closely by Gabe and his wife. Maggie and John are next, carrying flutes, a bottle of champagne and some juice. Clara and her boyfriend are last, but she beats everyone else across the lawn. She throws her arms around me with a squeal.

"I've always wanted two sisters," she whispers. "I'm so happy for you, Dee."

After Clara reluctantly lets me go, I welcome hugs from the rest of the Bowmans. Then they start doling out the champagne and the juice for the kids. When everyone is distracted, Luke takes my hand and pulls me away. We round one of the big trees, glancing over our shoulders to make sure no one saw where we went.

Luke's hands settle on my waist, and then he walks me backwards until my back is against the trunk of the tree. "Hi," I say.

"Hi." The moonlight illuminates his features, and I admire how relaxed he looks. How happy. "How early do you think we can kick everyone out?"

I laugh. "Considering they just got here, not very."

"How unfortunate," he muses. His hand slides into my hair, getting lost in the strands. "All day long, I've been thinking of which way I'll fuck my fiancée for the first time. I'm getting a little impatient here."

I hum. "You have, have you? And what if I said no?"

Luke shakes his head. "You wouldn't have."

I raise a brow. "You're confident."

"In you and me?" he clarifies. He presses a kiss to my lips and then pulls back, meeting my eyes. "Of course I am. We're a sure thing, baby."

ACKNOWLEDGEMENTS

Arguably, my favourite part about reading is getting to the acknowledgements page. I've even been known to flip to them first when I buy a new book. Even though these people are strangers to me most of the time, I love reading about how they each played a part in that author's journey to publishing. To be writing my own acknowledgements right now is quite surreal.

The Edge of Summer is the first real novel I've finished (we're not going to count the werewolf book I wrote when I was fifteen). I'm pretty stoked to be at this point. This book was truly an exercise in persevering when the self-doubt began to kick in. I've grown a lot since I began to write this book, and I've learned a lot of things. This process would not have been half as fun without the community around me, though.

To Cole and Maddie, thanks for being my besties for the past 20 years. You were the first people to see my writing in the very beginning, and I wouldn't be here today without your friendship and encouragement. Love you!

To my family, thank you for the support. Even though I'm still hoping you haven't read this, I appreciate you telling everyone you know that I wrote a book. Beneath the overwhelming embarrassment, I'm happy that you're proud of me.

To Karley, thanks for putting up with me. I slid into your DMs months ago and haven't left you alone since. Forever thankful for you and your slutty cowboys. We'll always be two fried pickles sitting in a basket together. <3

To my Baddies, thank you for the daily doses of laughter and light bullying. Here's to many more book releases in our futures. Hell yeah, brother!

My alpha readers: Karley, Mollie, Trinity and Gillian. Your interest in my novel in its rawest form gave me the momentum to keep writing. I'm so grateful for you.

My beta readers: Deidre, Malani, Ashley, Ada, Carly and Marina. Thank you for helping me make *The Edge of Summer* the best it could be. It truly would not be the same without your reactions and feedback.

And to my readers: Thank you for deciding to take a chance on a baby indie like me. I'm so glad I was able to share Luke and Delilah's story with you, and I look forward to sharing many more.

ABOUT THE AUTHOR

Bobbi Maclaren is an indie author from a small town in Ontario, Canada. When she isn't writing, she can be found reading, wrangling her mischievous black cat or booking her next trip to a new country. She also loves fall, dresses with pockets, and her emotional support water bottle. *The Edge of Summer* is her first novel.

Printed in Great Britain
by Amazon